# MONTANA
## In The
## Rearview Mirror

# MONTANA
## In The
# Rearview Mirror

# G.L. BARBOUR

ARPress
ILLUMINATING IDEAS,
EMPOWERING VOICES

**ARPress**
45 Dan Road Suite 5
Canton MA 02021
Hotline: 1(888) 821-0229
Fax:       1(508) 545-7580

Ordering Information:
Quantity sales. Special discounts are available on quantity purchases by corporations, associations, and others. For details, contact the publisher at the address above.

Printed in the United States of America.

ISBN-13:   Softcover    979-8-89356-509-6
                 eBook          979-8-89356-511-9
                 Hardback    979-8-89356-510-2

Library of Congress Control Number: 2024902490

Other books by G.L. Barbour

<u>Academic</u>

Quality in the Veterans Health Administration
Redefining a Public Health System

<u>Fiction</u>

**The Ron Looney Mysteries**
Death Unexpected
One, Two, Three Times a Murder
A Twisted Death
A Researched Death
Naked Death
Alibi for Death

# Table of Contents

# PROLOGUE

Eventually, of course, they did find the body. However, several days had passed before the search began, and everyone had focused initially on looking for him in places around town. That decision meant that the move to the countryside had been delayed another day. Even then, the hunt seemed futile after a full first day of looking without success. No one was feeling positive about the process, and the Sheriff was considering calling the search off. Instead, starting on the second day, he split the searchers into two smaller groups and mapped out a larger area for review. Then, in the afternoon of the fourth day, one group was alerted by a collection of crows spiraling in the air several miles north of town over open fields. Sensing the importance of the gathering of scavengers, they radioed the Sheriff and the other group.

The two groups converged their paths to arrive at the location at about the same time. The Sheriff stood quietly on the slight rise above where the body lay and stared. As with many things, even after locating the body, the circumstances were unclear. The body was on its back, sightlessly staring at the sun; exposed parts had been worked over by the crows.

"Wow!" one of the searchers said. "Those crows really did a number on him. Look at his face."

"Yeah," the sheriff commented. "But it's him. No doubt about that."

The men stood on the top of the little rise above the body and silently looked down, nodding at the sheriff's wisdom.

"Whadda ya think, Sheriff?" one of the men finally asked.

The answer came after a brief pause and stare down at the dead man. "I suspect that bloody mess in the front of his chest will turn out to be a shotgun blast. The question will be where did it come from."

After a bit, one of the searchers carefully slid down into the small ravine where the body lay. He stood next to the body for a moment, and then crouched without touching anything on the body. After a moment, he reached into the grass and picked up a shotgun lying beside the body. He stood and showed it to the sheriff. "His gun's been fired. Maybe he hit the other guy."

"How was it lying, Benny?"

"Uh. Butt down toward his feet."

Another man leaned over the body, holding his nose, and said, "Sheriff, I think there's stippling around this wound. The shooter was really close to him."

The Sheriff nodded, "Then, I'd guess it's possible that he got in a shot, too. Maybe even hit the guy that killed him." The Sheriff turned to the rest of the searchers and said, "We need to start looking for somebody showing up with a shotgun wound in the last few days. No matter how small."

"I don't see any other blood around here, Sheriff. Could be a shot and a miss."

The sheriff shook his head. "Nope. If the killer was that close to him, he musta been hit. Even just a little. Been too long out here for blood evidence to last. This scene ain't about to give us much help. Somebody get a picture, will you? We gotta start checking with the doctors in the county." Another man added, "And all the vets, too."

Everyone nodded at this wisdom and began making motions to move the body. Within minutes, the searchers became stretcher-bearers and started the long trek back toward their vehicles carrying their gruesome burden.

✕

# CHAPTER 1

## JULY 1957

Four days before the body was found, Walt Dell, recent high school graduate, returned from an unsuccessful rabbit hunt and announced to his parents that he wanted to join the Army. Walt's parents were immigrants from Ireland and were not initially comfortable with Walt's decision. He tried to explain that he had no promise of college and the Army would provide him training and a job with good pay, a retirement plan, and the G.I. Bill for college if he wanted to do that. His mother was concerned he would be shot, and Walt explained as a volunteer he would get to choose his field of expertise. He assured both parents he had no intention of choosing a combat role. Walt's father's concern was Walt might be deployed to some distant place and they would not see him for years.

Walt thought, *that's actually one of my goals in joining up.* But he convinced them that he would likely stay in the U.S. for most of his time in the service. Reluctantly, they agreed and he told them he would go to Billings for an entrance physical and swearing in ceremony,and then would likely go to Fort Leonard Wood in Missouri for Basic Training. After a little teary eyed response from his mother, a handshake with his father, the three of them hugged and Walt went to his room to begin packing.

One of Walt's favorite stories about the Army was what happened the day he 'took the oath'. He had to travel a couple of hours before arriving at the Armory in Billings. He arrived at ten minutes to eight in the morning and thought he might get back to Whealton for a late lunch. What he knew was going to happen was a physical exam and a swearing-in ceremony; he thought, *This won't take long.*

He swung open the heavy exterior door and stepped inside the Armory - joining the four hundred other young men also there for induction. Sharply at 0800 hours, a Uniformed Sergeant stepped up on a bench and began speaking. Walt had never heard such a commanding voice before. The Sergeant's voice was clear and quite loud, but the man was not shouting.

He said, "Good morning, recruits. My name is Staff Sergeant Miles. I am in command of the Armory today for your induction into the United States Army." At this point, the Sergeant was interrupted by several individuals, pumping their fists in the air and shouting, "Go Army". Sergeant Miles stared at them until they became quiet, then he addressed them and the group, "There will be more of that. From now on, do not speak unless you are spoken to."

Sergeant Miles laid down additional behavior expectations - no crowding, no jumping any line, etc. - and then told everyone to get into the locker room and strip off all their clothes except their underwear shorts. Sergeant Miles anticipated the next question from the crowd. He said, "Grab the leather bag inside the locker, put all your valuables in it and hang it around your neck. NOW!"

Of course, only two normal-sized doors were opening into the locker room, and they were on the other side of the room from where Walt was standing, a room packed with manly flesh attempting to beat all others through that doorway. Consequently, Walt found himself among the last few Valiant to get inside and face the impossibility of finding an unclaimed locker. Thus, Walt Dell was one of the last three individuals to stumble out of the locker room. He noticed everyone else lined up shoulder-to-shoulder in more than a dozen ranks, staring straight ahead. He and his trailing companions pushed themselves to the end of the back line and formed up.

Walt mumbled to the man on his left, "I hope that doesn't mean we're gonna get checked last."

Sergeant Miles boomed in their general direction, "I said no talking in the ranks. And I mean it!"

Immediately, a clear voice from the ranks could be heard, "Violators will be shot!"

Walt saw the Sergeant's nostril flare and expected an outburst. But, it turned out that Sergeant Miles thought the comment was funny, too. After suppressing his laugh, the Sergeant said, "Alright, that's enough. Now listen up. This is how your day is gonna go!"

Walt especially loved telling how the rest of the day went; four hundred nearly naked men standing in various lines in the sweltering hot Armory. Get your feet checked! Get your paperwork checked! (Walt had completed his Form 88 and Form 89, and one of the physicians on-site went over them with him.) Get your blood drawn! Get your physical exam - including a brief measurement of his blood pressure, listening to his lungs and heart, and checking him for a hernia. *Nothing embarrassing there!*

The last event of the day involved the swearing-in ceremony. Walt thought this part of the day most significant; four hundred naked men standing at some kind of pseudo-attention, reciting their name and pledging to support and defend the Constitution and to obey orders given to them by a superior officer. All the men in the room took one step forward as an indication of their acceptance of this pledge. Shortly after five o'clock, or '1700 hours', Sergeant Miles called out, "Recruits! Formation!" Everyone hurried back to where they had started initially. He explained their day was nearly completed, and that they soon could get redressed. One guy in the front rank asked, "What about the blood tests, Sergeant?

"What do you want to know?"

"I mean … uh, I noticed the blood samples were not labeled. Surely that was a mistake. How will you know who to call back?"

"We are the Army," Sergeant Miles said proudly. "We don't make mistakes. If one of you recruits has a possible positive test, we'll call the whole lot of ya back here and do this day all over again." That answer chilled any further questions.

Sergeant Miles waited a few seconds and then spoke in the voice that penetrated the rear rank, "Ten Hut!" Most of the recruits understood the command and everyone tried to form their ranks properly; this took several seconds for four hundred manly naked young men to get themselves into anything approaching a recognizable formation. As the recruits shuffled around, Sergeant Miles loudly whispered, "God help the U.S. Army."

Once the men in the attempted formation ceased juggling positions and the formation no longer resembled an anaconda swallowing a pig, Sergeant Miles again said, "Ten Hut" and everyone in the formation braced their back. The Sergeant waited for all movement to disappear and then said, "Recruits, you are about to be dismissed by order. The Army expects professionalism, order, and recognition in response to such commands. Here are two behaviors that will ease your entry into Army life. First, every command pertains to someone or some bodies. I just called you together as 'Recruits', but once you arrive at Basic, you will become Private So-and-So and members of companies and platoons. That unit leader will call you to order and formation by calling "Company" or "Platoon." Learn your place in the organization, and things will go well with you.

"Second, there is a correct way to acknowledge a command. You will respond in Army traditional language, isn't that right, Sergeant Blair?"

An Armory Command Company Sergeant, a light-skinned black man about 25 years old in Army uniform stepped out of formation at the rear of the Sergeant Miles. He moved to the side of the bench where Sergeant Miles stood, stiffened to attention, and said, almost without moving, "HUA!"

Sergeant Miles said, "That's exactly right, Sergeant. Thank you." He turned back to the formation of recruits and said, "The correct response to an order from a superior is 'HUA'. This phrase indicates you have Heard the command, that you Understand the command and all it entails, and that you Acknowledge your acceptance of the order."

He paused, and then said, "Recruits! Formation!" and ten seconds later, "Ten Hut". When the shuffling following that command had ceased, Sergeant Miles said, "Recruits, Dismissed!" A scattered calling of 'HUA' accompanied the command, and a rush to be first through the door began. But Sergeant Miles, anticipating this, called "Recruits!" and everyone stopped where they were; he went on, "Orderly and with Professionalism. Proceed."

Walt was in the rank closest to the locker room, and when no one pushed to gain an advantage, he was able to get in, get dressed, and out of the locker room in the first dozen. Feeling like he had escaped from a prison work camp, he found his car and headed home.

Ten days later, he received notice to show up for basic training and induction into the United States Army. His orders showed him appearing the following Monday at the Miles City Recruitment Center for transport to Fort Leonard Wood, Missouri.

# CHAPTER 2

## 1957 - 1960

Walt's recollections of events in Basic Training were colorful but turned out to be very few. His explanation was, "I was sleep deprived! For two months! I didn't pay a whole lot of attention or take notes or anything. But, there was this one time …"

Walt did remember those long eight weeks, and he did so proudly. He might join a conversation later in his career where old soldiers were swapping stories. He would hold back, though, and not push to tell a story until things seemed to slow down. Then, he would say, "Well, there was this one time …" and follow up with a story so funny and ridiculous that his hearers laughed until they cried. When asked why he didn't tell his stories earlier, Walt's explanation was simple and straightforward. He would explain, "My Daddy told me the first liar doesn't stand a chance."

Asked about specifics, Walt often said, "It was like in the movies, lots of dirt and mud, people yelling at me to do something faster, jerked out of sleep at 0500 hours every morning. The only good part was the shooting range. I liked that." With some prodding, Walt told the group that most of the guys from Midwestern and Southern states were already proficient with rifles.

All-in-all, Walt made it through Basic Training without compelling harm to his psyche and a host of funny stories that he rarely brought out. When he was given his choice of Military Occupational Specialty (MOS), Walt went with the Signal Corps (MOS 25) even though that decision committed him to additional Basic Combat Training and Advanced Training of 16 more weeks. Later in life, Walt would share stories about these training periods as times when he forgot the outside world existed and was at his most calm, especially on the Firing Range.

PFC Walt Dell blossomed in the Signal Corps. After completing his Advanced Training at Fort Gordon, he was assigned responsibility for coding in multichannel transmission systems and quickly established himself as a leader and productive member of his platoon. The work assigned consisted mainly of keyboarding on the base; Walt wanted to gain competency in fieldwork and pushed his platoon Sergeant to help him transfer to Signal Support within the first quarter after he became permanent party at Gordon. His request was finally approved almost five months later and explains why PFC Walter Dell was engaged that winter with Signal Support for a nighttime battalion infantry exercise with light infantry from the 1st Infantry Division out of Fort Benning, GA.

The planning for such exercises was supposed to be secret, but nothing spreads faster in the Army than an exercise rumor. So, on that cold night, Walt was not surprised when the horns began shrilling their mournful single-note alert. Already half-dressed, Walt was first out of the barracks and into the rear of the truck his platoon would load and ride to the edge of the firefight. Their responsibility would be to maintain contact with the field command officer and report the effects of his efforts in enemy territory. Walt was excited about the exercise, his first field-level action; he wanted it to get going quickly and decided to help his platoon load their truck.

Walt jumped out of the tarp-protected truck bed and started handing boxes of equipment into the rear until became obvious there was more need for him in the truck bed. He jumped up on the rear bumper and started grabbing material from others, and placing boxes in the truck in the order needed. Everyone was eager to get to the field, and the truck driver was particularly hyped. When the truck was about three-quarters loaded, the driver jumped into the driver's seat and revved the motor.

Bare moments later, with Walt trying to wrestle a large monitor over the rear bed edge, the driver's foot slipped off the brake, and the truck lurched forward a foot or so. This forward motion caused Walt to lose his footing and fall to the ground from the truck bed, pulling the large monitor down on himself.

Medics were immediately summoned. Other members of the Signal Support team got the monitor into the truck, and it pulled away to join the exercise. The medics stabilized Walt on a gurney in the ambulance heading for the base hospital. On arrival, Walt was semi-conscious and obviously in pain; he was administered several doses of morphine and lapsed into a stupor. A radiographic study revealed the injury that changed Walt Dell's career ideas forever: the fall and heavy monitor had created an unusual circumstance: his pelvis was fractured on both sides.

The fractures made Walt's pelvis unstable, and he faced immediate surgical intervention to obtain stability; in the operating room, his fractures were stabilized by internal pins and an external wire across his abdomen. Walt woke up in recovery with considerable pain, and no memory of anything about the accident. His pain was intense for the first few days; he was given morphine for pain control which left him with general narcosis helped to confuse him further.

His platoon leader visited him at the bedside and explained how the injury occurred. He also explained the injury was declared line of duty (LOD), meaning Walt would get some disability for the accident at retirement. Walt had no real concern about his retirement at that point and became suspicious of anyone who suggested he should take his recovery more slowly; he thought they might be pushing him toward leaving the Army. Resisting the advice to take his therapy slowly, Walt thought, *I need to complete this rehab as soon as I can. I can't be shipped back to Montana.*

Throughout his hospitalization, Walt was most troubled by his post-operative restriction on weight bearing. He was allowed to sit on the side of the bed for meals but otherwise, except for bed baths, remained on bed rest for almost four months with some passive physical therapy. Walt had not completely adjusted to the restrictions on his movement when his commanding officer came to his bedside one afternoon.

Walt knew that such visits were unusual and feared he was about to be discharged.

The Captain took off his cap, sat in the only chair in the room, and asked, "How are you doing here, Private?"

Walt thought, *I remember others saying that officers would ask the stupidest question,* but he said, "Just fine sir. Looking forward to getting back to work."

"I'm glad to hear that, for sure. But, I didn't come to encourage you to early recovery." He paused and looked at his lap.

"What is it, sir? You're not going to let me go, are you, sir? The doctors say I'm going to be well and will recover in time. I can still work in the shop here on base, I promise."

The Captain reached over and took one of Walt's hands. He squeezed, smiled wanly, and said, "I'm not here for that, soldier. Everyone says you are expected to fully recover. I'm here for another reason."

"What's that, sir?"

"I just received a telegram from the Army. Your parents were involved in a major automobile accident last night, Private. Both of them were killed!"

Walt felt his chest crumpling and being unable to breathe. He had a feeling of becoming very large while the room and its occupants seemed to be floating away and shrinking. One of the tiny figures raised his hand to touch Walt, and it seemed to grow larger as it approached his vision. Walt said, "Killed? You mean, dead?"

The Captain said, "Yes, son, that's what I mean. I know this as a shock."

Walt thought, *A shock? Really?* but said, "Yes, sir. Can you tell me what happened?"

"It seems they hit a patch of black ice at a turn. The driver lost control, and they went over a railing and rolled the car."

After a brief silence, Walt swallowed hard and asked, "Thank you, sir. What's going to happen next?"

"Are you asking about burial plans?"

"Yes, sir."

"I don't know what's going on at that end. But I would imagine soon. And you are in no position to return home to …" The Captain paused to re-read the telegram, "to, uh, Peck, is it?"

"No, sir."

"It's not Peck? What is it then?"

"It's definitely Peck, sir. I was agreeing that I would not be able to attend." *And I don't want to be back there, anyway. That's why I didn't give Whealton as home address.*

"I see. I'm very sorry this happened, son. I will keep you apprised of the circumstances." The Captain stood, and said, "Well then …" before turning to the door and marching out.

The nurse who had accompanied the Captain came to Walt's bedside and took his hand. She said, "Were you very close to your parents?"

Walt looked at her, thinking, *here's another fount of wise questions,* and said, "I guess so."

She said, "Look, if you have trouble sleeping tonight, I'll get you something to help." She patted his hand and left.

Walt felt it difficult to cry. The event was not completely real in his mind, and he tried to guess which turn in the road was involved. *Can't do that because I don't know whether they were coming from the North or South, or why they were out so late. The Captain said black ice, must have been after dark. Oh, yeah, he said it was after dark. He also called me 'son'. But, I'm not a 'son' anymore, I'm the oldest. Now I'm going to have to start acting like an adult.* That did make him cry.

When he woke the following morning, Walt felt some chest pressure and breathlessness when he considered he was the 'adult' of the family now. He waited for assistance sitting up for breakfast and considered his new relationship with the world. He remembered many of his father's pithy sayings and his advice on how to get along and succeed. He had a new 'family' now - the Army. He decided he would work to regain his position with the new family, get along and succeed. He knew he was the one to do it; after all, he was now an adult. *And this means I don't ever have to go back to Montana. That's good since I need to keep my distance from there anyway. Hell of a price to pay, though.*

From then on, Walt progressed so well with his recovery that his doctors thought he could start active physical therapy after three and a half months of bed rest. The physical therapy he most looked forward to was weight bearing, painful and uncomfortable as that was. After regaining weight bearing, Walt was most determined to get back to his assignment; he did every exercise as designed, not only in the clinic but also in his bedroom at night. He asked the therapist for clear measures of when he could leave the inpatient program. His approach to exceeding those measures was successful, and he was discharged back to the barracks on limited duty after five weeks of PT.

He still had a slight limp after discharge from Physical Therapy, so Walt went back to PT to address it; three weeks later his limp was overcome. He had never been a sprinter, but by the time he was allowed to accompany the platoon on a five-mile run before breakfast, he became accustomed to finishing last.

But those physical limitations also led to a major career change: he was placed on Limited Duty (LD) at work and given only desk responsibilities. Walt was disappointed by this action by his supervisor but understood when quick movement or heavy lifting was needed he would be unable to perform. However, the deskwork he was given involved more and more coding, using the 88-column cards and a punch system. And Walt loved it; he was allowed to join the programming office to talk with the Army's satellite system. Everyone could see that digital electronic systems would be the technological breakthrough in future conflicts.

And Walt Dell was going to be there and involved.

# CHAPTER 3

## 1970 -1980

Walter Dell's career in 19070 coincided with important changes in the structure and function of the service. Although Walt's recovery from bilateral pelvic fractures was sufficient to remove him from Limited Duty, he did not obtain a position to support any unit likely to see actual combat. So he developed a career path that had not existed before: Signal Force Consultant. His broad-based experience with the operations of the Corps and his willingness to learn the applications to combat allowed him to secure approval and funding for visiting nearby combat units for two-way consultation. Walt spent time on various bases near Fort Gordon explaining many of the Corps functions and how the field combat officers could best use these functions. He also spent time in a listening mode, hearing from field officers and experienced combat teams about how they would prefer to have their signal officer and mechanics work. Thus, Walt became a two-way consultant, reporting to his Corps about the field needs and helping field units best use the available tools.

Walter's brigade commander, a full colonel, summoned Walt to his office shortly after one of his visits to another base. As any enlisted man, when called to the commander's office, Walt had visions of doom and disaster regarding his career. He shined his shoes twice, checked all his brass for the appropriate level of luster, got a haircut, and showed up in the Colonel's office fifteen minutes early on the appointed day.

The Colonel came from behind his desk to shake Walt's hand and asked him to sit down for a chat. Walt was taken aback at this suggestion, and his answers to the Colonel's opening questions were terse. The Colonel noticed this and asked if Walt would like a cup of coffee. That seemed to melt any frigidity in the discussion, and Walt learned that the Colonel received laudatory letters from bases he had visited. The Colonel wanted to know the specifics of these visits, including what planning went into a visit, and how Walt performed his two-way communication.

The two men talked for over an hour and three cups of coffee. When the Colonel thought he had the information he needed about the job and the man, he said, "This meeting was very helpful; I have reached a conclusion about you."

Walt put his cup down and started to stand. The Colonel indicated he should keep his seat and continued, "I think you are a bright, dedicated, and clever NCO. And I think you have shrewdly overstepped the bounds of your job description and those of your superiors."

As he heard this, Walt's comfort slowly disappeared, and he began feeling again the pressure in his chest that seemed to prevent breathing. The Colonel went on, "I'd like to get you into the CWO program right away and build an internal consultation process around you and what you have already done. What do you think of that?"

Walt's anxiety did not dissipate, he remained somewhat confused between being told he had overstepped his bounds and consequently was considered for a significant promotion; none of that sounded like the Army way. He swallowed hard and cleared his throat, and then he asked, "Sir, would you mind repeating that question in different words?"

The Colonel smiled and said, "Sergeant, I am asking you to advance a big jump in your lane. I would like you to become a Chief Warrant Officer, and to develop a Brigade-wide program of this two-way consultation."

Walt understood this request, and he nodded. But he also asked, "When?"

"Now. And before you tell me what works against that happening, let me tell you that I have looked into your EPR folder. Every rating has you listed as a numerical 5 in all categories. And, those grades are accompanied by a written addendum about some particularly outstanding work you did. And, everyone includes a recommendation to promote."

Walt had seen these performance reports and had signed off on them; this was not news. Nonetheless, he started to say, "But …"

"Not so fast, soldier," the Colonel interrupted. "I have also matched those performance ratings against your medical records and service time. You already have the required Secret Clearance because of the material you handle on the satellite system."

"Yes, sir." Walt waited for the rest of the story.

"I will have someone in my office help you put together an application, you will have to pass the combat fitness test, and this can happen within a month or so."

Walt smiled at the Colonel and said, "Thank you, sir."

The Colonel stood and said, "I would prefer to hear your acceptance of this offer."

Walt swallowed again and said, "Sir, yes sir, I accept the offer and will do my best to bring honor and success to this mission." He saluted the Colonel, who smartly returned the salute, stuck out his hand, and asked, "Anything else you want to say, Sergeant?"

Walt replied, "HUA, Colonel."

One of the First Lieutenants in the Colonel's office took charge of the application process. He and Walt met twice and reviewed all the criteria to make Warrant Officer. As the Colonel predicted, the only missing items were the formal completion of the Combat Fitness Test and paperwork indicating a choice of Military Occupational Specialty. Walt's choice, of course, was Signal, and he and the Lieutenant crafted a thorough defense of this choice by enumerating Walt's duties throughout his career and his proficiency in that regard.

When the package was complete, Walt again met with the Colonel, who pronounced it ready for submission. He also indicated he would submit a cover letter of endorsement and bare outlines of the proposed new activity. Numerous handshakes followed; Walt returned to his regularly assigned duties to await the decision of the Board. That decision came six weeks later; a relatively thin envelope with a single sheet of paper inside setting a date soon when he could pin the eagles on his collar. Even though that date was more than three months away, Walt made a trip to the commissary and purchased a set of CWO eagles, and put them away in his sock drawer.

The next few months were difficult for Walt; his immediate supervisor knew of the promotion, but no one else in the company did. Whenever Walt was working on a problem with another sergeant and thought the solution was months away, he tended to give the other NCO more responsibility for the project, believing the other man would benefit more from understanding the program after Walt had moved on. Some of them interpreted Walt's action as shirking responsibility; when that occurred, the Captain arranged for Walt to work on a different project.

Once the promotion was public, even though not in effect, Walt's coworkers were pleased about it and started calling him 'Sir Walt' in fun. And when Walt was allowed to pin on his new rank, everyone wanted to join the new outreach activity. Smartly, however, the Colonel took upon himself responsibility for selecting individuals to staff the activity; his choice was to put NCOs on this function that had not served directly with Walt. The Colonel explained his reasoning to Walt, "Son, it's hard enough to start a new activity without criticism from former bunkmates."

Once the assignments were approved and a workplace identified, Walt called his coworkers together. Quite apart from usual, instead of giving orders, Walt talked only about the Colonel's expectations and goals for this new group. Then he asked them to take a long lunch and discuss how to approach and attain those goals. Feeling rather strangely emboldened about such a request from a superior officer, the NCOs returned with ideas, plans, and a surprise. One of the NCOs had formerly worked in the Colonel's office and knew of actual communication measures between combat corps and Signal Corps - and the Brigade did not have good marks.

Walt and that NCO met with the Colonel's Executive Officer and obtained the source of information that went into these measures of communication. Then Walt's group spent time rethinking their goals to support these measures; they found process gaps in the information sharing up and down the chain. Rather than suing the Colonel to change the measures, the Flag Group as they started to call themselves, added thought to their own goals and created supplementary steps to make the connections to the Brigade's measures.

These NCOs knew their jobs and were able to quickly develop two plans for their work with the combat groups: one involved what and how to teach the best concepts for sharing information and how to collect opinions of their 'product' from the direct users; the second focused on including a combat command briefing each time they met with individuals from combat groups.

Some of the Lieutenants and Majors in command of the combat groups resisted taking time for the briefings, and Walt found it necessary to call on the Brigade Colonel for support. The Colonel's support was given, and meetings and briefings began to happen. Flag Group personnel tried to include at least one point in every briefing that was a surprise to the audience, and build on that to improve two-way communication that included criticism of the way Signal Corps operated. These 'customer' complaints were circulated upward in the chain of command as they were obtained.

Four months after beginning the Flag Group, scores on communication had left the bottom ranks, and six months after that, the scheduled reporting time revealed the Flag Group had effected a major change in the Brigade's score, with the organization ranking near the top across the Army. The Colonel told Walt he intended to award him a Commendation Medal, but Walt refused, saying the effort was Flag Group's; he indicated that everyone gets a commendation or nobody gets one.

The Colonel agreed, and after the award ceremony, the Flag Group created a new tradition: Dinner, drinks, and dancing by the Group whenever their scores were in the top 10% of the Army.

# CHAPTER 4

## 1977 - 1980

Madeline Heusner always seemed to attract attention, mostly from men, of course, because of her looks. But she always had a cluster of women around her, too, discussing and arguing something - politics, secondary education principles, and always some discussion about how they would do things better.

Madeline was born in Springfield, Illinois, in 1943. Both parents were glad they had left Europe before it became a possession of the Third Reich. Her mother, tall, blond, and Scandinavian, was a high school mathematics teacher. Her father was of northern Germanic extraction and was a lawyer. Each contributed genetic treasures to their daughter, as Madeline was tall with an oval face and almond-shaped eyes framed by long, light brown hair. Her face was nearly symmetrical with slightly sunken cheeks, thin lips, and fair skin. The total picture was reminiscent of a beautiful model on some magazine cover. And Madeline, who took little time to do make-up or try a different hairstyle, could not possibly care less about her looks.

She was a champion of the downtrodden, beginning in the third grade when she campaigned to her father about the unfairness of city rules prohibiting Joey, who lived just down the block, from having a lemonade stand. Her father found the relevant city statute and tried explaining its intricacies to her; she remained adamant that the rule might be necessary to address the activity of scofflaws, but it did not apply to Joey's venture. She remained convinced, even after long discussions with her father; her pivotal argument was, "I don't like it." her father's legal opinion was Madeline was being weak and unpersuasive. Madeline finally realized her reasoning was beyond adult comprehension and ceased her campaign.

Madeline's next crusade of significance began in seventh grade and persisted throughout high school: bad teachers should not be in the classroom. During the eleventh and twelfth grades, she organized small learning groups in Math, Chemistry, Physics, and Biology for students with subject matter difficulty. She even identified other students who understood the material well enough to help her oversee learning in the groups. Madeline discovered much later that the principal and many teachers were aware of her activity and supported it without touting it.

Consequently, Madeline's decision to attend Augusta University and major in Innovative Educational Techniques was understandable. Her parents were also not puzzled by her desire to obtain her Master's degree there, also. She fit in well with the other undergraduate students, studying together, lying on the lawn on lazy days, and imagining innovation for their future classrooms. And, of course, they occasionally decided on an evening of fun and frivolity together. And that's why Madeline Heusner found herself, on a critical evening, at one of the restaurant's round tables, staring at a distinguished soldier in uniform at the next table. Madeline had seen many attractive young men in her life and never could explain why this one intrigued her. Perhaps it was how he carried himself: assured without cockiness, interested in his surroundings without being obtrusive and a man highly regarded by the others at the table. But what she mentioned most often when asked why she was attracted to him was, "Because he was looking at me and wouldn't look away."

"Honey," her mother would say, "men have always been staring at you."

"Not like this. He wasn't just staring. He was assessing me."

"And what did you do?"

"I winked at him. Guys caught staring are usually embarrassed."

"Ah, and what did he do?"

"He winked back, got up, and came over and asked me to dance."

"And how did that go?"

"He continued assessing. I found out his name was Walt, and he worked at Gordon, but that's all. He didn't talk much about himself, but he wanted to know everything about me. Parents, where I grew up, why was I in Georgia? What is Innovative Teaching, and how would it pertain to adult education in the Army?"

"All that in one dance?"

"Oh, no. We danced the rest of the night. All our friends left, and I had no ride. So, Walter took me home and asked if he could call on me the next night. I liked him, but I said, 'No, that was when I do my hair, and I look awful', and he said, 'I don't care, I want to talk with you. You can talk with your hair done up, can't you?', so I agreed. And I think we have talked to each other every day since then."

As the mother and daughter talked, probing each other's feelings, they came to an unspoken agreement: This Walter Dell from the Army base was different from all other suitors Madeline had dated.

That spring, as Madeline finished her requirements for the Master's degree, she and Walt were a constant pair. He proofed the first copy of her thesis, revealing for the first time that his limited formal education had not limited his education. Walt read widely, mostly about politics, history, and philosophy, and was a proficient editor, catching misuse of the passive voice, and when Oxford commas were needed. But their discussions not concerning the thesis had taken a serious turn: they began to talk about their future.

"C'mon Maddy, be serious about this. You're going to graduate in two months, and you don't have a job. What're you going to do?"

"I've told you, Walt, if I don't find an assistant position at the University, I'll go home to Springfield to look for work."

"Yes, you have told me that. Many times. And I have let you know that you leaving here when I cannot follow will do serious damage to my internal organs."

"You have never said that before, silly. What do you mean?"

"I've looked this up, Maddy. It's science."

"What are you talking about?

"Medical problems that accompany depression, anxiety, loneliness, fear, separation, and Grade four heartache."

"Really? What ailments?"

"Broken heart, gastritis, ulcers, tearful and cloudy vision, mental distraction, hypertension and possibly artifactual Addison's Disease, weight loss, night blindness and probably toe fungus, although the research on that last one is inconclusive."

"Walter, you are making that all up."

"Am not." A pause, then, "Well, not the broken heart thing."

The admission was usually followed by some kissing, and the subject, unresolved, changed to something else.

The circumstance of Madeline's location after graduation was unresolved, although frequently discussed in the next month. One afternoon, three weeks before graduation, Walt showed up for a usual session of round-the-rabbit-hole discussion, and Madeline handed him a crisp, white envelope. She sat on the couch, and he sat across the room. She indicated he should read the letter. He pulled the single sheet from the envelope and opened it to read, "Dear Miss Heusner, I would like to personally congratulate you on your Master's degree from Augusta University and offer you a position on the faculty here at Heritage Academy. We are, of course, aware of your work through your extension classes with our teachers and the presentation you made at the faculty meeting last year. If I have the acceptance of this offer, I should like to introduce you to the current faculty at the Faculty Awards Banquet in June. Signed, Patricia Harding, Principal and Dean, Heritage Academy.

Walt looked up and said, "You're surely not going to take this offer are you?"

Madeline smiled primly, "Probably not. It would mean I had to stay around here for another year, at least. And I can't think of a thing that interests me enough to stay another year."

Walt stood and said, "Right. I certainly see your point. I'll just throw this away then." And he made to crumple the letter.

She jumped off the couch, "Oh, you silly. I've already accepted the offer." Madeline snatched the letter from him, threw her arms around his neck, and kissed him vigorously.

Walt said into her hair, "I don't want to go through all this a year from now."

She pulled back and asked, "What do you mean?"

"I mean, would you marry me?"

Later, they would tell friends it took Walt almost a year to decide that he wanted to marry her, two months to get around to asking her, and two seconds for her to say 'yes'.

At the urging of the Brigade Colonel, the Dells had a military wedding in the base chapel that fall. Usually, the planning, getting invitations, and arranging all issues with the chaplain at the chapel took several months; the Brigade involvement shortened that to less than three. And a glorious wedding it was. Madeline's parents knew very little of the Army traditions and were impressed by the number of officers in attendance wearing dress blue. Madeline's father was particularly captivated by the saber arch. Her mother appreciated activities that welcomed her daughter into the U.S. Army.

Walt had been living rent-free in the Bachelor Officer Quarters, but with Madeline's agreement, put their salaries together with Walt's housing allowance and purchased a house in Augusta. This meant Walt was the one driving to work through the gate every morning, rather than Madeline coming through in the evenings. They found a small bungalow with easy access to the Fort using a short search. Within three months of marriage they were homeowners. Part of Walt's long-range plan was to use the equity they earned to get a larger house when they added children to the family.

# CHAPTER 5

## 1980 - 2000

Both Walt and Madeline were forward-looking individuals and their planning for the future with two salaries created a stable financial basis for their marriage. Unfortunately, Walt and Madeline did not succeed in having children, and they remained in the bungalow until they left Augusta in 1980.

Walt had 23 years of service with the Army, and Madeline had published several papers on her innovative teaching techniques and was becoming known in the discipline. They might have stayed in Augusta after Walt retired, but Madeline wanted to be closer to her family. So, they took their equity in the bungalow and searched for the 'right' house in Springfield, Madeline's hometown.

The search was neither quick nor easy; there were hardly any houses that appealed to them, or the house was located where they didn't want to live. But, perseverance paid off. Walt found a new ad for a 'fixer-upper' in a neighborhood near a middle school. He called and learned from the agent that the house was the once popular Sears Woodland two-story with a corner yard and garage. The price was right, and he made an offer on the phone. When Madeline came home and heard of the decision and offer, she felt somewhat anxious. Normally, she and Walt would have discussed the opportunity and all the options in great depth; this time Walt gave her the ad, a picture of a

Sears Woodland, notes he had taken, and a folded piece of paper concealing the price.

After reading about the house, Madeline asked, "How much 'fixing-up'?

"Probably whole house wiring, a recurrent issue with the roof leak in the rear upstairs, and the garage will not pass inspection."

"We're going to need a garage, winters are often hard."

"Yep."

"So, what's the deal, here, Wally? Why are you acting so smug?"

"Have you obtained all the information you need to make a decision?"

"I know enough right now to think we should continue looking.," she said, folding her arms and staring at him. Walt slid the folded not to her across the table. She gave him a quizzical look and opened it.

"What's this," she asked. "Cost of removing the garage?"

"Nope. That's the bid I made on the property. The agent said she imagined the family would accept it."

"Really? We have that and enough to do all the repairs."

"Yes, ma'am. And it's empty, and we can move in anytime."

"Wait a minute. Why is our bid so likely to succeed? There's lots of people in Springfield who could afford this price."

"According to the agent, this is an estate sale, the last owner was the grandmother of the clan, and the children are interested in getting their money. Every bid they have received has been contingent on selling other property, but our bid is cash without contingency."

"My heavens, how lucky."

"Right, my dear. All it took was each of us saving for the last 16 years."

The Dells were in the new house in Springfield within two months. They might have been there sooner, but for all the parties their friends held for them in Augusta and at Fort Gordon. But finally, they were packed, and moved, and unpacked and standing in their new front yard.

Madeline took Walt's hand and said, "I think I've seen several things other than the garage that need repair or replacement."

He nodded, "Sure. Isn't it exciting? I'm retired and have some experience in the things we need to have done. I admit I'll be busy, but I'm looking forward to it. By the way, did you ever hear from that principal?"

Madeline moved her hands up Walt's arm and leaned against him before saying, "Heard today, and it is also exciting for me."

"Really? Come on, babe, tell me."

"The principal over at the Middle School has already said she wants me on her faculty, and today she said the Superintendent agrees. I'm to go in tomorrow for an interview."

"Honey, you da bomb!"

"Don't know what that means, but I'll assume it's good."

And, of course, it was good. Madeline was hired to teach Social Studies to seventh graders and was approved to introduce her innovative techniques. Within a couple of years, she was promoted to assist the faculty in developing and integrating innovative techniques across the spectrum of the seventh and eighth-grade curricula. She also took the job of mentoring new faculty.

Meanwhile, Walt went to work with a small company, LRD, that wanted to get into the computer business and used Walt's expertise to help guide business decisions. Over the next twenty years, he successfully directed their programs into supporting the company in becoming a market outlet for the external disc storage items made by Seagate. Later, he was the foresighted individual that encouraged LRD to support the concept of the personal computer that brought an enormous boost to their business.

Walt and Madeline were settled and happy in Springfield until, in 2000, she began having difficulty stumbling and falling several times. Her physician referred her for special testing and the diagnosis of Multiple Sclerosis was confirmed. Soon thereafter, Madeline had to resign from teaching as the disease progressed rapidly to near paralysis and a bed-bound status. Walt took a leave of absence from LRD to care for her at home. Her disease progressed quickly, however, and two years later, she expired from pneumonia.

Walt formally retired from LRD and his world of contacts shrunk dramatically. His few regular acquaintances were limited to Ben at the meat counter and Janelle in the check out line at the nearby Kroger, Jack, the mail carrier, Henry, the barber whom he visited every month and Dennis, the manager of the nearby Ace Hardware store.

Springfield, IL

# CHAPTER 6

09/16/2019, MONDAY

Sandra Postella watched the students come into her classroom and select a desk. She had learned to observe this activity at the beginning of each year; students' behavior in this unguarded moment gave clues to their connections to other students and indicated whom they liked to be near and, often, whom they would prefer to avoid. Sandra often used that insight to defuse certain situations before they began, usually without the knowledge of the involved participants. But she also used her knowledge to make assignments across the friendship barriers. Her success in these pairings over the years continued to surprise the other teachers at the high school. The most puzzling aspect was how often she not only got away with those unlikely pairings but how often students in those groups did some of the best work in her class.

Sandra was a Social Studies teacher of some renown. Winner of Teacher of the Year a few years back and a runner-up twice since, Sandra Postella was secure in both her job and the results in her class. As the last student was settling into a desk, she began to speak in her usual below mid-range pitched voice. Her consistently low volume was intentional; it forced the students to quiet themselves to hear her.

"Good morning," she said, in a friendly tone.

24

"Good morning," the students echoed, unevenly.

"I am Ms. Postella, your Social Sciences teacher. It is my pleasure to be with you this year." She paused to let a pair of unruly boys in the back row settle down before continuing. "There are several text books available for reading assignments," here she indicated with her hand a shelf toward the front of the room with more than a dozen such volumes, all of them thick. She paused again and allowed the usual groans to be heard. Then she brightened as if hit by a new idea, and said, "I believe it might be best if you tell me what you expect to learn in this class." She walked to the front of the room, picked up a piece of chalk, and turned to the blackboard as if to write. When there was no response from the class, she turned back to face them and said, "Class participation is a key component in your final grade in Social Studies." She paused for a moment, then put chalk to the board again while saying, "Now, don't all talk at once."

"Culture?" one girl said hesitantly.

"Culture," Sandra repeated, writing the word on the blackboard.

"Maybe some history or something," mumbled a boy in the front row.

"History," Sandra said, scribing that word on the blackboard.

Then the dam broke, and, over several minutes, virtually everyone in the class made a comment or suggestion. Sandra needed to write quickly to transcribe everything. As the suggestions began to taper in frequency, they also became redundant. Sandra stopped writing, put the chalk in the chalk tray, and turned to face the class.

"Originality is also a major component of your grade in this class," she said with a smile and was rewarded with a giggle from several students, recognizing her point.

"Well, that was refreshing and fun," Sandra said, turning back to the board and viewing the many entries. "What you just completed is an exercise called 'brainstorming'. Can anyone tell me some unusual characteristics of what just happened here?"

Almost immediately a boy in the rear of the room raised his hand.

"Yes. What struck you as different?" Sandra asked.

"You actually wrote down everything that anybody said. I mean, you didn't correct anybody. And some of that stuff is stupid. I mean, that was weird." Several other students nodded and looked around the room to get agreement.

Sandra nodded and said, "Good point. That is the primary rule of brainstorming. Let the ideas flow. Get everyone's best ideas and take all ideas. Make no judgment. Stupid or not." She smiled at the class and went on, "You all did very well on that rule of brainstorming about not judging. I didn't hear applause or booing from you about any of these ideas. While we are 'storming' for ideas, we make no judgment; all ideas are considered worthy of putting on the board. Good job to you all."

A girl on the far side of the room said, "But that's just a mess up there. How are we ever gonna study all that?"

Sandra nodded, "Another excellent question. We are now going to go to a different step in this exercise. We will group all these things that are alike and see what we have." She then spent ten or so minutes with several students assigned to keep track of what the class decided. At the end of the ensuing vigorous discussion, she asked each of those students to explain how they had grouped the blackboard terms.

With possibly sixty or more terms on the board, the students agreed they should be clustered together into five major groups: History, Government, Economics, Culture, and Geography.

Sandra said, "You have done remarkably well on these exercises. Now I would like a show of hands. Do you individually agree that these are topics we should study and learn about this year?" Every student raised a hand.

"All right then, you have chosen your curriculum for the rest of the year." They beamed at her and at each other.

Sandra lightened her voice and commented, "Since these topics are your choices, I will not be assigning reading from a textbook." More shows of approval, including a short smattering of applause.

"However," she added, "that will require that you read a daily newspaper every day before coming to class." Moans and headshaking. "Because we will use what is in the newspaper to learn the background of the concepts of the issues you identified for your class curriculum. But that's not all."

As she paused and looked at the clock on the wall above the door, the students became very still. There were only a few minutes left before the end of class. Sandra folded her hands in front of her and quietly said, "A major part of your final grade will involve a team report done by student groups. That report must review in-depth how our major topics, history, geography, economics, governmental civics, and culture of the time affected the national response of the United States to a major historical event. I will provide a list of such events for your consideration. Each event occurred before your parents' birth, so they will not be your primary informants. Your report must include first-hand information obtained by interviewing someone alive and aware of things at the time of the event."

The students, all of whom had been thinking about how easy this class was going to be, suddenly were struck by the enormity of Ms. Postella's requirements for a passing grade. She wanted them to read the newspaper every day, participate in class discussion, act like ladies and gentlemen, and to put in many hours researching something from a hundred years ago by interviewing someone like their grandfather. Why did all the students from previous years say this was their favorite class?

Just before the bell rang, and into the shocked silence of the students in the room, Sandra said, "I will have the team assignments ready to hand out in class tomorrow."

The bell rang, and the students, still quiet and thinking about what they just heard, slunk between the desks and out the door. The last student turned at the door and mutely asked if she wanted the door closed. When she indicated yes, he closed it, and the room fell quiet.

Sandra Postella, an attractive, if slightly overweight 62-year-old unmarried teacher, smiled to herself. That class exercise went about as she expected. She took the class roster and put it in her purse; team creation would occur later, with a cup of tea while sitting on her porch after school.

She walked to the filing cabinet in the front corner of the room, and opened the top drawer, labeled 'History', and placed the class worksheets in a folder at the front marked with the academic year. She noted that the drawer was nearly full of folders containing multiple newspaper clippings, each folder labeled with a calendar year. She closed the drawer and glanced at the remaining drawers, one for Civics, one for Geography, and another for Economics, and the bottom one for Culture. Those drawers were full of similar folders and newspaper clippings from classes in the past. Each year, students added salient clippings, and Sandra would refer students with questions to this filing cabinet throughout the school year. She smiled about how this group of students had, without her involvement, developed a list of the same five major categories for their Social Studies yearlong curriculum, as had so many senior classes before them.

# CHAPTER 7

## 09/20/2019, FRIDAY

The three students were sitting on the Henderson's front porch right after school was dismissed that Friday. They were at the Henderson's for several reasons: Bella had volunteered to host, and her mother agreed to make some cookies; plus, the Henderson home was close to the school, and Joey Symes passed it every day on his way home from school. Such agreement about the meeting place, however, did not immediately generate a consensus on the reason for their meeting, which Bella had decided was to agree on a topic for their group report to Ms. Postella's class.

As promised, Sandra had presented the class with a lengthy list of events from early in the twentieth century. The teams were to choose one and discuss their plan for a report with her before proceeding. The task, however, was not accomplished with cookies and minimal commutes.

Bella Henderson, the putative hostess for this meeting at her house, came prepared and ready to make a decision. Her black hair was cut in a pixie style with a prominent forelock hanging down over her left eye, and she repeatedly tossed her head to move it back. Bella had a very open face, rounded and carrying a smiling mouth exposing very even teeth. Her voice was almost melodious. She planned on a singing career. When pressed, however, she was uncertain about how that type of career would ever turn into a salaried job or consistent income. But, at this moment, all she wanted was agreement on a topic for their group.

"Come on, guys, this is not brain surgery," she said urgently.

"I don't know, Bella," Joey Symes said, slowly munching on his third chocolate chip cookie. "I think we need to have a topic that got a lot of coverage at the time, you know. So we'd have a lot of material to go on."

"Yes, Joey, I heard that the second time you said it," she replied. "What I don't understand is why?"

"So we would have a lot of material we could read, that's why. Then we wouldn't have to rely so much on talking to some old geezer with memory problems."

Hal Bingham, also deep into the cookies, made a mumbled noise and followed that with a gesture shoving a closed fist out toward Joey. Symes ignored the invitation for a fist bump and said, "I propose - again - that we address the Kennedy Assassination."

Joey, formally known as Joseph Perlin Symes, was a tall, nice-looking young man. He wore his six-foot, two-inch frame well, carrying over two hundred pounds discreetly. He was blond and also had a long forelock that overhung his face, covering the right eye. He cleared his visual field with his hand every few minutes. Joey was uncomfortable in this grouping; his father owned the largest bank in town; he spent most of his non-school-related activities at the local country club. Before being placed in this group, Joey's knowledge of Hal Bingham and Bella Henderson was limited to recognizing them as in the other half of the alphabet in the class. He was annoyed that Bella was unconvinced by his argument and only slightly mollified by Hal's ridiculous agreement.

Hal looked at each of them, hoping one would give in to the other. Hal was a 17-year-old Black kid who had successfully avoided challenge and confrontation for years. He simply didn't like confrontation and would prefer to ride along with whoever wanted to drive. Neither of the others seemed to be budging, so he took another cookie. Harold Bingham, Hal to his friends, was a solid five-foot, ten inches tall and 195 pounds with medium to dark café-au-lait colored skin. This physique had allowed him to play football as a lineman in high school, but he knew he was too small to play in college. He didn't understand the whole college interest anyway. It was more schooling and that was of little interest to Hal. He actually liked learning but not from reading a book; he was more comfortable learning by doing. He had a squarish head with prominent eyebrows and a crooked smile as if he were making fun of something. He knew who Joseph Symes was, but he didn't care. He also knew Bella but had never talked to her before this meeting on the porch. He did, however, like the idea of the Cuban Missile Crisis, but was not ready to stick that idea in front of the others.

Hal thought he knew something about that event and agreed that the newspaper coverage would have been intense. That meant that the 'readers' in his group, Bella and Joey, would do most of the work in getting the group project a high mark.

Bella wasn't having it. She thought the whole idea of the process was for them to have content in their project that did not come from traditional library sources.

"Look guys, I went and talked to Ms. Postella. I worried about all this, too. I mean, you know, what's the reason to talk to Grandpa. So I asked her. And she said that was the real point of the project in her mind."

This comment puzzled Hal. "What do you mean, the real point of the project?"

Joey turned his head to face Bella, leaned toward her, and asked, "Exactly what did she say?"

Bella tightened her lips a little and said, "Just what I said. She expects every team to spend time with an older person in the community and get that person's viewpoint on some historical event."

"But, why?" asked Hal.

"Broaden our understanding, she said," answered Bella.

"Hmmm," Joey said, "Maybe we should take two possibilities to discuss with her. One that's big and important and another one that probably no one remembers. She will end up approving us to work on the big issue and we will have a lot of background to use."

"So what, Joey? She is still going to want us to talk to some old person."

"Yeah, Bella, I know. I just think we can get by with very little from the ancient one if we have a big event to read about."

Hal chipped in, "I'm good with that plan."

Bella thought for a moment and then commented, "I bet you already have the two topics already picked off the list, don't you, K.I.A.?"

Joey answered quickly to get past the nickname. "Well, yes. Making a choice here isn't brain surgery, as you reminded me recently. I suggest we choose the Kennedy Assassination and the Hungarian Revolution."

Hal sat up and asked, "Wait. What's this Hungarian Revolution about?"

Joey nodded, somewhat dismissively toward Hal and said, "My point exactly. We'll get assigned to the assassination and hear all about the 'two shooters' from someone who was 15 at the time and we'll be golden for the project."

"I'll second that," Hal said. This was a plan he wanted to endorse.

Bella thought a moment and replied, "I don't think it's a bad idea. But I'm not sure it will work."

"Okay, then. Done." Joey exclaimed, grabbing another cookie and heading down the steps. "I'm going home. You write something up for us to show Postella, and I'll go along with it."

Bella turned her back to the riser behind her and leaned back. She looked at Hal, who looked back and said, "What?"

"He's planning on volunteering for the reading and letting us do the interview, isn't he?" Bella asked.

Such an idea had not occurred to Hal. He said, "I don't know. I just want to get this thing over with. And I truly ain't interested in the reading."

Bella's head slumped onto her chest; she had been concerned about the workings of this team from the beginning. Now she began to worry that she might not get a passing grade hooked up with one player that didn't want to interview and another that didn't want to read. She let out a deep sigh that brought immediate attention from Hal.

"What's up?" he asked.

She smiled at him, relieving some of the tension and said, "It's gonna be fine, Hal, just fine. We'll divide up the work and we'll be just fine."

Hal nodded at her with growing concern that this project was mostly reading, talking and writing and he did not immediately see where his strength would be of assistance. But, he smiled at Belle and said, "Right, we'll be just fine."

# CHAPTER 8

09/17/2019, TUESDAY

Walt Dell was finishing his grocery shopping for the week. Walt had lived in Springfield for nearly forty years but still thought of himself as a Montana boy. Now, at 83 years old, he is shorter than when he actually was a boy. His forward slump gave him the appearance of frailty. But Walt Dell was not a frail man. A widower, he still handled his own activities of daily living, including grocery shopping, laundry, and housecleaning. He was on a first-name basis with managers and clerks of the local grocery and sundry store and the girl at the laundry. Walt's wife, Madeline, or Maddy, died several years before with complications from her multiple sclerosis. Maddy had instructed Walt on all critical household chores, and she was as proud of his independence as he was.

Walt loaded his two sacks into the car and took the cart back to a reserved area before starting his car and heading home. His home was several blocks away and down a spottily populated street and Walt thought about the call he had taken from Sandra Postella earlier that day. He had known Sandra for most of the time he lived in Springfield; she had been mentored in her early years of teaching by Maddy and had been in their house many times.

Sandra's call and request were not unexpected. For five years, she had asked Walt to be a 'community resource' for her social studies class. When she had first asked him to be a resource, Walt was hesitant and quite negative about the prospect. He envisioned traveling to the school, sitting in an uncomfortable chair, and being asked by students ignorant of history about his role and memories of his European experiences in World War II and the peacetime right afterward. Walt even reminded Sandra of his total service time being CONUS (Continental U.S.) Sandra had anticipated his resistance and quickly described her expectations for 'community resource people'. Her idea was in-home interviews by small teams of students whose questions would center on a particular historical event. She wanted Walt to provide them with a mental Rembrandt of mid-America in the 1950s and 1960s to help them understand events, perhaps differently than they might tend to react in the early 21st century. She said she wanted the 'Whealton picture', not the viewpoint of troops in Central Europe.

Walt remembered thinking her re-described request was an easy one, and he agreed. Two times over the next four years, teams from Sandra's class made appointments with him and trekked to his house for interviews three or four times. Walt had not been happy with the students' knowledge of history and was short and hurried with the first group. Sandra visited him after their report was finished and discussed with Walt how he could be more helpful for future student groups. Again, he wanted to back out of the commitment, but Sandra promised she would send a team that he would find more amenable to his stories; he agreed to another try. That time was last year, and Sandra sent a team, two girls and a boy who wanted to talk about how the erection of the Berlin Wall was perceived by folks in Montana. Their interviews had been based on significant reading, and his answers were usually short. The team came three times, and Sandra graded their report as an A.

Now Sandra wanted him to participate with another team. She described them as intelligent, likely to have read widely about their topic, and politely thorough. Walt realized that Sandra had not revealed what they had chosen as a topic; he thought that omission odd but did not call back to enquire.

At home, he put the car in the garage behind the house and took the two grocery bags through the back gate and into his backyard. Walt's backyard was comprised of raised-bed garden beds through which meandered a chipped gravel walkway. He took the shortest route to the back door, appreciating the effect of the oncoming winter on his vegetables. Inside, he put the groceries away and sat at the small kitchen table where he and Maddy had shared most of their meals. With the grocery task out of the way, Walt thought more deeply about Sandra's call. She seemed very upbeat about the team she had assigned to discuss something with him. At the same time, Sandra cleverly dodged every opportunity to disclose the topic this team had chosen. Walt remembered that he had not directly asked about the topic; he then wondered if he should call Sandra before the students came. He certainly didn't want to rely solely on his sixty-year-old memory, did he?

Walt sat at the table as the sky darkened, considering a call to Sandra. Then, he thought, *Wait a minute. Did he really need a head start to discuss the 1950s with high school students? Would Sandra think he was losing his ability? What ability? Memory? Conversation? Maybe calling her is not a good idea.*

Finally deciding he would not contact Sandra to inquire about the topic, Walt made his traditional evening cup of coffee and went out on his front porch to watch the end of day. The sunset was spectacular that evening, every color of the spectrum palleted luminously on scattered cumuli overhead against a black foreground of sentinel trees. Walt was relaxed, and any concern of what topic he might discuss vanished gently and unhurriedly from his thoughts.

# CHAPTER 9

## 09/24/2019, TUESDAY

Immediately after class that Tuesday, Bella corralled Hal and Joey to meet with Sandra. Bella had done as Joey asked and written up a good plan for a project covering the assassination of President Kennedy. Joey and Hal both liked it. However, she knew that Ms. Postella would not fall for the trick Joey had proposed, so she also wrote a similar proposal for the Hungarian Revolution, based almost entirely on one Wikipedia entry. The boys expected a shorter and less impressive presentation of the Revolution, but they agreed to put it in front of Ms. Postella.

Sandra smiled at them as they approached her desk. "Is the team ready to make a proposal?"

Bella answered, "Yes, ma'am. The three of us actually were interested in two topics on your list." She laid the two packets she had produced on the desk in front of Sandra.

Sandra did not open the packets but looked at the two boys. "Harold, Joseph, what were your reasons for each of these projects."

Both young men looked away and shuffled their feet somewhat. Bella started to answer, but Sandra stopped her and continued looking at the two boys on the team. Joey finally decided he would have to speak, "We all liked the idea of covering the assassination."

Sandra raised her eyebrows, "Oh, is one of these about that topic?" She opened one of the packets and saw that it was, and she began to flip through the proposal. At one point, she looked up at Bella and smiled, then she turned to Hal and asked, "What was it about the assassination that intrigued you, Hal?"

A little taken aback at being asked his opinion directly, Hal stammered a bit, then answered, "Well, that was a really big shocker for everyone, you know. It had the government turned upside down and all that." He opened his eyes wide to indicate fascination.

Sandra smiled slightly and turned to Bella, "Bella, what did you use as a source in crafting this proposal?"

Bella fell for the crafty question and promptly answered, "I looked things up on the internet and found several long articles about the controversy."

"Controversy?"

"Yes, ma'am. Some people thought there were two shooters, and we thought that was very interesting." Bella shifted her feet.

"Hmm. I see. Was there anything else about the assassination that you found interesting, Harold?"

"Ah, no. Uh, not exactly. Like Bella said. Maybe a second guy with a gun somewhere." He was stumbling through this sentence, and everyone knew it. Sandra asked, "Joseph. How about you?"

"About what?"

"What, other than the idea there may have been a second shooter, made you interested in the assassination?"

"Oh. Well, like I said, the politics and all, you know."

Sandra leaned back in her chair and asked, "Did any of you watch the special on television about the assassination last Fall? It was on over three nights on Channel 7. They covered all the issues about why Kennedy was in Texas, the two-shooter controversy, how the government changed, and all that. Did you see that?"

All three students looked at their shoes and shook their heads.

Sandra went on, "And they spent a considerable time on the possibility that the assassin was a communist Russian agent." All three heads popped up and Joey began to grin, thinking that would be a great part of their project.

Sandra slowly closed the packet and pushed it away from her. She looked into the eyes of each of the three students and said, "I'm certainly glad that you are interested in knowing more about one of the great tragedies of American history. That is laudable on your part. That event, and the aftermath, however, have been the subject of many television specials, books, and editorials in national newspapers since then and including as recently as last year. The topic has been worked to death."

All three students noted how they had stopped breathing and were now feeling a heavy weight sinking in their stomachs.

"Plus, I have had teams make their report on the assassination twice in the last five years. And I am aware of the widespread information there is about the provable events and even more about the controversial ones." She slowly shook her head, "One of the reasons I ask to approve your project at the beginning is to ensure that your work will not only teach you something you didn't already know but that it would also be of that same value to your classmates."

Sandra leaned back in her chair again and ruled, "I cannot approve of this subject for your team."

Three pairs of shoulders sagged at the decision and Joey started to raise his hand to object when Sandra leaned forward and picked up the other packet. "Fortunately, you put in time and effort on a second possible subject. Let's see what that one is."

She leafed through the project proposal carefully while Bella stood wishing she had spent more time on the writing. Finally, Sandra looked up and winked at Bella, and announced, "Now this is a good idea. No student group has ever been interested in the Hungarian Revolution and I look forward to seeing your final product. This proposal is approved."

Hal made a twisted grin, first at Bella and then at Ms. Postella and started to scratch his head. Joey took a deep breath, used his hand to move his forelock out of his face, and said, "Yeah, Okay." Bella looked down and bit her tongue to prevent herself from smiling. Ms. Postella had seen right thru their ploy and turned it back on them.

Sandra closed the packet and handed it to Bella. "I also have the name of someone you can interview about this topic. He was in high school at the time and probably remembers it." She reached into her purse and took out her wallet and contact list. She flipped quickly to a page and with a brief reference to the contents, wrote a name, address, and telephone number on a sticky note and handed it to Bella. "He's also an interesting man. His wife was a teacher here for many years."

The boys nodded, and sensing a break in the conversation, turned and started for the door. Bella didn't move but asked, "Why did she leave?"

"Who, dear?"

"This man's wife."

"Oh, she retired. But she went home and died a few years later."

"So, this man is a widower?"

"Yes, Bella, he is. Lives alone. Had a cat once, but it died, too."

"How come you know so much about this guy?"

"His wife was Madeline Dell, a highly-honored teacher in this system. She was my mentor when I did my practice teaching here. We have been friends for years."

# CHAPTER 10

## 09/30/2019, MONDAY

Back on the Henderson's porch a week later, Joey was still unhappy that their preference for a project had been denied. "I still don't get it," he said, waving one hand.

Bella and Hal had accepted the decision by Ms. Postella long before and were wanting to get into the business at hand - agreeing on what they needed for their assigned project to go forward and get a good grade. They saw Joey's recalcitrance as not only unneeded but distracting.

"C'mon, Joey," Bella said pleadingly, "we need to get our thoughts straight about what's next, not moan and groan about what was."

Hal took another cookie and said, "She's right, man. Sit down and help us."

Joey sat down, took a cookie, nodded, and smiled briefly at them both. He was only halfway intending to get involved.

Bella brought them to a starting point, "I'm hoping you both read the Internet article I pulled about the Revolution. I sent it to your email. I think we should start with what's known and build some questions for this Mr. Dell. Okay?"

"Hmm," Joey offered.

Hal, his mouth full of cookies, just nodded.

Bella went on, "This Revolution seems to have started with some University students protesting in the streets. They had a list of things they wanted changed, starting with removing Russian troops from the country and giving everyone more freedom and a national minimum wage, right?"

Hal said, "Sounds a lot like those crazies out in California!"

Joey said, "I didn't know it started with University students. That's kind of interesting. But it wasn't Russian troops; it was Soviet troops."

Hal was puzzled by this comment. "What's the difference?"

Joey was happy to be the expert on something and explained. "After the Second World War, Russia controlled a lot of former European and Middle Eastern countries and had a dozen or so countries linked together in a 'Soviet Union', and they required men from all those countries to join their 'Soviet Army'."

"So, some of those soldiers in Hungary could have come from France?"

"No, Hal, France was not part of the Soviet Union. It included countries like Ukraine and Latvia, and it was soldiers from these places, and Russia, in the Soviet Army."

"Huh."

"Yeah, that might be something to ask the old guy," Joey said to Bella. "What does he know about where those soldiers were from?"

Bella stared at Joey, not writing down his suggestion until he said, "What?"

"We are not going to ask a highly specific question like that to a 15-year-old student at the time. Plus, it doesn't matter. Our project is to connect the event, that's the Revolution, to the culture and economics of the time."

Joey stared back. "Okay. What should we ask? How did the Revolution affect the culture of your town?"

Bella made an eye-roll before replying, "Well, yes, something like that but a little more subtle."

"How long were those students in the streets?" Hal wondered.

"Oh," Bella said, "that was all covered in that article I sent. The Prime Minister sent the police to shut down the protest and they shot guns at the crowd, and, of course, that made everything worse. In one day, the protest spread around the country. The Soviets thought they could cool things off by putting in a new Prime Minister, but the guy went along with the protestors and negotiated the leaving of the Soviet Army from the country."

"Wow," said Hal. "That sounds like a win."

"And then the Prime Minister tried to leave the Warsaw Pact, so the Soviets went in with tanks and put the revolution down."

Hal was interested in her explanation and asked, "What's this Warsaw Pack?"

"Pact," Bella answered, emphasizing the 't' at the end. "It was what the Russians wanted to balance NATO."

Hal nodded, making a mental note to look up this NATO thing.

Joey asked, "Any idea why the Prime Minister did such a crazy thing?"

"Yes," Bella replied, acutely aware that only she had read the material she had gathered and circulated. "The Prime Minister thought he could get support from the United Nations and countries in Europe like France and Germany and, most important, from the Americans." Her choppy speech drew both young men's attention to what she was inferring.

"Hah!" Hal exclaimed. "We can ask the old guy why he didn't join the army right then."

Bella said, "He was 15, Hal."

"Oh. Well, still."

"I agree that's a good area to probe. 'What were the attitudes of people in your town about whether the United States should support the Revolution?' "

Joey nodded and said, "That's a good start, and we should see why people thought different things. We can probably tie that to culture and economics somehow, right?"

"Wait," said Hal. "Did we go help the Hungarians? Americans, I mean."

"No," said Joey and Bella together. She added, "That's another area we can probe with the old … with Mr. Dell."

"Why not? I mean, we're the good guys aren't we?" Hal asked.

Joey looked at Hal with new insight. He thought to himself how difficult it was going to be for Hal to read a newspaper every day. Joey said, "That's another very good item to ask the old guy."

Bella quickly wrote that in her notebook. They talked and suggested and argued and rated each other's ideas for another hour, ending with five superior questions and six secondary ones. Each of them agreed to take a couple of the highest ranked questions, with Hal taking only one. Bella insisted that they should study their question and be prepared to ask a follow-up question. Their discussion earlier had emphasized concern with Walt's tendency to stray from the initial answer and they wanted to keep him on track.

Fully prepared for their next interview and full of Mrs. Henderson's cookies, they separated.

# CHAPTER 11

## 10/01/2019  TUESDAY

Walter Dell, 83 years old, had lost some height since his youth and was now only five foot nine inches tall, and, he was stooped in addition, which made him appear even shorter. But he weighed only 179 pounds and had a very modest waistline increase, less than the average for his age group. His head was covered with unruly white hair, a little too long on the sides and his jaw jutted out from his head, already extended by his spinal curvature. Walt didn't shave every day; white stubble often accentuated his chin.

He watched the three students slowly come up his front walk and he gave them a tight smile

"Mr. Dell? I'm Bella Henderson. I'm the one that called you about an interview."

Walt nodded at these words, but sat still in his rocker. The students stood at the bottom step, somewhat unsure of their next step. Walt sat in the rocker, as he did most afternoons, drinking coffee and staring at the sunset.

After a few uncomfortable moments, Walt addressed the girl. "Are you going to talk to me from down there?"

"Ah, no, sir. May we come up?"

"Of course, of course."

Two other chairs, both straight-backs, were on the other side of a small table from Walt. He indicated the students should sit for the interview. The girl took one and the tall blond kid the other. That left the short Black boy to sit on the top step.

"Like I said, sir, my name is Bella Henderson and this is Joseph Symes and Harold Bingham."

Walt nodded at each as their name was mentioned.

Bella cleared her throat and said, "I told you on the telephone about our project. We are assigned to learn how a historical event was affected by the culture of the time."

"And I am to be your historical observer, eh?" Walt asked with an uncommitted look on his face.

"Ah, well, I guess that's right," Bella said.

"And do your accomplices have a speaking role in this interview?"

Both young men looked somewhat surprised and sat up a little more straight. Joey answered, "Uh, yes, sir. Each of us are interested in your memories and have questions for you."

Walt nodded, thinking to himself that the blond boy's answer was fakery and made simply to preserve face. He moved his attention to other boy, sitting on the top step and leaning against a porch column.

Hal looked at Walt directly and said, "Well, it's a team project so …, you know."

Walt recognized the honesty of the answer and looked back at Bella. "How long is this going to take, Bella?"

Somewhat surprised at the use of her name, Bella responded, "Uh, we thought we might need to meet with you two or three times to get the information we need for the project."

"I see. Is that because you think it will take that long for me to remember things from way back in my childhood?"

Each of the students looked at him with a shocked look on their face. Joey spoke first. "Uh, no, that's not why. We will need to meet and talk over whatever we learn from you and that will raise some additional questions, that's all."

Walt looked at them solemnly for several seconds and then said with a straight face. "It may take much longer than that if your sense of humor is so absent you don't know when I'm pulling your leg." When he grinned at them, all three students let out their breath and smiled.

"How long are you planning on staying, then?" Walt turned back to Bella for an answer.

"Ah, we can only stay for an hour. Hal has football practice and I have basketball."

"Well, well. A little athletic club, eh? And what sport do you play, Joseph?"

"I'm on the basketball team, sir."

"Good thing with that height."

"Yes, sir."

The conversation died at that point. Everyone looked at Bella, Walt leaned back in his chair and took a swallow of his coffee. Bella said, "Uh, sir, Mr. Dell, we can only come to see you on Tuesdays, and those are the days we have practice. So we can only stay an hour. If that's all right with you."

Walt scratched his chin and thought about what she said. *They were being very careful about getting too involved with an old man*, he thought. They picked a day they can only stay for an hour. No long entanglements and a perfect reason for getting up and leaving. That was actually smart. But he was not going to let them know he was on to their plans.

Walt nodded and said, "Yep, that will work. My Tuesdays are pretty clear. I will note it in my calendar."

Bella cleared her throat, "We can't come every Tuesday. I mean we have other class work to do and we will have to get together to discuss our findings after every meeting. So we were hoping we could arrange for us to meet maybe every other Tuesday."

"Starting today, then?"

"Yes, sir. If that's all right."

Walt knew they were not interested in much that he had to say. But he wasn't surprised. At their age he had very little interest in comments or advice from his elders. They wanted to ask a general question and get a useful, quite specific answer they could use from him and be done with the interview. Walt did not intend to play their game. But he maintained his smile and nodded again to agree with their schedule; he winked at Hal.

Bella said, "We discussed our topic with Ms. Postella. I think you know her." Walt nodded as Bella continued, "She agreed we should talk with you about the Hungarian Revolution. Do you remember that?"

Walt tried to maintain a look of dispassionate interest but almost laughed at their choice of historical event choice. Sandra must have had a hand in that choice, or in sending them to talk with him about it. He had some quick memories flitting across his brain of the discussions at their dinner table involving Sandra and Maddy, his wife. The Revolution was one of those intense topics the three of them never really resolved among themselves. Now Sandra arranged for him to 'advise' these young students about those distant events. Walt wondered how she was going to grade their effort and whether his opinion would get them in trouble..

He nodded a positive response to Bella's question. "Yes. I recall that."

Joey pressed the point, "What did you and others think about it, then?"

Walt smiled and said, 'Well, son. You can't quite grab hold of other people's feelings about things like that without knowing their background and their raising."

"Maybe you could tell us how many people …"

"Nope. Can't do that right off the bat like that. People did have different opinions and some of them changed. But I bet Ms. Postella wants a little more depth in your report than just numbers, right? She definitely wants you to understand the times."

Joey wilted under the steady gaze from beneath those grizzled bushy white eyebrows. He looked down and nodded. "Yeah, she does," he agreed. Walt could see Hal from the corner of his eye and saw that young man slump as his partner gave in.

Walt said, "I guess you know that Revolution happened in 1956, Right before Christmas. Nineteen-fifty-six was not that long after America had fought a major war both in Europe and the Pacific. Lots of people had personal memories about war and particularly about soldiers who did not come back home."

The students sat quietly as Walt talked. He spoke softly but clearly. He did not ramble and he did not talk quickly. Over the next thirty minutes or so, he quietly sketched the reality of small town America and its 'awareness' of war and its lingering consequences. He explained how people felt when a certain pew was empty on Sundays or how odd it seemed that certain young men were not available to help at the grocery store or the filling station. These missing were young men known to the people of the town who were aware of their absence, not as closely as did their families, of course. There were a few, of course, that did return. Some stayed in Europe or Japan. But far too many would never come home. And no one in town knew how to say anything about it.

He mentioned how people visited the cemetery more frequently, leaving flowers and messages at gravestones labeled 'PFC. Killed in action. France 1943." Sometimes people could close their eyes and not see the absent young men. But when they opened their eyes, they saw the ones with missing limbs or prosthetic feet and they were reminded again that no matter how far away a war occurs, it has an impact on small town America.

Walt had just started talking about the rationing of foodstuffs that occurred during the war when Bella held up her hand. "Yes, Bella, what is it?" Walt inquired.

"Uh, we've got to go. Out time is up, you know."

"I see. Are you planning to return in two weeks, then?"

"Yes, sir," they all said, hurrying down the steps and down the walk.

"Good," Walt called after them. "Then I can finish telling you about how the wars affected my little town." He watched them scurry away and smiled a little to himself. Sandra would not let them fail to return. And if they were going to stick it out, there was so much more they needed to hear.

Sandra had sent other students in years past and they didn't want to hear the story. This girl, what's her name? Bella. She's faking interest, at least. The two boys seem not only less interested but incapable of faking it. I bet she's a linear thinker, Walt thought. And at least one of those boys is a visual thinker.

Walt went back into the house for another cup of coffee, thinking that this group would be no different than the others.

# CHAPTER 12



After the students left, Walt went to his kitchen and turned on the flame under the water kettle. He rummaged around in the cabinet and brought out a small foil package of Guatemalan coffee someone had gifted him the Christmas before. While the pot was heating up, he found his Chambourd French Press, sat it on the edge of the stovetop. When he could hear water bubbles forming in the kettle, he poured some into the French press and returned the pot to the stove. Then he sat down at the kitchen table and stared out the window.

Walt had known Sandra Postella a long time, and he was certain she sent these students to him because of a conversation he and Sandra had at that very table many years before. Sandra appeared for dinner at their house often in those first few years she was teaching. Walt remembered how his wife, Madeline, had taken the young woman under her wing, even beyond the formal year of 'observation'. Madeline was a dedicated teacher, with very sharp skills in handling 7th and 8th-grade students. Those skills were not always transmitted to the student teachers she mentored, but Sandra grasped them and made those skills her own, and Maddy appreciated that.

The water kettle began to whistle, and Walt pulled it from the flame, turned off the burner, and sat back down. He remembered how much Maddy enjoyed the conversations over dinner with Sandra. They talked more about the mechanics of teaching than about any subject matter. Their interest was in what 'worked', what got the students interested and invested in learning. And they enjoyed hearing about each other's different successes.

Walt took the press to the sink and poured out the water, then spooned in several teaspoons of the coarsely ground Guatemalan beans. He poured some water from the kettle to cover the grounds, then he stood staring at the now submerged grounds. At the magic moment in his mind when all was right, he filled the container with water, stirred it once, placed the filter and top on it, and put it on the edge of the stovetop.

Walt went to the refrigerator and extracted a small container of half-and-half and a partially empty tin of cookies. He sat back down and thought about that particular night when Sandra brought up the Hungarian Revolution, and Maddy had started to laugh. Remembering her laugh brought both some pleasure to Walt's mind and some warmth to his ears as he still blushed to remember his response that night. Sandra was telling how some of her students were agitated about the events of the Revolution, especially the first few days, and were talking about how they would have gone over there to fight when Maddy couldn't contain herself and started laughing out loud, and pointing at Walt.

Walt glanced at the press and determined it had steeped sufficiently. He slowly pressed on the filter, pushing it to the bottom over about 45 seconds. Then he grabbed his large mug from the cabinet and filled it briefly with more water from the kettle to warm it up, then dumped that in the sink.

Walt slowly decanted the contents of the press into his now-warmed cup, halting near the top with just enough room for a tablespoon or so of half-and-half. Then he grabbed the tin of cookies, his cup and went back out on the porch.

He took his seat and looked out at the gathering dusk, realizing that the shortening of days was happening again, his own like those of the calendar. He took a bite of cookie and a sip of the coffee and wondered what he had been thinking about. Maddy's laugh came back to him, and he recalled the discussion that night. Sandra had been so proud of her students for wanting to go join the Hungarian Revolution that Maddy had to interrupt to tell her how Walt had been exactly the same. Except he was in high school when the Revolution occurred and had been very angry that America and American troops had not gone to the aid of those students. Sandra wanted Walt to explain his feelings so she could understand her students better, but Walt was not willing to do so. That time was embarrassing for him, and he was irritated that Maddy had brought it up in front of someone outside the family. As Walt looked back on that evening's discussion, he was again embarrassed by how he had acted. He had refused to explain his thinking at the time but did note quite emphatically that his opinion was quite different when he and Maddy married. Walt remembered that she giggled her agreement with that statement. He also thought both women were making fun of his militant thoughts of young manhood. He had rejected dessert and left the table.

Sipping his coffee and watching the horizon darken, Walt was still embarrassed by his behavior that evening. He guessed he always would be. Then he thought of how his meeting with the students had gone just a short time before. He wanted them informed of the nation's grief and attitude toward war, at least in a general sense. He knew he would have to make the story more specific to get across the point that Sandra would want them to learn. Walt knew he would have to relive his youth at that time, that he would have to recall some, perhaps many, of the painful memories from the 1950s back in Whealton, Montana.

His cup was about half empty when he came to that realization, and he stopped with that cup halfway to his mouth. Whealton, he thought. How long has it been since I even thought about that little place? Or the people there? How will I ever be able to convey a sense of that place to these students Sandra has sent to me if I can't recall the people, and places, and events of that time for myself?

Walt sat quietly for several minutes and his coffee got cold. But during that time he decided to consciously put his mind to the task of remembering. Remembering Whealton, the small little burg of 3000 people in Northern Montana, where he began to learn both the English language and the American way of life. The language was difficult enough and compounded by the profuse use of idioms by his peers. He knew he would never have made it through English classes without help from his buddies, Andy Steward and Charlie Tatum. And, of course, Jan Berryman. Walt knew much of his recall of that time would proceed through the memories of those three friends and their adventures together. But, even as that reality became clear, Walt began to feel a cold, sinking feeling of dread deep in his stomach. He knew he didn't want to think too deeply about those times and events; some things would be too painful, would cause too much heartache, too much fear. He determined that his recollection of those bad times and things would not get his attention; he would steer clear of them, and when these students were finished and had left, he would not think of them again. *I ran away from my actions and these memories once and I can do it again.*

To seal that deal with his conscience, Walt downed the last of his cold coffee and set some mental parameters for further discussions with Sandra's students: he would tell them about Whealton and some, but not all, of the people who lived there in the 1950s. He closed his eyes, leaned back in his chair, and tried to reconstruct his small town of Whealton. He visualized the plain two-street intersection on Highway 117 that comprised 'downtown' Whealton and was able to retrace his usual path from the drugstore to his home barely four blocks away. A vision of the school building came into view, a two-story central building for the high school with one-story wings for the elementary and junior high classes. Walt thought he could see the ball field behind the school with the ten-level bleachers on only one side. He tried to pull back his vision but instead discovered he was looking at the homes of Charlie and Andy and Jan. They were actually scattered several blocks apart, Jan's was on the outskirts of town, but somehow his vision of them placed each of them on the same block.

Walt's vision jumped suddenly to the outskirts where the main road ran north toward Highway 2. He saw the small truck gardens where he and his father grew vegetables, the dirt tilled and appearing ready for planting. And his line of sight quickly included the small back road heading away from the highway and ending in an angled descent to the Missouri River downstream from the dam. He could hear old man Hutchinson saying, "That ain't a river, it's barely a crick." But the water was deep enough to swim in, and a sandbar protruded into a bend of the river that allowed for picnics and such. Walt thought about the puzzling Milk River joining the Missouri farther downstream. Lewis and Clark had named the river for its color like milk tea. The color came from suspended clay and silt coming all the way from Canada.

Most of the visions Walt saw were either neutral or comforting, although he did feel anxious about the sandbar. He pulled away from that image and looked northward, toward the vast open prairie that extended to Canada. And that was when his anxiety increased, heart beginning to race, breath coming short, and he opened his eyes and willed the mental picture of Whealton and surroundings away. Walt automatically grabbed his coffee and found the cup empty, so he sat still and waited for the anxiety to ebb away. When it had, he thought about other, disconnected recollections of Whealton; snow figured prominently in those mental events, incredibly cold weather, and a north wind that could pierce any and all layers of clothing. He also thought of days he worked without a shirt, sweating in the garden, or mowing lawns in ninety-degree heat.

Walt knew these present-day students, reading some cold history, would have difficulty grasping the culture and the times. He realized when he was their age, he didn't appreciate the differences in people's beliefs and attitudes very well. Walt scratched his head and wondered if it were even possible for Bella, Joseph, or Harold to understand the mixed reaction to the breaking story of the Hungarian Revolution in the Whealton population some sixty-plus years ago. He also realized that, unknowingly, Sandra had involved him in an effort of remembrance that included some dangerous steps for him. Walt had long known that he needed to resolve some issues from that time; now, Sandra's intervention seemed to be the catalyst to starting that task.

Walt wasn't sure whether he should thank her or curse her.

# CHAPTER 13



Bella explained, "Look, we have to talk to him about this stuff. We have got to get this information into our project for a decent grade. You both know that. So, why are you so burned up?"

"I don't know," Joey admitted. "I'm just uncomfortable around him."

Bella looked at Hal, who shrugged and said, "Me too. I mean that place of his is kinda weird, isn't it? Out there by itself and all."

Bella was exasperated at them. "You are just making stuff up. It's not like he could be a serial killer or anything. Ms. Postella has known him for years, and she says he's a good guy."

Joey frowned at Bella, "And you know this how?"

"She told me, that first day when she gave us his name."

"But you didn't tell us, Belle. Why not?" Joey reverted to Bella's childhood nickname that he knew would irritate her.

"Because I didn't think it would matter, that's why, Mr. K.I.A.," Bella bit back at him. Hal was not interested in the disclosure about Mr. Dell's friendship with Ms. Postella, but he wanted to know about the name-calling.

"What's the K.I.A.?"

"Joey's nickname since the fourth grade," Bella said.

"Cut it out," Joey said, turning away.

"What's it mean?" Hal persisted. Bella said, still staring at Joey. "He always knows what anybody should do or say in any situation. And he has the answer to any question, right, Joey? Mr. Know It All?"

"I said, cut it out."

"No, you are the one that has to change this time. We are a team, and if you don't pull your weight, other people will be affected. And one of them is me. So, I won't 'cut it out'. I intend to push us to get the information we need for an outstanding project." She almost stamped her foot, and her fierce stare made both boys cautious about saying anything in response.

After several minutes of uncomfortable silence, Bella said, "As I mentioned, we have to talk to this old guy. And we are going to do it as a team. We have already set things up so we don't have to worry about getting away. We chose a day when we have practice so we can't stay more than an hour. If we get him to focus on our questions, we can get his data in the next couple of visits."

Hal said, "I'll go with you, Bella. I kinda feel like he's judging me. So, don't ask me to do much with the questions and all. But, I promise to listen and help you write the project."

"All right," she said. Then, turning to Joey, she asked, "Can you at least do the same?"

Following a brief pause, Joey nodded, but added, "But, we have to make him stay on topic, you know. We ask a question, and he wants to give us the background on everyone in town. We've got to channel him better, Bella. And you're the one to do that."

"Maybe so," she agreed, "but I need help from both of you. Follow-up questions to things he says that will move the conversation back on the topic would help."

Hal asked, "Can't we just get a few questions that will get us what we need? If we can push him to answer those, we can let him ramble a little on some others, right?"

Bella and Joey exchanged looks and nodded. She said, "Let's get those important questions down on paper, and I'll try to think of ways to reword them if he doesn't come right out with answers."

Thus directed, and fueled by Mrs. Henderson's cookies, they redirected their energy and focus to constructing Bella's list.

Half an hour later, Joey looked up and asked, "Did Postella tell you where the old guy was in high school? It's gonna be weird if it was here in Springfield."

"She didn't say."

Hal said, "But his wife was like her monitor or something, right?"

Joey sniffed at Hal, "Her mentor, Hal. That's a teacher for a teacher."

"Yeah, okay. But what's the difference anyway?"

Bella didn't raise her head but answered the question, "A teacher teaches you facts, a monitor checks that you did that, and a mentor teaches you how to teach."

"Oh great," Joey moaned. "It just dawned on me. Postella has assigned us to her mentor's husband. He's gonna try to mentor us and we want him to teach us some facts for the project. We gotta figure some way to get to what we need quickly."

Hal agreed, "I think you're right, Joey. And, let me tell you, sitting on that top step is not comfortable. I can't take that for a long time."

Bella raised her head and commented, "Look if we don't get most of what we want this next week, I'll ask him if we can sit indoors, okay?"

The boys nodded, but when Bella bent over her work again they each rolled their eyes. When they finished that afternoon, Bella had developed a short script for their next meeting with Walt Dell. Each of them had an assigned question and a follow-up question and knew that clear answers would move them very close to what they needed for an outstanding project.

# CHAPTER 14

## 10/15/2019 TUESDAY

Bella started up the walk to Walt's house but turned and spoke to the young men following her. "Remember, try to keep him on topic. And remember your questions. I don't want to be the only one talking in there."

"Gotcha," Joey said.

Hal nodded.

As they approached the house, they noticed that Walt was not sitting on the porch, as he had been the last time they came. Bella slowed her approach and only had her foot on the bottom step of the porch when the front door opened, and Walt stuck out his head.

"Hello," he said warmly. "Welcome back. Come right on in." he opened the door widely and gestured.

The three students dutifully tramped up the steps and into the house. They entered directly into the front room, each expected a dreary interior, but were surprised to be in a brightly lit area, with yellow walls, open curtains, and with white bookcases everywhere. The bookcases were filled with books, filed not in the sense of a library, upright with vertical binding, but lying on their sides and stacked up toward the next higher shelf. All the titles were easily readable in this manner, the colors of the covers vivid against the white background.

They stopped just inside the doorway and looked around, stock still.

Walt said, "Come on in, then. I've made cookies and some lemonade. Wasn't sure what you would want."

He noted that they turned toward him at the sound of his voice and looked as if they were unsure of their surroundings. He smiled and said, "I didn't think you were all that comfortable out on the porch last time. And I thought if you were coming, there should be refreshments." He gestured toward the front of the room, and they noticed a two-seat love seat and some armchairs arranged around a low coffee table. On the coffee table were two plates of cookies, one chocolate chip, and the other peanut butter. There was also a large glass pitcher of lemonade and several glass tumblers and coasters.

Walt gestured for them to take a seat, and they quietly moved to the love seat and chairs. Walt seated himself opposite the love seat and picked up a tumbler, "Who would like some lemonade?" he asked, glancing at each of them.

In short order, everyone, Walt included, had a glass of lemonade in front of them, resting neatly on one of the coasters. Everyone but Bella also had a cookie. Bella sat up straight on the front of the cushion of the love seat, looked directly at Walt, and said, "I hope you recall that Ms. Postella sent us to get your impressions of the impact that the Hungarian Revolution had on the people you knew at the time."

"Oh, yes, I definitely remember that," Walt agreed.

"The last time we were here, you told us that we needed to understand how people would respond because that time was so close to the end of World War Two."

"That's right. The war was constantly in everyone's mind at that time ..."

"We understand that, sir," Bella said, interrupting him. "We would like to hear how people responded and their opinions."

"Uh-huh," Walt said. He slowly nodded and took a bite of the cookie he was holding. "Well, I guess I did give you a heavy dose of the war fatigue related to that big war," Walt went on. "But I think you have to understand there were two other factors, both related to each other, that also caused people to think hard about American involvement in Hungary at the time'"

"Two other things?" Hal asked. Bella swung around to stare at him, willing him to remember they had agreed not to encourage the old man with follow-up questions to his ramblings.

"That's right, Harold, two other factors and both were big ones."

Walt paused, and the three students stared at him. Walt could tell they wanted both to ask 'what factors?' and to skip over his lead and get the answers they came for. He let the silence drag on a bit and then said, "Of course, if you just want the shallow picture, I can do that, too." He sat back in his chair and gazed upward as if struggling to remember something.

Bella sighed and said, "I'm sure Ms. Postella is anticipating that you will give us the big - and deep - picture of the times." Then she grabbed two cookies and leaned back in the love seat next to Joey, who gave her a sidelong glance.

"Well then, you probably know this, but let me remind you that when the Soviet Army rolled into Hungary, the United States was already fighting a war."

He could tell from their look of surprise that this information was new to them, so Walt backtracked a little and asked, "What do you know about Korea?"

The boys looked quickly at each other, eyes wide. Bella looked down at her notes. No one spoke.

"Okay," Walt said soothingly, "this wasn't supposed to be a test. How about I tell you about Korea?"

Each student nodded and sat back against the cushion of their seat.

Walt took a long drink of his lemonade and put his hands together to crack his knuckles, then said, "You see, after that big war, Korea the country ended up divided into two parts. The Northern part was connected to China and was Communist, and the South was a democratic republic. But in the middle of 1950, the North Korean Army invaded the south ..."

"Why did they do that?" Joey blurted out.

"Well, there's still some controversy about that, but most people then, and now, think they were put up to it by Stalin."

"Why?" Hal wondered aloud.

"Now see," Walt said pointing at each of the boys, "these are very good questions. I must tell you, those same questions puzzled a lot of folks at the time. Most now think Stalin was testing the new president of the United States. Wanted to see what Truman would do. He had only been President since April and this happened in June."

"And …" Joey's question lingered.

"And President Truman responded by sending troops and getting other countries involved in pushing the North Koreans back into their own country. But along the way, Communist China got involved, and there were some major battles, and some more of our soldiers were killed or wounded." He let that thought hang in the air for a bit.

Hal jumped in, "But that war is over, isn't it?"

Walt nodded but said, "Funny thing, and this bothers a lot of people even today. We were never in a legally defined war. Congress never declared war and the whole shebang goes down in history as the 'Korean Conflict'. But we still had men, and boys, that died over there, and everyone knew about it."

"When did it end?" Bella asked.

"Technically, it never did. We have been in a stalemate and an armistice since mid-1953. And the north keeps rattling their sabers and menacing the south, so ever since the mid-1950s, people have had the threat of another hot, shooting war over in Asia hanging over their heads. And recently that threat has included nuclear war."

Joey raised his hand and asked, "Did that have anything to do with Vietnam?"

Before Walt could do more than nod his head, however, Bella jumped into the conversation and said, "Remember we need to understand about the Hungarian Revolution."

Walt nodded and smiled at her. Hal jumped in and said, "Wait. You told us there were two issues." Bella's glare at Hal was poorly concealed.

Walt smiled at him and said, "That's right. And the second one affected people's attitude toward Korea and Hungary even more than the risk of a shooting war."

Another short pause occurred while Walt took another drink. Bella said impatiently, "And what was that, Mr. Dell?"

"Communism," he said, grabbing another cookie.

The students looked at each other, puzzled.

"Oh, yeah. " Walt repeated. "Truman was determined to keep communism bottled up in Russia and China and not let them gobble up their neighbors. America hated communism because it looked like an economic system that would destroy our country and freedoms. For a while after the war there were some people - including major newspapers - that praised communism as a 'better way to govern', but by the 1950's Truman knew it was a godless system that had killed millions of people and he was dead set to prevent its spread. The American foreign policy became 'contain communism at home and abroad'."

"That's why Korea, but then why not Hungary?" Hal asked.

"Again with the great question, young man. Therein lies a thorny reality and …"

"And we are out of time again, Mr. Dell," Bells said, grabbing her notebook and standing. "Thank you for your time - and the refreshments."

The boys stood, too, and started moving toward the door.

Walt got up and got to the door before them, opening it and nodding at them as they left. "See you in two weeks," he said, and the students nodded.

As they went down the walk, Hal and Joey were discussing something. Bella walked without paying any attention to either of them.

Walt closed the door and returned the remaining cookies and lemonade back to the kitchen.

# CHAPTER 15

## 10/15/2019 TUESDAY

Walt stood in the kitchen for a few moments, rubbing his face with both hands, thinking about his conversation with Postella's students. He had talked almost automatically about the political scene and the concerns regarding Communism and extended war. He had kept talking to prevent other thoughts from intruding into his presentation. He allowed himself to think about those things as he turned to the ritual of preparing his coffee.

Once he was safely seated on the porch with freshly prepared coffee and the remainder of the peanut butter cookies, Walt allowed his recall to flourish. Among his prominent memories of his high school time, after the Korean Armistice, was the philosophic discussions he had with his close friends, usually at dusk, while lying on the grass and staring at the stars.

As Walt thought about his friends, he realized there were similarities between them and the three students that Sandra had directed to his door. He did not recall discussing his high school friendships with Sandra; maybe the resemblances were the result of some cosmic parallelism that clustered young people by an invisible inner sameness. Walt could certainly see some characteristics of Harold in his friend Andy.

Andy Steward was somewhat shorter than Harold, Walt thought, but built almost identically. Squarish of body and of head, Andy played football and was a steady 'B' student. Unlike what he had seen of Harold, so far at least, Andy was outspoken, and that was an understatement. Andy's indoor voice projected at least a block in every direction; Walt and Charlie were continually reminding him their discussion was not intended for everyone in town to hear. Andy was gregarious, talked with everybody and was always able to keep their small group up to date on all the gossip in town. In some mysterious fashion, Andy's blond crew-cut hair never seemed to change; he never mentioned getting it cut and it never appeared long.

Walt tried to remember what happened to Andy. They were in the same grade and graduated together. He remembered at least one of their 'Philosophy Group' sessions after graduation but not exactly what Andy had said about his future plans. The Philosophy Group sessions had no set address, usually occurring in the freshly mown lawn of one of their family's back yard or in front of the school. Walt sipped coffee and munched on a cookie trying to remember that last conversation. Instead, he recollected an undated conversation where Andy held forth on a topic and everyone in the group repeatedly shushed him. Andy's neighbor had a daughter two years older than Andy and she was a beauty. Although polite enough to Andy, she was not interested in his attentions and that hurt his feelings. This girl, Barbara Something-or-Other, was known to enjoy sunbathing in her back yard and Andy seemed determined to get a peek. He had tried over the past couple of years without success, as the Philosophy Group knew well from his stories. Barbara used some large cardboard carton partitions to shield her private space, frustrating Andy no end.

Walt also remembered how Charlie kept needling Andy about his failure in this regard. Charlie Tatum was six-foot-one in height, played center on the school basketball team and towered over the five-foot-six Andy. So, he would tease Andy about being too short to look over the cardboard barrier and too white to jump high enough to see over it. Charlie himself probably weighed about 150 pounds; in a game he was a fair shooter, decent rebounder and a lousy defender. But he was balanced about the team's lack of success, never complaining and always emotionally calm. That calmness was at some odds with his dark and always unruly hair atop a triangular head, small chin and nearly hairless face.

Remembering Charlie, Walt also pulled up the memory that Charlie was a year ahead of him and Andy, and was not present at that last meeting of the Philosophy Group. In fact, Walt recalled, he and Andy had talked about

Charlie and his absence. Andy had mentioned that Charlie had gone to the University of Montana after graduation and they had lost contact because his father, an engineer on the Fort Peck Dam construction project, had moved away after Charlie graduated.

Walt suddenly remembered more about Andy. Their discussion about Charlie and the University led to Andy mentioning his interest in going to Montana Teachers College. *Andy went off to become a teacher,* Walt thought, realizing that he had not thought about Andy and his post-high school life at all since leaving Whealton. Walt wondered, for about three seconds, why he hadn't been interested in what happened in Whealton or to his friends after leaving; then he recalled why and the hard knot in his stomach appeared again. The last cookie and the end of the coffee helped Walt to shift his thoughts and to partially relieve the knot, but not completely.

And, of course, the knot made Walt think of the third member of their Philosophy Group during their high school years: Jan Berryman. Jan, who resembled a pixie as a freshman, never taller than five foot-seven and 125 pounds. Memories of Jan flooded Walt's mind and caused the stomach knot to spin around. He focused on the memory of her as a freshman, lying on the grass with him and Charlie and Andy and thinking about existential questions. Walt easily recalled her oval face, engaging black eyes, tapered nose and that small mouth - until she laughed and it widened across her face. Jan was energetic back then, almost bouncy, and certainly 'tomboyish' that year. Walt remembered that Charlie had commented on how strange it seemed that Jan could lie with them on the grass for such long periods, calmly discussion the edge of the universe without bouncing to her feet and running off.

As he leaned back and allowed his memory to pull wisps of recollection into recognizable events in his mind, Walt thought of how odd it was that the four of them, Charlie, Andy, Walt and Jan, became more than friends over those years. They were almost confidants, aware of each other's thoughts and needs, never becoming competitors. Even after Charlie graduated and it was only the three of them, they still met and talked about deep feelings and thoughts, and life goals. Walt marveled briefly at how such a close-knot group could have passed the life-threshold of high school graduation and then completely lost contact - and interest - in each other.

But Walt hadn't lost interest in Jan. He remembered she was good student, all As and a few Bs. Clearly someone who could have succeeded in college. He also remembered that she had mentioned interest in a career as a psychologist because she had a distant cousin or something married to one. Walt wondered if she ever got to college and the knot in his stomach grew larger.

So, to relieve that knot, Walt consciously turned his thoughts away from Jan and the others. He tried to pull up thoughts about events they had discussed. There was the Hungarian Revolution, of course. But that was later. Early on the group had discussed other issues. What were those issues? And what had they decided? Walt considered it might take a second cup of coffee to get into those depths. Then he remembered Eisenhower.

For some reason, the Philosophy Group had spent more than a couple of sessions talking about the surprise announcement by the General of the Army that he would run for the presidency. And that he would run as a Republican! Walt thought of the public display that President Truman made at Ike's announcement. Truman had been expecting Ike to be a Democrat and had lauded him highly in every public offering; when Ike announced he was a Republican, Truman looked liked he wanted to eat his own tongue.

Walt also thought the election would be close because the Democrats ran Adlai Stevenson, famous as the UN Ambassador, an obviously intelligent man, even though one with a hole in the sole of his shoe! Walt almost laughed aloud as he thought of that.

The Philosophy Group had varying opinions about the fitness of each man for the job, plus considerable opinion about the 'rightness' of a five-star general becoming the civilian head of government. Walt recalled the history-based discussions about the variable successes of previous presidents who came to the office as successful generals. He also thought that the vote was split on Jackson, Johnson and Hayes. But the group was completely in favor of Ike, perhaps mirroring the feelings in their household and the probable voting pattern of their parents. Walt thought it more likely had to do with the degree of information, including some negative, about the earlier general/presidents that made a determining factor.

Walt felt the stomach knot dissolving and turned his thoughts to what he remembered about headlines and the Korean 'Conflict'. Although the conflict is now referred to as 'the Forgotten War', current-day headlines were graphic and not easily forgotten. Walt remembered seeing the movie 'The Steel Helmet' at some time in high school and thinking at that time how unfair war was and yet he began to think of enlistment. Walt's mind wandered and he thought of the television series MASH about medical care near the frontlines in Korea. Comparing that to 'the Steel Helmet' and the way the television series was made into a comedy had always puzzled Walt. Why would major armed conflicts with widespread death be considered fodder for a television comedy series? He realized he had never answered that question satisfactorily in his own mind.

Then Walt remembered taking Susie What-was-her-name out parking in his father's car on a bluff overlooking the river. He reclined in the chair and closed his eyes to facilitate memory. The pretense he used, like other boys in the high school, was telling Susie they were on 'submarine patrol', watching the river, in case Korean or Chinese submarines decided to attack Whealton and Fort Peck by water. In those days, all automobiles had bench front seats and 'submarine watching' usually involved sitting very close together and doing some hugging and kissing. But then everyone got home by curfew and the Fort and the Dam remained safe another day from foreign submarine forces.

Walt opened his eyes and began brushing cookie crumbs from his clothes. He got up and took his cup and the cookie tray back inside and to the kitchen. Thinking about the military questions concerning Korea, Missouri River submarines and generals in the White House had toggled another minor memory in his head. It involved a nice looking young man with a crew cut two years ahead of Walt in school; he played guard on the basketball team. His name was something that started with a 'C'. He graduated and Walt didn't know him or keep track of him until a year later when Life Magazine ran a cover story about West Point. Their cover picture was taken at a dress ball at the Point and prominently featured that crew cut Whealton graduate with a young lady dancing at the ball. The Whealton graduate had gained admission to West Point. That had definitely impressed Walt and again stirred some thoughts about enlisting.

# CHAPTER 16

## 10/18/2019  FRIDAY

This time Joey started the discussion.  "Have we gotten any information about the Revolution?" he asked rhetorically.

Hal said, "I think he's about ready to talk about that."

Bella was skeptical. "Oh, really?" she barked. "What is the clue that makes you think that, Sherlock?"

Hal answered, a little defensively, "Well, it just seems like he's told us about everything that was going on back then. Maybe he's run out of side issues."

"Maybe," Joey said, 'but maybe not either. Who knows what stories he's still got in his head. We have got to be more direct."

"Absolutely," Bella added.

"Okay," said Hal.

"Not 'Okay', pal. You kept winding him up with those follow up questions of yours."

"I said, okay. And I wasn't the only one asking questions that kept him going. You two did it, too."

Joey stopped whatever he was about to say and agreed, "You're right. So, let's all just agree to keep the old guy on the topic of the Hungarian Revolution, okay?"

# CHAPTER 17

## 10/29/2019 TUESDAY

Walt watched them come up the walk from his front window. He noted that their steps were trudging and their heads were down. They weren't talking to each other, either. He shook his head slightly, recognizing their attitude was a reflection of disappointment with their progress toward their goal. He also knew that he was at fault and before he opened the door, determined he was going to confront the issue.

Walt was smiling broadly, however, when he opened the door and ushered them into the living room. They entered quietly, not subdued, but with a purpose. They noted that this time the coffee table held a large platter of brownies and a pitcher of milk. Walt saw them look at each other and shrug their shoulders.

Bella took the same seat she had at the first visit and the boys followed suit. Walt indicated they should get a brownie and a glass of milk and that activity took the first few minutes. Walt had remained standing and when he thought they were somewhat settled he said, "I've been thinking about our discussions and I think they have not gone as you would like."

The students froze in position and cast sidelong glances at each other, unsure of how to respond. They, of course, agreed with him but were uncertain whether their opinion might lead to their loss of a source of information. They waited for him to continue.

"I'm pretty sure that bright kids like yourselves are aware that you can get on the Internet and find out all the pertinent facts about the Hungarian Revolution that you need to write a pretty good story about it," Walt said with a sly grin. The students each nodded briefly.

"And that just might do for most teachers, I would guess," Walt continued, encouraged by their agreement. "But Sandra Postella is a very different teacher. She's going to expect that you will drill beneath the surface of whatever Mr. Google could tell you about the facts of the Revolution. Am I right?"

Bella reluctantly nodded and the boys went along.

"So, I'm going to give you the inside story on the impact of the revolution in Mid-America. I'm going to see that you understand how people felt when they heard of the riots in the streets and why they acted - or didn't act - they way they did. I promise to give you all those stories and the insight to write the project that Ms. Postella wants from you. And I will also give you an inside look at a 50-year later perspective. How about that?"

Joey spoke first, but only because Bella had a brownie in her mouth. He said, "That would be terrific, Mr. Dell. That's really what we want."

Hal added, "Yeah, that would be great. We've been a little bummed that you were talking about other things and ..." He tapered off into silence.

Bella, stepped in, "Mr. Dell, we appreciate your time and willingness to talk with us about things. We were expecting to get your take on expectations and attitudes right from the beginning. We want to get to work on this project as soon as possible and not get caught up in the holidays."

Walt clapped his hands and sat down in the remaining chair, saying, "Well, I'm glad we are in some kind of agreement, here. But let me be clear. I'm about to tell you many more things about people and events before we get to the meat of what you want to know. It's not going to happen today. I don't think you, here in the first quarter of the twenty-first century can grasp why people did certain things seventy years ago without knowing more about them."

Hal asked, "Are you going to tell us war stories?"

"Not exactly. The men I knew didn't want to talk about it. Even when I asked them directly."

Hal grinned, "Sorta like what you're doing to us."

Walt grinned back, "Not exactly the same. But it likely appears that way."

Bella had opened her notebook and asked, "Well, what will we talk about today?"

Walt leaned back, let out a big sigh, and said, "Let's talk for a minute about who these people were. Most of the families in Whealton and throughout Northern Montana at that time were not native to that area. My own folks came from Ireland. Bet you didn't know that."

Joey looked puzzled. "What do you mean?"

"I mean, most of the families in that area were immigrants. There were a good number of Swedish families, some other Irish like us, fair number of Germans. All immigrant families."

"So what does that have to do with the story of the Revolution?" Joey persisted.

"Well, son, in my mind it has a lot to do with the reaction and the attitudes of those people. You came here weeks ago telling me that you were interested in how Americans reacted to the news of the Hungarian Revolution, right?"

Joey said, "I don't recall specifying 'Americans'?"

Walt looked at him with a sly grin and said, "I'd guess you are headed for a career in the law, Joseph?"

"I don't think so, sir. I'm actually more interested in Business and Finance. Why did you think I wanted to be a lawyer?"

"Because you were nit-picking my interpretation of your intent. No, I don't think any of you said you were interested in the attitudes and culture of 'Americans', but that's what you meant when you wanted to know about small town America, isn't it?"

Bella said, "Of course that's what we were thinking. And your point here is that …"

"That these people in my small town were not raised up American. They came from widely differing backgrounds and cultures of their own. So, you may have to factor into your project that some of them were exhibiting reactions of European origin, not 'American'."

All three students frowned and glanced quickly at each other. Bella spoke first, "Were you born in Ireland, Mr. Dell?"

"Yes. Yes, I was. Came with the family when I was about six. We came because my father couldn't get land to farm in Ireland but was offered fifty acres if we immigrated to Montana."

She smiled at him tight-lipped. "And did you and your family consider yourself Irish or American?"

Walt nodded at her, "Very good, lass, very good. My family, like most of the immigrants that settled in Montana, came through Ellis Island."

"Where's that?" Hal wanted to know.

"It's an island in New York harbor. For a long time it was the official entry point for immigrants who wanted to become American. Most of the time, the naturalization process happened right there, as soon as you got off the boat. My family left Ellis Island for Montana as naturalized American citizens the same day we disembarked."

"Wow. I didn't know that," Joey said. "Are we still doing that?"

Walt made a lop-sided grin and said, "No, Joseph, the process is much more complicated now. And a lot of people come here to visit or for school and not for the primary purpose of becoming a citizen."

Bella said, "Well, if that were true for most of the immigrants in Whealton, then they were 'Americans', right?"

Walt grinned widely and answered her, "Absolutely correct, Miss Bella, they, we, were all first generation Americans. But my point is, most of us had not been raised in this country and did not have the background or personal history connecting us to the history of the country. We were labeled 'American' but we lacked a common language. I mean, my family spoke 'English' and we couldn't be understood by native English-speakers."

"That must have been a mess," offered Hal.

"Oh, it was, lad. But we weren't alone. And since there were so many having difficulty, the school in Whealton started a night class to teach English. Most everybody got up to speed within a few months."

Bella again asked, "And how does this affect our project?"

"Well, think about it. The Germans might have a basic prejudice against Hungarians. The Irish might be so tired of fighting with the British that they couldn't stomach another shooting war. People of different backgrounds might well bring very opposing views to the same question. That's how this pertains to you and all of us here in the early twenty-first century."

The three students nodded sagely. Bella checked her watch. Walt noted the movement and said, "So, let me tell you about how that diverse group of first-generation Americans, from a variety of European nations, handled two American holidays: Memorial Day and Veterans Day."

Hal chimed in, asking, "Why those holidays?"

"Primarily because they are uniquely American, Harold. There is no carry-over for either of them from any similar celebration in Europe. What I want you to know is that every Memorial Day I can remember in Whealton, everyone took a holiday. Work stopped, parades occurred and families went to the two cemeteries, Protestant and Catholic, and put flowers on the graves of their family members who had died in the Great Wars. Speeches were made from the steps of the biggest local government building in town and nearly everyone attended. Frequently, fireworks displays were set up at dusk."

When he paused and looked at his audience, Joey spoke up, "Meaning that these immigrants were acting like Americans?"

Walt nodded, "Exactly, Joseph. Acting like patriotic Americans after being in the country for a very few years. And it was the same with Veterans Day."

Hal interrupted again. "What's the difference between those two anyway? I never really understood that."

Walt looked at Hal somberly and replied, "Memorial Day is to remember those who died in wartime in military service. Veterans Day is in honor of all who put on a uniform and served, wartime or not."

"Uh-huh," Hal offered.

Walt went on, "And my point is that these recent immigrants all knew someone who had done exactly that. Put on a uniform, picked up a weapon and went off to defend the nation's priorities. There were more speeches, big cookouts on the downtown square and everyone felt part of a nationwide party."

Joey pointed out, again, "Acting like real Americans!"

Hal said, "We kinda do some of that today, don't we?"

Walt laughed and said, "Well, they both are holidays still, mostly for mattress sales events, however. You have to look hard to find the speeches and the memorials."

Bella stood up, taking another brownie as she did. "Thank you, Mr. Dell. That was a good history lesson. I'm looking forward to learning how that ties into our project."

Walt made a wry grin, recognizing her sarcasm and ushered them to the door. With his hand on the door handle, Walt turned and asked, "What about the big holiday coming up? Are you dressing up and going out to collect candy?"

The students looked at each other and muffled their laugh, "Oh, no, sir. We're all too old for that. Halloween is for little kids," Bella said.

"Except for Joey," Hal said, pointing at Joey, who promptly blushed.

"I'm not dressing up and asking for candy, Hal, and you know it!" he said. "I'm providing Overwatch for my little brother. And that's all."

"And getting all his Butterfinger bars as payment, right?"

"Well, it only seems reasonable," Joey said, looking at Walt with a question in his eyes.

Walt nodded solemnly in agreement and smiled broadly, aware that the students were now comfortable making light-hearted fun in his presence.

He stood in the door as they exited and watched them till they reached the end of the walk, then closed the door and cleaned up the sitting area, smiling to himself.

# CHAPTER 18

## 10/29/2019 TUESDAY

Walt puttered about with his coffee that evening, forgetting to turn on the kettle and being surprised when he filled the French press with cold water. He was thinking about Halloween, and it was distracting him. He stopped what he was doing, looked out his kitchen window, and forced himself to think of something else.

The memory he came up with was connected to Halloween, but it involved Charlie Tatum and their attempt to steal watermelons from Mr. Herfindorf's farm just outside town. Once he was no longer distracted, Walt focused on preparing his coffee, grabbing a brownie, and moving on out to the porch.

Sitting and watching the sunset, Walt let his memory run with the recall of Charlie and the watermelons. The Herfindorf farm was well demarked on the road north to Highway 2; there was a thick growth of chokecherry bushes all along his property line. Chokecherries were common in Montana, their bright red berries attracting attention from all sorts of fowl during the summer. But the real fun came in September, about the same time that school started when it was time to harvest the cherries. Small, full of their single seed, clothed in dark purple colors, the cherries made excellent jelly. Charlie's grandmother used to send him and the other boys out to find bushes full of the fruit and she would make jelly jars for the neighborhood.

Old man Herfindorf did not allow his bushes to be harvested, however. No one was ever sure if he used any of the cherries from his boundary line; late in the fall, the ground under his bushes was littered with overripe fruit. He was the same way with his watermelons. He had two large garden plots in his front yard, one given over solely to the melons. He grew them for the market in town and often gave a few to the church for one of the fall potluck dinners.

One year, the three boys were discussing whether to get costumes for Halloween and considering dressing as ninjas. Then Charlie had the idea that the chokecherry bushes would give cover to pirate a watermelon apiece on a moonless night if they were dressed as ninjas. Walt remembered how they had giggled and laughed at the prospect and how they all managed to arrange for an overnight stay at Andy's because his bedroom was in the basement and he had a door they could sneak out. That night, dressed all in black, the three of them walked from Andy's out the highway to Herfindorf's and then crawled across the front of the property to get in position. Separated from the melon field only by the bushes, they began to squirm their way through the barricade.

All of their experience harvesting chokecherries in the wild had not prepared them for the dense closeness of the cultivated border bushes. They could not find an open path through the bushes large enough for them to pass through and had to return home defeated. Andy's rationalization of the night's failure was, "I don't think there was enough room in there to get one of them melons out, anyway." From then on, whenever someone suggested a hair-brained scheme, one of the others would say, "Or, we could go steal some watermelons."

As the oldest of the four, the others deferred to Charlie as the leader. Andy was a natural follower, but his role often was to say or do something odd or silly to make them laugh just before they started a dangerous or unlawful adventure. His comments usually made them desist and likely kept each of them from having a police record before graduation. Charlie would ask the odd question while the four of them lay in the grass watching the stars at night during the summer. One of his questions was, "What do you think is at the end of the universe?" And he followed that with, "And what's on the other side of that?"

By the time they were in seventh and eighth grade, they no longer went out trick-or-treating. Walt recalled the first year that they abstained and had a recollection that their discussion about costumes somehow never really occurred and how Charlie finally said he planned to stay home that Halloween to help hand out candy. That turned the tide; from then on, they did not participate in the candy game on Halloween.

High-schoolers, on the other hand, had their own tradition: a bonfire on the sandbar with some music and intermittent dancing. Many went as couples, but there were always some unattached boys and girls, especially in the younger grades. Walt's memory of one such event caused him to sigh, lean back in his chair, and close his eyes. It happened during their sophomore year in school. The four of them went together to the sandbar, and Walt had recently realized his interest in Jan was more than simply a friend in their group. He planned for several days how he would get with her on the sandbar and talk to her about being more than friends, whatever that might mean.

But, Walt remembered that his plan went awry from the outset, as he couldn't stay close to her walking from the car to the sandbar. Jan was skipping around, changing position in the group, and was impossible to keep up with. Once they arrived where the bonfire was located and found the other students, Jan disappeared, and Walt spent the next hour or so with his two friends, poking the fire and telling jokes. Later, when Walt got up to walk around, he noticed Jan lying with Billy Parks outside the circle of light from the fire. Their bodies entwined, they were totally engrossed in each other. The mental image of the two of them stuck in Walt's mind for years and came back to him on the porch. With that image came the feeling of hollowness in his chest and the sinking sensation in his stomach. He tried to stop thinking about the image, but only succeeded in pulling to the forefront his recollection of what the image meant to him at that time: Jan's opinion of him, Walt Dell, was as a friend but certainly not as a boyfriend. He thought he might cry, but instead moved away and counted all the couples enjoying each other outside the firelight. And that also made him sad.

Walt snapped his eyes open. "I can't be thinking about that again," he thought, forcing his mind away from the bonfire. He settled on thinking about one fall evening a month or so later when all four of them were again together. They were lying on the school lawn, watching the Northern Lights dancing above their heads. The famous Aurora Borealis that evening took on the appearance of a giant iridescent curtain of gray, blue, and blazing white waving in the sky. Charlie said, "I wish we had a movie camera to catch this."

After a brief silence, Andy said, "Or we could go steal some watermelons."

# CHAPTER 19

## 11/12/2019  TUESDAY

That Tuesday was cold. Fresh snow had fallen on four days of the previous week and the temperature had not risen above twenty degrees. Neighborhood kids had cleared Walt's sidewalk for him each time it snowed; he always rewarded them with some cookies, hot chocolate, and their twenty-five dollars. Walt was aware that school had not been closed so he was not surprised to see the students coming down the street toward his house at the appointed time.

He watched with interest as they skipped and hopped up the walk and lightly took the porch steps two at a time. That was so different from how they had approached the house that first day: slowly, heads down, almost unwilling to go forward. Instead of opening the door for them, he waited until they knocked and after they had stomped all the remaining snow off their boots.

"Come on in," he called in response to the knock and they burst through the door, shaking their heads and clapping their gloved hands.

"Whooiee," Hal said, "And I thought the weatherman said there was a chance of sunshine today."

Joey kicked off his galoshes and dropped his gloves on them, "At least there aren't any mosquitoes."

Walt smiled at their light-heartedness and said, "Come on over here. I've got the fire going, and I have hot chocolate."

They all hurried to get their heavy coats piled on the staircase or bannister and shuffled over to get in front of the fire."

Walt started pouring hot chocolate into cups and commented, "I wasn't certain you would be coming today."

Hal nodded and said, "Yeah, we considered not coming and going to the park to play some touch football."

Bella gave him a glance and said, "Oh no, we decided early in the day that we would come no matter what."

Walt poured himself a hot chocolate and pushed the tray of store-bought cookies toward her. "Well, I'm glad you're here. I couldn't drink all that hot chocolate by myself. What are the questions today? But first, can I get a report on the Trick or Treat business?" Walt asked this, looking at Joey.

"Ah, well. I guess it went well. I mean, it was okay."

"How many Butterfingers?"

"Oh, I see what you mean. Three. Only three, and they were the little ones. I really should have negotiated after we got home rather than before."

Walt nodded, "That was right after the first snow, wasn't it?"

"Oh yeah, and many of the sidewalks weren't cleared off yet, and it was colder than … ah, well, it was cold, and we didn't stay out very long."

"Well, you can have all the hot chocolate you want today."

"Thank you, sir. But would you first answer this question, "Can you tell us about the specifics of how people in town reacted to news about the Revolution?"

Walt looked at the other two students and noticed they were watching him closely. He figured they had talked beforehand and perhaps had chosen for Joseph to make the overture about specifics. Walt nodded in response to the question but continued to stall for a moment.

He reached for the cookie plate, picked out a chocolate one, leaned back in his chair took a bite and slowly started chewing. He gave the appearance of a man slowly contemplating a serious question. The reality was, Walt had become happy with the every other week intrusion of these kids into his home. He enjoyed their laughter and their maneuvering to get him to talk about his high school days. He even realized that, in the main, he enjoyed recalling some events and certain people's reactions to events, and he was reluctant to have their questioning end.

But, he knew that end was coming. They had a school deadline, and he couldn't drag this out any longer. Besides, if he cut off the memories now, he might not have the nightmares again.

Walt took a deep draught of his chocolate and said, "Well, truthfully Joseph, the specifics were very variable. You want to know how people reacted to hearing about a revolution happening in Europe just a few years after we had concluded a World-Wide War over there, right?"

Joey swallowed hard, looked Walt in the eye and said, "It's Joey, sir. Nobody calls me Joseph except my mother. And, yes sir, that's my question."

"Joey, then. I'll tell you and remind you, at that time I was a high school kid. I didn't sit around in the barbershop and chat with the men, and I didn't have a job on the construction site to listen to the conversation of the guys digging holes and pouring concrete. So, what I'm about to tell you comes from what I heard in two specific venues - my civics classroom and talking with some of my close friends after class."

"Okay."

"Will it be 'okay' with you two, then?" Walt asked, looking at Hal and Bella.

Hal nodded and said, "Hal. Never Harold."

 Bella nodded also.

Walt stood up, adjusted his sweater, and took a position behind the chair where he had been sitting. "The source, and it was mostly a secondary source, for the opinions of the towns people was my Civics class. That means about twenty-five students, more girls than boys. We were well-educated about the structure and functions of our government and the responsibilities of office-holders." He paused to look at each of them.

"I don't know whether you have had a class on civics or government or even a deep discussion of the Constitution and the Bill of Rights, but we had. And our teacher, Miss Wayle, was determined that this question of whether the United States should get involved in Hungary be thoroughly discussed in the classroom."

Walt paused to grab his cup and take a swallow. He found that his chocolate was now cold and not so tasty. He returned the cup to the table and began to sketch in the air the discourse as he recalled it.

"In my class, there were probably a third of us with family members who had served in the war. Uncles, older brothers, fathers. Most of them were Army soldiers in Europe, but two were sailors fighting Japan in the Pacific. For us in that classroom, everyone who went to war had come home, with one exception; the uncle of one boy in the class who was killed in Europe. The rest of the class had no personal experience with someone close to them in danger halfway around the world."

Walt looked at Bella and recognized the light in her eyes. Hal did not have that same look but was watching Walt intensely. Joey was looking at the other two students, perhaps to judge what his response should be.

Walt continued, "I said this was a secondary source, and I mean it's a secondary source as far as you are concerned. But much of what got said in the classroom was also secondary. Comments often began with, "As my dad told me…" from one of those with a veteran in the house.

"And I can tell you," Walt said firmly, "there was no consensus, anywhere. About half of the boys held an opinion we should help these college kids rebel against their government. The other half were hesitant to jump in so quickly, like the first day or two after the riots started.

"Even the girls were divided. More were against American intervention than for it, but even they said they would agree with going in if the revolution spread further.

"And the odd thing was the report from the absent veterans was that they, too, were split. Some of those who had been in Europe were familiar with the Russians and Communism, and they wanted the U.S. government to get into Hungary immediately; they were angry at any delay.

I remember one boy saying that his uncle, a veteran, was incensed at a photograph of Eisenhower playing golf when tanks were rolling down the streets of Budapest." Walt stopped speaking to put a fist against his chest and say, "And I felt that way, too."

Hal said, "But you were a veteran, too, weren't you?"

Walt grinned, "Yes, Harold, I was. Many years later."

Hal continued, "My Dad and I went to the VA Clinic last week for their Veterans Day Party."

Walt looked at Hal and asked, "Interesting. Why?"

"Dunno. I mean, you told us it was a holiday and all. But they were celebrating on Thursday, and that was on November 7."

"What did you see?" Bella asked, obviously unaware of this visit by Hal.

He answered, "They had some food set up, and there were a lot of guys in uniforms and funny hats and some speeches about military service."

Walt asked again, "Why did you go?"

"I asked my Dad if he'd ever been, and he said no, and we just decided to go. I learned something, though."

Walt nodded, still grinning at the young man. "What did you learn?"

"I learned we're supposed to say, 'Thank you for your service' to veterans when we see them."

"That's very good, Hal."

"So, thank you for your service, sir."

"You're very welcome, Hal."

In the ensuing pause, Bella looked at the two boys and, with their unspoken agreement, took the lead in asking, "So, there really wasn't a split of opinion by age or sex or military service? Is that right?"

Walt nodded and retook his seat. "Yes, that's right. Miss Wayle let this discussion take over our classroom time for several days. Everyone had the opportunity to discuss the issue at home and bring that discussion back for the whole class to hear. Lots of kids did that, too. We heard pacifism from the preacher's kid, arguments for immediate war against Russia, or the Soviet Union, for their indiscriminate actions of firing cannons into buildings and lots of other positions. There was no single position on either side and certainly no majority opinion."

Walt leaned back in his chair. He imagined his recounting of that classroom discussion was as unsatisfying to these students as it had been to him and his classmates. He watched as Bella furiously took notes, as Hal and Joey watched. No one seemed interested in the cookies anymore.

After a few minutes of quiet, Bella became aware that everyone was watching her scratch out notes. She stopped, raised her head and said, "Is that it?"

"Basically, yeah, that was it. The newspapers told the story of the attempt by the prime minister to leave the Soviet arena of influence and how the tanks crushed that idea and jailed lots of people, and then the whole thing just died. Churchill had already noted how the Soviets could shut off information using their 'Iron Curtain'. It really came down on this; within a week, local newspapers were on to other things. But some of us felt betrayed by our country for some time."

Hal asked, "But weren't you in the Army yourself? Why would you join if you felt betrayed?"

"That's a a very good question, Har … uh, Hal. But a much longer story and not relevant to your project. Let me say, I matured a good deal between the time of the Hungarian Revolution and when I enlisted."

"Huh. Okay," Hal said, unconvinced.

Bella stood up and said, "Well, out time is up, and we need to scurry off. We will be back in two weeks to see if there's anything else you can remember."

"All right, then," Walt said, walking to the door with them. He watched them quickly don their galoshes, coats and gloves, and wind their woolen scarves tightly around their neck, leaving a slightly loose portion in front where they could bury their nose. Then he opened the door and exchanged goodbyes with the muffled group as they scooted out the door, allowing him to close it quickly behind them.

Walt went to the front window and watched them down the sidewalk and turn toward the school. He shivered and moved to stand in front of the fire. He watched the flames and coals shifting in the fireplace and, remembering he hadn't been able to sit on the porch at sunset for along time, added two more logs and replaced the screen before taking the cups to the kitchen to fix his evening coffee.

# CHAPTER 20

## 11/12/2019 TUESDAY

Walt took his freshly made coffee back into the living room and sat where he could reach the plate of cookies he had left on the coffee table. His memories of the class discussions came even more clearly in his mind. Each student had an opinion, and Miss Wayle insisted it be voiced. She did not allow personal attacks, but she certainly encouraged vigorous dissent with any position taken.

Charlie and Jan were in that class, and Walt had difficulty remembering their positions on the question. Oddly, though, he remembered that Jan was wearing some burgundy colored corduroy pants and a yellow sweater. As he thought about it, Walt realized he remembered more about how tight her sweater was than about her attitude concerning the Revolution. On the other hand, he did recall Charlie standing by his desk and quoting Patrick Henry's speech to the convention of Virginians meeting to decide on actions to take against Britain in 1775.

Charlie said, "A famous man once stirred this country by saying 'Give me liberty or give me death' and America was forged. Now two hundred years later, we apparently say 'If they get liberty, that's okay.' But I say we should stand beside these brave young men and help them to gain that liberty!" Then, he sat down.

Walt thought the whole speech was contrived to mimic the mental picture of Patrick Henry's pronouncement, but it drew some scattered applause from the class. Walt wondered why he remembered that corny presentation at all. Probably because it was at the end of the week of discussion, and seemed to sum up a minority opinion.

Of course, all the opinions were minority, just as he had explained to Bella and the boys. Almost immediately upon recalling Charlie's impassioned speech, Walt remembered the class discussion just days later when the Soviet tanks rolled into Budapest and began indiscriminately blowing down buildings and shooting protestors in the streets. Student dialogue then devolved into various permutations of 'I told you so' from all sides.

Those who argued for American intervention claimed that if Eisenhower had only followed their advice, the slaughter of innocents would not have happened, and liberty and freedom would be established in Hungary. On the other side, the 'hands off' crowd was emphatic about the terrible consequences certain to occur if the Soviet tanks had encountered American troops or armor. Just as before the Soviet invasion, everyone held tightly to their belief and scenario of the 'what if'. And, just as before, no one was persuaded to change their opinion.

Walt leaned back and let his memory float back to his time on active duty. Because he was a senior non-com, Walt had been included in a strategic session. Thinking back, Walt couldn't remember the exact reason for the briefing, but his mind was clear on the simile the speaker made to the Hungarian Revolution. The presenter that day was a combat colonel with gray hair and possibly was telling a personal story. As Walt recalled, the colonel's simile pointed out that at the time of the Revolution, Hungary was solidly in the Soviet orbit, behind the Iron Curtain, if you will.

Consequently, in that circumstance, American intervention would almost certainly engage our country in an active war with the Soviets, and President Eisenhower wanted to avoid that. However, the colonel further stated, when the Revolution broke out, army units in Europe were told to prepare for invasion if needed. Almost immediately, those plans were blocked by Austria, who denied the Americans either a land route or an air corridor into Hungary. That information was not widely known or publicized. Additionally, the colonel said, military command in Europe did not have a plan for assisting in any uprising behind the Iron Curtain. The absence of any such plan had led to stationing army units at some distance from the Hungarian border, and land movement, even if it had been ordered and initiated, would have taken days to reach Budapest.

Walt remembered how he felt when the colonel explained the lack of American intervention. He had been both embarrassed and relieved. He had sat quietly in the strategic session, thinking of his outburst in high school doubting his national leaders; now he understood their lack of action. And, he wanted to call Charlie and tell him why things happened the way they did. But he never did. He didn't know where Charlie was. Walt shook his head at these clashing memories. But, he didn't move from in front of the fire. Instead, he grabbed another cookie and dunked it in the last of his coffee.

Walt's Philosophy Group had met later that week for some further cogitation about the Revolution and possible outcomes. Jan expressed her firm resolve against having the country involved in another war; Charlie was still a little stiff about the President not taking his advice. But it was Andy that made the most sense with his comment that he didn't see that it was America's business to "go poking the bear in his own backyard." And that closed the discussion.

# CHAPTER 21



Following their custom, the students met at the Henderson's home to discuss their progress on the Social Studies project. Bella's mother supplied some hot, spiced apple cider and sugar cookies, and the three sat around a low coffee table.

Joey repeated a remark he had made earlier at school. "I think we have it. We've got the information the old guy can give us. Let's organize our thoughts around Bella's notes and write it up."

Similar to the response he had received earlier at school, Hal and Bella did not comment for a few seconds. Then Hal said, "Yeah, I see your point, Joey, but really he just gave us the first cut at any real data."

Bella added, "It's still really shallow, I think. We need more substance. Maybe more about the composition of the town. I mean, most of the workers at the dam construction were from somewhere else, right?"

Joey leaned back against the sofa cushion, "Now you're just making stuff up. Everybody is from someplace, aren't they?"

"Don't you want to know why some of these people were ready to get back into war?" Bella asked.

"Not really. I mean, what difference does it make now, anyway. That was what, almost seventy years ago. Today Hungary is out from under Russian - or Soviet - control, and so what?"

Hal frowned at Joey, "C'mon man, you're not being serious about this project. We're not doing a science fair project on the Effect of Sunlight on Sunflower Seeds. This is a serious project, and we need to have a deep understanding of that part of the nation's reaction to a major history event. And so far, all we have is one brief memory from a high school class discussion. Ms. Postella expects more."

Bella looked at Joey expectantly. "Right, Joey?"

Joey made a clownish frown and stared at the other students. "You know," he said, "methinks you do protest too much."

"What does that even mean?" said Hal.

"Oh, that's rich." Bella noted, "Now you're the great psychoanalyzer?"

"Yeah, that's right. I'm seeing right through you two and your 'its too shallow' complaint."

"What's he saying?" Hal asked Bella. "I didn't say shallow, I said 'brief memory' or something like that."

Bella continued her stare at Joey. "Go ahead, Joey. Tell Hal exactly what you're saying."

"Come on, guys. You know what I mean," Joey said, reaching for the cookie plate.

"Oh no, you don't," Bella said, moving the plate out of Joey's reach. "Make your case."

Joey leaned back and contemplated the lack of sugar cookies. He checked a quick glance at the others and noted they were sitting on the edge of their seats, eyes firmly on him. He took a breath and said, "You know what I mean. You both just want to go back and spend more time with the old guy. I get that. I simply don't think we need it for the project."

"What?" Hal said, looking first at Joey and then at Bella.

"He thinks we are enjoying ourselves at the old guy's house, Hal."

"What?"

Joey smiled briefly at Hal and said, "Can't you say anything other than that?"

"What?"

Joey shook his head and leaned across the table to pull the cookie plate closer to him. He picked one of the cookies, took a big bite, smiled at Bella, and mumbled, "I'm right, aren't I?"

Bella didn't answer but instead asked him, "Are you that uncomfortable up there? Do you wish we didn't have to go to his house anymore? What's your real reason for wanting to stop interviewing the old … Mr. Dell?"

Joey swallowed and drank some cider before answering. "No, I'm not uncomfortable in his house. I'm just frustrated at him wandering around the point. Really, Bella, think about it. We've been going up there now for more than a month and only this last time did we get any data for the project. We need a grade from Ms. Postella, and at this rate, it may be another year before we get anything more useful. I just want to get this done. That's all."

Bella sniffed, "No, that's not all, Joey. You are accusing us of liking those trips that you find boring and unproductive. You think we are having a good time while you are itching to get out. Isn't that right?"

Joey shrugged, "Well, maybe a little." He turned to Hal, "And you can't stop asking him follow-up questions, can you? Every time he is about to talk about something we can use, you ask some question that he uses to run off like he's chasing a rabbit."

"Hey, I'm interested, that's all. And when he answers me, we get more useful information for the project."

"Really? Give me an example."

Bella interrupted, "Stop it. We all know that it's possible to use everything he gives us. And the more he does give us about the town and the people and their thinking, the more we have to choose from to make a really good project. So, the more time interviewing Mr. Dell, the better. That's my position."

Hal addressed Bella while staring at Joey, "When do we have to have this project done, anyway? I thought we had months."

"We do. The final project isn't due until spring, but we are supposed to have a proposal for her to look at right after Christmas Break."

Joey tried to press his point, "If we take what we've got and start working on the proposal, we can have our break free of classwork."

Hal said, "He's right. If we keep going up and getting more information, we won't get started on the proposal until Christmas Break, and I don't want to do that."

Bella shook her head sadly, "You guys are so linear. Ms. Postella did not say our fact-finding had to be completed before we could start planning the final project. There is no reason we can't spend the next couple of weeks planning, and then whatever time we need after that, we go back to see Mr. Dell and get him to fill in parts we need."

The boys looked at Bella with new respect. They each nodded, and she continued, "Personally, I'm enjoying hearing him talk about 'the good old days' the way he does. My grandparents are all dead, and I don't have a source to hear about those things."

Joey said, "Actually, I have an idea about the project and how to present this stuff we're learning from the …Mr. Dell."

# CHAPTER 22

## 11/26/2019 TUESDAY

The weather was still cold, and a recent snowfall had covered sidewalks and streets with a light coating of white. Walkways were discernable by the piled-up snow on the side; the walk up to Walt's house, however, had been swept clean earlier in the day, and the bright sun had removed the last vestige of snow. The students stomped their snow-clad boots as they approached the porch and went quickly up the stairs.

Walt was at the door to admit them. There were some mumbled greetings, but everyone was more interested in getting rid of their winter wear and moving into the living room, where a fire burned cheerily. They took their usual seats and noted that Walt had provided a chocolate cake and a large pitcher of milk.

Hal engaged Walt, "What's the story about this?"

"It's a favorite of mine," Walt explained. "As a kid, one of my favorite things was to have chocolate and milk when it got cold. I like the taste of chocolate mixed with cold air, I guess. And, of course, one can't have chocolate cake without milk. Am I right?"

Joey asked slyly, "Do we have to go back outside to enjoy the cold air with our cake?"

"As you wish, Joey. But we're not going anywhere," Hal said as he took a piece of cake and began pouring a glass of milk.

Walt smiled at the rhetorical question, "Certainly not, Joey. I wouldn't put you out in this cold."

Each student put a piece of cake on one of the small saucers provided and took a glass of milk before settling in their seats. Walt noted that Bella put her saucer on the arm of the sofa and pulled her legs up to sit cross-legged. He thought that indicated her degree of comfort at the moment and thought she might be about to open the discussion with a question.

Walt derailed any such opportunity by saying, "I think I owe you an apology and an explanation for things we discussed last time you were here."

Bella paused in eating and cocked her head; both boys continued to eat. Walt waited for a few seconds and then said, "It's about the reaction to the President not taking action to support the Revolution in Hungary."

They looked at him without comment. Walt thought perhaps the boys were being polite since they had chocolate cake in their mouths, but he was surprised that Bella didn't say anything either. He nodded at them and got up from his chair.

"It's not a terribly long story, and I didn't think of it for some reason when we last talked. I guess I was stuck remembering what we had discussed at the time." He began slowly pacing toward the fireplace and back to his chair as he continued, "You know that I went on from there to have a long career in the Army, right?"

All three nodded, their eyes fixed on his movement between the chair and the fire. Walt nodded in return and continued, "What you probably do not know is what I did in the Army. I was originally a supply clerk, and I worked in small warehouses for a couple of tours. But, when I began to comment on how the Army should make improvements in our storage, record keeping, and retrieval systems, they promoted me. I was transferred into a new unit in support of something called SAGE. I'm not going to bore you with all that military stuff, but SAGE was part of the military system designed to provide warning of a hostile attack by air."

All three students sat almost immobile, transfixed by the story. Walt noted this and paused to pick up his coffee cup and take a drink.

"SAGE was a big project involving military and private industry and was handled by ARPANET." He paused to see if that term registered with his audience. It apparently did not, so he went on, "The whole basis of the operation was to hook together a whole series of long-range radar detectors with a network of computers to recognize if any adversary - and we were really only thinking about Russia at that time - had fired a missile at the United States. The computer network was linked to the detectors to analyze the trajectory and predict where such a missile would land."

Walt paused to sip his coffee again and noted how the students followed his movements closely. Pleased that he had their attention, Walt quickly moved to his major reason for bringing the topic up.

"As you likely can guess, that system of linked computers gave rise to the Internet. But back then, this was all pretty hush-hush and required a top-level clearance. And, I had that kind of clearance."

The students did not initially react to this information as Walt had expected. They continued to sit quietly and watch his every move.

Slightly puzzled by the students' apparent lack of interest or understanding of the importance of his clearance level, Walt explained, "Because of that high-level clearance, I was present at several critical briefing sessions during the next several years. And I want to tell you about one of those sessions in particular."

Joey seemed to rouse from the entrancement. "So, what you're saying is that you were working on the Internet way back when?"

Hal said, "You heard that right. This is big."

Walt said, "Hold on. I did not claim to have anything to do with the creation of the Internet. I was working in a small shop, one that supported radar recognition of distant objects, doing some computer data entry. That shop was a small part of the military research and development program called ARPANET and that eventually turned into the Internet."

"Still ..." Bella said, spreading her hands.

"Nope," Walt interrupted, "that is not the point of this story - or any story. The point here is that because I had this high-security clearance, I was invited to a briefing session where I learned something about the Hungarian Revolution."

"What?" said Hal, "I thought that was while you were in high school."

"Very true, Hal. And the story I'm telling today happened more than a decade later." He took the last swallow of his coffee.

Joey said, "Come on, tell." Hal and Bella shifted to the front of their seats.

Walt smiled at the exuberance. "I don't remember what the briefing was all about. What I do remember is that the briefer was a full-bird colonel who spoke like he had personal experience with the time of the Revolution."

"What did he say?" Bella blurted.

"He was explaining something else at the time, defensive troop movements in Europe, I think. But he said something like, 'This is an attempt to not be out of position like we were for that uprising in Hungary'."

"What did he mean by that?" Hal wanted to know.

Walt held his hand up to the students, asking for time to tell the story. He went on, "So, someone asked what he meant by that, and the colonel said at the time of the student uprising, the Revolution, if you wish, there were no American troops in Europe stationed anywhere near Hungary. That meant an immediate ground force support effort was not possible. The colonel did mention that those troops in Europe were put on alert, however. But, almost immediately, Austria refused to allow the United States to use its land or their air-space for transit to Hungary."

Walt noted the obvious jaw drop as the students absorbed this fact.

"Now, it is true that the United States could have used some tactical nuclear missiles to wipe out Russian supply lines, but Eisenhower was concerned this would touch off a nuclear war between us and Russia. And nobody wanted anything like that, then or now."

The three nodded somberly. Bella was the first to recover, asking, "Did that change your mind? About the President and things?"

Walt said, "Yes, it did. My first reaction as a seventeen-year-old was that we should go fight for them, in Hungary, I mean. But ten years later, seeing the difficulties of the military situation, I had to agree with Eisenhower's assessment of the circumstances. He was right not to do anything."

"Wow!" Hal said. "Do you think if you knew then, what you know now that it would've changed your mind?"

Walt smiled and pointed at Hal. "What a great question, Hal. I don't know for sure, but I suspect I would not have changed my mind. I was seventeen and thought I knew pretty much everything that needed to be known."

"Hey," said Joey, "we're seventeen."

Walt pointed at Joey. Bella responded, "And that may have been exactly his point, Joey." Walt winked at her and returned to his chair.

"Hal said, "So you were one of the first computer programmers?"

"Yes, I suppose so. Although today you think of that as writing code on a keyboard and seeing it on a screen. That's not at all what I was doing at that time. See, back then someone else, in a completely different room, wrote down stuff in a code language like FORTRAN and handed me and some other guys sheets of paper with instructions. We sat at little tables in the refrigerated rooms where the computers were kept and key-punched those instructions."

"What do you mean, key-punched? Isn't that coding?"

"Well, maybe as an intermediate step. There was no direct keyboard connection to the computers; everyone talked in a foreign language, and our job was to covert those instructions into something the computer could understand."

"And that was cards with holes in them?" Joey asked.

"Yep," Walt answered. "Each card represented a line of code; the holes in the card allowed light to pass through and hit a screen that convert the holes to letters."

""I knew it," Hal said raising his arms to indicate a score. "You coding

"No sir, it was not. We just followed the directions on the instructions and typed into our little machine what we were told to. The only thing our little machines did was punch holes in these 80-column cards. These cards were like index cards but longer. When we finished with a card, it slid off to the side, and a new one slid in. We kept all the cards together in a deck until all the codes were entered and all the cards had been punched.

"Then we took the card decks and fed them into the computer and waited several hours to see if we had done it right."

Bella was puzzled, "Why hours?"

"Because the machines were pretty slow back then. Big and slow."

"That's amazing," Bella said. "But we had some follow-up questions from last time. Could we talk about those things now?"

"Absolutely. Fire away."

"Well, she said, looking at her fellow students for confirmation, "we would like more information about why people had such different opinions at the time of the Revolution. Can you explain that?"

"More than likely, not. Remember, I was a high school kid. I didn't go around questioning people and taking notes. I heard the different stories from classmates, but mostly we tended to tell each other the same things, over and over."

"But you must have some idea."

"Hmm. Well, yes, I guess I do. It always seemed to me that anyone who had been shot at or who knew someone who died in the war wanted nothing to do with another conflict. The rest of us were know-nothing teenagers, at least in heart. Let's talk about something else, like what your family is going to do on Thanksgiving."

Walt listened carefully to their answers. Hal's extended family was going to his grandmother's for dinner, Joey and his parents were staying home, and Bella's parents had invited some elderly singles from church to eat with them. In the discussion about what constituted the 'proper' dishes for a Thanksgiving meal, the students forgot to ask what Walt would be doing.

Then Bella noted that their time was up for the day, and there was the usual scramble to don their galoshes, scarves and heavy coats. Then they said their goodbyes and were gone. Walt stood at the door after it closed for a moment, mentally contrasting the sudden silence in the house to the recent chatter of excited teenagers.

Then he went to the kitchen to make his coffee.

# CHAPTER 23

## 11/26/2019 TUESDAY

Walt sipped on his coffee, enjoying the flavor and aroma. He sat in the same chair he used when the students were present, leaned back against the high back, and rested his neck. His neck had been bothering him more recently; stiff on his awakening each morning and then tight and aching in the evenings. He had started taking some Tylenol in the evenings, and it seemed to help. The aching and the stiffness reminded him of his time in rehabilitation.

Walt let his mind wander; he thought more about his memory of the full-bird colonel standing in front of the crew and making an off-hand remark about the Army being so poorly positioned in Europe in 1956. Even ten years later, he was surprised at such an admission. But the revelation was also an eye-opener for him. At seventeen, of course, he had no concept of logistics or manpower maneuvers. He realized that, even now, he did not know where the Army had stationed its strength in Europe after Germany surrendered. He was aware that, right after the armistice, several units were assigned to the Pacific, but he didn't know who remained, or where they were.

And, there was that business with Austria. What was that all about? Were the Austrians so frightened of Russia and the Soviets that they just stood around and let the Hungarians get crushed? Apparently so. The concept of the Soviet Army having that kind of effect on neighboring countries made Walt's neck hurt even more.

He got up, poked the fire, and added another log. Watching the flames jumping around the fresh wood, Walt remembered times when he and his fellows went on alert status. Often, that meant sitting around a fire, poking the wood, and hoping the siren would not go off. It also meant they had to sleep in their clothes and to see that their weapon was clean, loaded, accompanied by at least two loaded spare clips, and the safety was on. Such alerts were not rare, but Walt only remembered being rustled into mobilization twice. And one of those turned out to be significant for him.

The first mobilization came with the notice of the Berlin Wall construction in August 1961. Someone misread the defensive posture of the Wall and thought the Russians were fortifying the city in preparation for an attack on the Western sector. Walt and company spent three days in their clothes, eating and sleeping in or around their vehicle until some officer far up the chain of command ordered them back to regular duty.

The mobilization for the Cuban Missile Crisis in late 1962 was quite different. The interpretation of the situation was an imminent shooting was and probably the use of nuclear weapons. Everyone thought the main focus would be in the Gulf of Mexico, but anyone present in Europe could feel the Russians breathing down their necks. This mobilization involved moving troops into bunkers and bomb shelters and called on Walt and his unit to handle supplies. In that instance, 'supplies' meant more than just food and water; it also meant weapons and ammunition.

Walt was finishing the loading on a transport vehicle and about to give the order to drive when he noted a case of bazooka rockets loose and wobbling on the top tier of the load. He jumped on the rear tailgate and reached up to steady the case when the driver allowed the truck to lurch forward. Walt fell backward, pulling the heavy rocket case down with him. Both landed on a concrete drive, the case hitting beside Walt and spilling its contents over the driveway.

*Déjà vu* ran through Walt's mind of his previous injury and he held his breath waiting for the call for 'Medic". Several seconds went by and then the assistant quartermaster, who was overseeing truck loading, was hollering at him.

"What's this, Dell? Is it your nappy time?'

Walt ran his hands over his body carefully and then quickly and found no injuries.

The assistant quartermaster was not appeased by Walt's grin of happiness at finding no bones broken, he yelled again, "What're you feeling yourself up for, Dell? This ain't playtime! Get on your feet!"

Walt scrambled to his feet, brushing the dirt off his uniform. He faced the assistant quartermaster and said, "Sorry, Sergeant. Just checking for injuries!"

"If you ain't injured, get back in the game!"

"Yes, Sergeant." Walt ran around to the front of the truck and told the driver to put the vehicle in park, then gathered some help to round up the rockets. Once the full box was secured in the truck Walt jumped down from the bed and signaled for the driver to move out.

Later that night, secured in the field and poking a small fire, Walt recalled that after his first injury the only person in Whealton that communicated with him other than the funeral director was Charlie Tatum's mother. Walt never understood how she found out where he was and how she got through the Army communication system to get him on the telephone. But, he was glad to hear her voice and news that the funeral was 'nice and comfortable'. Mrs. Tatum also conveyed his parents were buried without trouble or fuss. Walt told her that he didn't have anything there in Whealton and that somebody could sell the house and belongings and use the money to pay whatever debts existed, and just send him the remainder. She had arranged for him to give power of attorney to a lawyer in Billings.

A few months later, as he was finishing his rehabilitation, his commander told him that he had a deposit in his post account of several thousand dollars from clearing his parents' obligations and selling their goods. He remembered thinking that money didn't seem very much for what his father had worked all his life.

Walt poked his fire again, evoking a shower of sparks that reminded him of another time of showering sparks from a fire - on the sandbar one summer. The football team had been gathered there by the coaches for a pep talk before the opening game of the season; Walt thought it was his junior year. Coach asked the starting player in each position to stand up and make a short speech about teamwork. Walt remembered very little of what others said that night, but he could not forget what Billy Parks had said. Billy was the starting right guard, and Walt was his backup. Billy's comments were about how he depended on the center and the tackle to do their jobs on the team so he wouldn't get hurt. Because he knew if he were hurt, the team would have a huge hole at right guard when Walt had to fill in.

Everyone laughed, but the comment hurt Walt's feelings, and even though the coach corrected the impression that the exercise was to embarrass other players, Walt just wanted to leave. Later, when the coaches were passing out some cold drinks, Billy sidled over to Walt and said something like, 'She's the one that said it, you know.' Walt asked who 'she' was, and Billy said, "Jan, you goofball. She sees you hanging around and watching us. She's the one that said you wouldn't be able to take my place."

Even decades later, remembering those words brought tears to Walt's eyes and a sinking, hollow feeling in the middle of his chest. Of course, he hadn't wanted to believe it, but it still hurt. He remembered how angry he felt toward Billy Parks for saying that. Walt was holding a piece of firewood, poking the fire when Billy came up to him and made his comment. Walt remembered how his grip tightened on the wood, and how he had considered smashing Billy in the face. But he didn't, and Billy had walked off, snickering.

Walt returned to his chair, noted his cup was empty, and sat down to stare at the fire. He didn't want to dwell on these negative thoughts and feelings. He preferred to think about Jan when she was part of the Yard Philosophy group, energetically pushing the discussion, staring at whoever was speaking with those engaging black eyes, teasing Andy about his semi-obsession with Barbara Mingo.

Mingo! That was Barbara's last name. Walt wondered how he could have ever forgotten that. Barbara Mingo, sunbathing behind the cardboard barriers, driving her neighbor, Andy Steward, crazy. And creating a point of drama for both Charlie and Jan to tease Andy. As he remembered some of those teasing sessions, Walt had a sudden insight: Andy wasn't hurt by all their teasing; he had been reveling in it, enjoying being the center of attention even as the butt of the jokes. Walt thought to himself how typical that was of Andy - class clown and doing anything to attract attention.

# CHAPTER 24

## 12/03/2019 TUESDAY

Joey sat in a large overstuffed chair in the Henderson's living room. He stretched out his legs and said, "Well, you've got to admit, that was a great interview. Lots of good stuff." He showed his notebook to Hal.

Bella agreed, "Oh yes, we got some great insight into our question."

Her tone was not completely in line with the mood Joey had been trying to set. He said, "Whoa. You're not saying it's not enough, are you?"

Bella shrugged her shoulders and looked at Hal.

Joey interrupted any comment, "Wait a minute. You two are talking about this without me, aren't you?"

Hal explained, "Look man, we've got study hall together right before the final bell. Mr. Arnold lets us sit at the back table and work on the project. That's all."

"Well, it feels like I'm being cut out."

"Nobody's trying to cut you out, Joey," Bella said, trying to soothe ruffled feathers. "We're prepared to tell you everything we talked about. But, yeah, we did agree that maybe a little more information would be helpful/"

"Information about what?"

Hal tried to justify their thinking by saying, "Depth, maybe. Or nuance."

Joey snorted, "Nuance? Now you're just making stuff up. You're enjoying listening to the old guy … excuse me, Mr. Dell, talk. Aren't you?"

Bella started to speak but Hal interrupted. "Yeah, we are. Or, at least, I am. I think he's a lot more interesting than I anticipated. Some of his stories are great. Like all that stuff about early computers and stuff."

Joey smiled at Hal and said, "I knew it. You like the old …Dell."

Bella said, "That's not a crime, Mr. K.I.A."

"Oh, I know that, Bella. The fact is, I kinda like the old guy myself. My grandfather is about that same age and he has some interesting stories. Dell also has some stories. And, I'm finding that I enjoy listening to him tell about things."

"So, you're not against us going back to meet with him again?"

"No. Of course not."

"Then what were you getting all bent out of shape about over us talking without you?" Hal asked.

"Cause this is a team project, right? I want to be part of the team, Hal. That's all."

Hal nodded and shrugged, "Okay, Joey. But I got to tell you, that's a complete surprise to me and probably to Bella, too."

"What do you mean?"

"We both thought having to work with you on this project would be like fighting snakes."

"Why?"

"Because we thought you would try to tell us how to think about every aspect of the project."

"Hey guys, I thought we were getting along…"

Bella held up her hand to stop Joey from speaking any further. "That's right," she said, "we are getting along on this project famously. In fact, both of us think your idea about how to display our findings is golden."

Hal stepped in, "It's just that, we maybe thought our luck was going to run out and you would drag your feet about talking any more with Mr. Dell."

"Really?"

"Well, you suggested exactly that just two weeks ago."

"Oh, yeah. I guess I did." Joey looked down at his feet for a brief moment and then looked up and said, "Well, let's forget that. But I do think we need to get him to talk more like he did this last time. More details will 'flesh out' out project, right?"

Bella and Hal looked hard at Joey and Hal asked, "Are you being for real right now?"

"I am."

"All right, then, I say let's focus on what we want more details on. We've got a couple more visits."

"At least," Bella said.

# CHAPTER 25

12/10/2019 TUESDAY

No more snow had fallen since their last visit to Walt's house, and the sidewalks were clean.

Hal worried out loud, "If we don't get another snowfall we might not have a white Christmas."

Bella nodded, "With all the climate change, having a white Christmas is becoming one of the fables of yesteryear."

Hal wrinkled his nose at her and stopped at the bottom of the steps to Walt's porch, "Are you one of those Global Warming nuts, Bella?"

She did not take offense, but said, "It's Climate Change, Hal, not Global Warming."

"Today and this week, maybe. But what's it gonna be when the sunspots cause a new Ice Age to Appear?"

"That's climate change," she replied.

"Well, my point is that mankind doesn't have that much to do with it. It was warm before there was an Ice Age, and then everything warmed up again. And it was a sorta little Ice Age back in the 19th century."

Joey jumped in, "That's reasoning a little backward, Hal. The warming since then has occurred as mankind has done a lot of things to the atmosphere."

"I'm not convinced," Hal said, turning to the steps. "Those things may be happening together, but I still don't think one caused the other."

Joey said to Bella as they went to the door, "I'm glad we didn't choose a project on Climate Change."

Walt answered their knock at the door wearing house shoes. He stared briefly at them and then stepped back to allow their entry.

"I'm sorry," he said as they kicked off their galoshes and heavy outer garments. "I didn't expect you to be here today."

Bella stopped and checked her notebook calendar. "It is Tuesday, isn't it?"

"Yes, of course. But I rather thought you had all the information you needed from me when we last spoke. That's all. Please come in." He waved them toward the living room.

They noted the absence of a fire, and Walt apologized for not having refreshments. He clarified again that his thought had been the series of interviews was over after he explained the different attitudes of people toward the Hungarian Revolution.

Bella took on the task of explaining why they had returned. "That explanation was a major part of our data-gathering, sir. But, really, we also want to have a deeper understanding of the people in Whealton for the project to have more than just a single dimension."

Walt looked at her and then at the two boys and said, "Dimension, eh? You want some depth about the people in Whealton? That's interesting, you know. Whealton doesn't survive anymore. The only Whealton that exists today is in the minds of people who were there, at some time in the middle of last century."

Hal asked, "Really, Whealton is no longer there?"

"It is not, son. Look it up on one of those Google map things. Some of the streets are still there, and one or two of the buildings are, but basically, Whealton died and disappeared when the construction on Fort Peck Dam ended. No construction, no need for construction crews and engineers and earthmovers and lawyers to handle land deeds where the lake would be. Without all those families, there was no need for stores, or gas stations, or schools, or movie theatres. And so all those things went away. There are still farmers in the area, of course, but the Whealton of old is now only an intersection on a map."

Bella recovered and said, "All the more important that we conserve those memories, then. And that's what we want to do. Joey has a really good idea about how to exhibit our findings in this project, and the more you can tell us about Whealton, the more real it will appear in our project."

"Huh," Walt said. Then he asked Hal to accompany him to the kitchen. "Sounds like we're going to need some refreshments, Hal." They returned a few moments later with glasses, a half-gallon bottle of milk and two tins of cookies that Walt put on the coffee table.

"Joey," he said to the young man, "why don't you get the fire going, it will be too cold in here for me very quickly."

Joey found some newspaper, kindling, and split wood in a basket next to the fireplace and had the fire burning well within minutes. Meantime, Bella and Hal had helped themselves to cookies and were ready to begin discussing Walt's memories of Whealton.

Hal began by asking, "Did you ever go back there after you joined the Army?"

Walt shook his head, "No, I did not. There was only one time I had any reason to, but I couldn't go then, and so it never happened."

"What was that reason for not going?"

Walt told them his story about the Infantry drill with 1st Infantry at Fort Benning and the mobilization of his unit. He explained how the drill was preparing for a shooting war, complete with missiles, involving Russia and so they were mobilizing armaments and communications gear and how he fell from the truck and the radar monitor case had landed on him and broke his pelvis.

"Yikes," Hal said, "that had to be painful."

"Yes. Yes, it was Hal. For quite some time, it was very painful. The repair involved two different surgeries and absolute bed rest for several weeks. And that was possibly the worst."

"How's that?'

"I was not allowed any weight bearing on my pelvis, so I could only sit to eat but not to do anything else."

"Such as?"

"Think about it for a moment, son."

"Oh. Wow. That has to be hard."

"You don't know the half of it. And, it is extremely embarrassing, too."

Bella interrupted what was becoming embarrassing for her, too. "And that was why you didn't go back to Whealton?"

"Yes. My parents were in a fatal automobile accident less than a week after my injury. Their funeral and burial took place while I was lying in a bed in the military hospital."

"Why didn't you go after you recovered?"

"There was no reason. I sold everything after their deaths, and most of the people I knew had already left by then."

"Wow. What a sad story," Joey said.

Walt looked at them and said, "What could I tell you about the town and people that we haven't already discussed?"

Hal said, "Maybe you could just tell us what went on there over your time in one school year. Maybe tell us about your classes, what about any sports, things like that."

"My goodness, young man. That's a very ambitious set of topics. Are you sure you need all that?"

The three students sensed an eagerness in Walt to talk about those things; they encouraged him, saying, "Oh, yes" and "That's exactly what we want to hear."

Walt talked first about small-town football in the 1950s. Whealton High School was in a conference with other towns with a history of competing against each other. Whealton was the 'new' school and became a target on every other school's sports calendar. The fall football schedule had to begin play almost as soon as school started; the first game was on the Friday of the week classes began. And the outside temperature might be in the 90s. Games were played on fields where little grass grew and so were mostly dirt. But by the end of the season, several heavy snowfalls had covered those fields. Deep snow required the fields to be cleared by snowplows, and teams kept a sideline barrel with a fire to warm players who were not on the field. Everyone's breath was visible, cheerleaders wore three layers of clothing, and any cheers from the stands came muffled through scarves, high collars, and ski masks.

Hal started shivering just hearing the stories. He got up, moved to the fireplace, put two more pieces of wood on the fire, and then stood with his back to the flames. Hal changed the subject slightly at that point. He asked, "What about the military?"

Walt countered, "What about it?"

"Well, I wonder what people thought about the military at the time."

"Oh, well, I guess they didn't think much about it at all. I don't remember a lot of discussions."

"Did you know anyone planning on joining the military," Joey asked.

"I don't recall. Certainly not anyone in my small group. Remember, the military service at that time was completely done through the draft. Every able-bodied man had to register when they turned 18. A lottery then assigned a number from one to 365 to the sequential days of the year. Men with birthdays on dates drawn by lottery were the first to be drafted. I think we all knew what our number was, but I don't remember people talking about volunteering."

"But you said you volunteered."

"That's right, I did. The military has always been open to volunteers. I had been considering going into military service for a year or so. I had discussed it with my Dad, and he was okay with that decision."

"Why did you decide not to go to college?"

"Remember, back in those days not everyone came out of high school aimed at a college degree. Although college was not highly expensive, it was out of reach for many, and they ended up working in a plant or industry."

"Then why did you choose to join the Army?"

Walt looked at Hal closely and asked, "If you're thinking about that, Hal, you can ask me straight out."

Hal blushed but said, "I'm interested in your decision."

Walt took a breath and said, "Well, there were reasons I wanted out of Whealton, and I knew I could learn some skill in the military. I didn't have any idea about what to do to earn a living, and I didn't have any particular interest. That felt like I needed some time to think about things, and I knew the Army would pay me a salary and feed me while I spent that time thinking. Plus, the Army let volunteers choose their line of work."

"So you would recommend the military for someone who didn't have a clear life plan?"

"You've been talking to a counselor, haven't you?"

"Yeah."

"Let me tell you, every Master's degree program in the country tells applicants to have at least two years of experience before going for their degree. I have been telling young men to take a couple of years to serve the country before making up their minds about a career. I say that to you, too. Hal."

Joey said, "I'm going to college and plan on attending law school."

Walt nodded, "I'm not surprised, Joey. And I would still recommend a couple of years in uniform before beginning law school."

"Why?"

"Mostly for the experience and the maturation that it brings."

"Hmm, I don't think I want that experience."

"You're probably a lot like the young men in Whealton. They thought being in the military involved wearing the same clothes every day, parading around, guarding some building or charging up a hill under gunfire."

"Isn't it?"

"Sometimes, but not often. Mostly it teaches discipline, teamwork, and diligence and provides college funding through the GI Bill."

"I don't know what that is."

Walt nodded at Bella and commented, "Bella is putting up her notebook, so it must be time to quit. Are you planning on dropping in any more?"

Bella answered, "Yes, sir. We want to keep coming for a while. We are learning a lot."

"Fine. Then we'll do the GI Bill at a later time. Two weeks?"

"Uh, Mr. Dell. That's Christmas Eve, and …"

"Absolutely correct, Joey. We should definitely not meet on that day. The elves and I have far too much to do at that time. Two weeks later?"

"How about one week after that?" Bella asked.

"That will be wonderful," Walt said.

He walked them to the door and sent them off, saying, "See you next year!"

# CHAPTER 26

*12/10/2019 TUESDAY*

That evening Walt sat and watched the fire die down while he sipped his coffee. He recalled the bonfire on the sandbar and Billy Parks' nasty comment again, this time without the hurt. Walt considered that the wound had hurt so much the previous recall because he had forgotten all the months he had spent after that bonfire thinking what he should have said in return. He had thought that "No one has any big gains on your side anyway" was more than a little weak, but "At least I remember to pull on the correct play" was a direct hit. That comment would have reminded everyone Billy had failed that assignment previously. And, when he missed the assignment, their quarterback was sacked for a loss.

Over the years, Walt had thought of perhaps twenty smart comebacks to Billy's insult. He had laughed out loud at one or two of them, all now forgotten. The effort had allowed him to heal up the bruised ego but had not assuaged the desire to strike back, hopefully causing the same amount of laughter and injury at Billy. But, years ago, Walt had realized that the art of the winning comeback was the same as the secret to excellent comedy - timing. And he did not have such timing that night on the sandbar. As he thought more about it, staring into the dying fire, Walt realized he still didn't have that kind of timing.

The Whealton football team also did not have the correct timing. Walt recalled that, in spite of Billy Parks' suggestion of prowess, the offense made precious few first downs during those last years. And the defense, where Walt was a starter at linebacker, couldn't seem to stop the other team from piling up first downs. Walt tried to remember the number of times his defense had caused the opponents to punt; Over his last two years, that number couldn't be more than five or six times. Not surprising, then, that Whealton went 0-8 each year.

Walt grinned into his coffee. That wasn't the case in basketball, though. Walt was the point guard on the team both in his junior and senior year and had several fond memories of those contests. The most memorable involved the opening game of the season his senior year. Whealton was up against the team favored to win the conference. But the opponent's point guard consistently failed to make good decisions and turned the ball over several times. Meanwhile, Walt hit three shots from the top of the arc in the first half - he had never hit three in a whole game before. So the second half Walt faced some double team defense, which opened his teammates up in the middle for their points. The game ended with Whealton ahead by three, and the other team was hopping mad.

Walt recalled their anger, first expressed as cussing on the floor, then threats about violence when the team boarded their bus for home. And, he remembered, they showed up a couple of hours later at the Canteen, ready to 'rumble'. The Canteen chaperones had prevented any fighting, but the incident became a major story within the school for the next week.

The Teen Canteen was a weekend affair. Open only on Friday and Saturday nights, there was dancing, Ping-Pong, and a gathering space for the high-school kids. The building was not very large, and half the floor space went to dancing, closely observed by the chaperones. The chaperones were one or two couples with children in the mix. Walt's memories consisted mostly of Jan dancing with Billy and things he didn't want to think about. He did recall that no one slipped out to sneak a drink because the chaperones would almost certainly catch them, and ban them from the Canteen for a month. But they did sneak out to smoke.

Smokers would post a sentry on the front steps while they went to the back to partake. If a chaperone came outside, the sentry would engage them in loud conversation, tipping the smokers to douse their cigarettes. In time, Walt understood that the chaperones would not detect recent smoking because they, too, were smokers. Of course, chaperones changed every weekend, but most people were smokers back then, so the system rarely needed any tweaking.

As he thought about the Canteen dancing, Walt's memories always involved him watching Jan. By the time they were rising seniors, Jan had 'developed' as the women would say. The waif of two years previously had a clear waistline, long tapering legs, and definitely filled her sweater up front. She had let her hair grow to shoulder length, and she had started tossing her hair with that tinkling laugh. Walt felt he couldn't stop looking at her, no matter what Billy Parks had said.

The fire was down to coals and ashes, and the room was beginning to cool. Walt switched his thinking back to the basketball court. But the scene that played out in his mind was the bus ride home from away games. Jan was a cheerleader and rode on the bus with the players. Billy Parks was a substitute - no jump and poor defense - but he was always on the bus too. The two of them sat together in the back and were always wrapped up in each other, kissing and running their hands over each other. Fortunately for him, Walt sat closer to the front of the bus and was not forced to watch that display. Unfortunately, his imagination made that interaction seem greater than it likely was.

Walt shook his head, left the room, rinsed out his cup, and headed for his bedroom. He was disappointed with himself for pulling all those painful memories back into the foreground of his thoughts. He had made peace with his departure from Whealton and with the associated decision to never contact Jan again. That decision did not stop him from thinking about her, however. He had endured several years of "what ifs" before being able to tamp down those painful memories; he didn't desire to go through that again.

Since Maddy's death, Walt's nighttime routine was preparing for bed and then sitting in his favorite wingback, reading the old classics and new scholarly treatment of history for an hour or two before turning out the light and crawling into bed.

In the bedroom, Walt quickly dressed for bed, brushed his teeth, and took his nighttime medications. Then he sat in the wingback chair by the window and picked up the book he was reading, *The October Horse'*, and buried his thoughts and memories of the saga of Caesar, Cleopatra, and the rising influence of Augustus. Walt had long been fascinated by the political intrigue in the Roman Republic and how the system ultimately became an Empire. Several modern historians were publishing theses comparing the

Roman experience with the government to that of the United States. Most foretold doom from existential threats associated with the rise of a dominant single class. Walt, at 81, wanted to know the outcome for America that he was unlikely to live to see, so he read everything he could on Rome and the history of its fall as an empire., secretly hoping America was not heading down a similar path.

# CHAPTER 27



On that first Tuesday of the New Year, Walt again met them at the door, pleased that they had returned. The students parked their coats, scarves, and boots near the front door amid scattered "Happy New Year" greetings, and moved into the living room without urging. Walt had again put out some refreshments, this time homemade cookies and a pitcher of milk. First in his seat, Joey assumed the responsibility of pouring a glass for each of them before they began any discussion.

Bella said, " Mr. Dell, something came up this past week in class that made us think about racism in Montana when you were in high school. Can you tell us about that?" She opened her notebook and leaned forward.

Walt looked steadily at her for a moment and asked, "Perhaps you could start this conversation by telling me what you discussed in your class?"

"Uh, sure, I guess. And Joey and Hal can help out, too."

The boys did not look at her, having become intensely interested in the plate of cookies.

Bella took a breath and said, "Well, one of the teachers was encouraging those students who did not score high on the SAT last fall to retake the test next month. She said that colleges were impressed with improvement on the examination."

Walt agreed, "My wife would have agreed with that."

"Well, one of the students said he didn't think it would matter because colleges are racist in their acceptance decisions anyway. And someone else agreed and said their older brother didn't get in where he wanted to go because the college was biased against white males."

Walt frowned at this and noted, "You remember my wife was a teacher for many years in the public school system. She heard some of those rumors, too. But she was convinced that every college worth attending would admit students with the best scores on their SAT."

Joey raised his hand to disagree. "Some places, like Harvard, are trying to use racial quotas, Mr. Dell. They are already admitting more Asians than there are in the population."

"Oh, I see," Walt said, "You mean they are choosing not to admit one minority group because they have so many."

"Yeah, I guess it does sound odd when you put it that way. But that's what they are doing."

"And that upsets you? Why? Are you applying to Harvard as an Asian-American?"

"No. Of course not. It's just that … well, it's unfair, that's all."

Hal said, "What Joey is really concerned about is those colleges deciding that what they need are not white males like him. He may get left out if these colleges decide to admit more minorities, just minorities that are different from the ones they already have."

"Hmm."

"So, what was the racist issue when you were in school?" Bella pushed. "I think you graduated before Brown v Board of Education, didn't you?"

Walt grinned at her and said, "Oh, yes, I did. But I want you to know that our Montana school did not have a problem with blacks trying to get in class."

"African-Americans," Joey corrected.

"And they weren't hyphenated Americans then, either. Montana did not have a significant black population in the 1950s, and there were no blacks living around our school district."

Bella sank back into the sofa. "So, you really can't tell us anything about racism back in your time in high school." She was disappointed because she had hoped to bring a fresh perspective to class discussion.

"Didn't say that, now did I?" Walt asked. He leaned back in his chair and folded his arms.

Bella seemed confused; Joey was no better. He said, "I thought you said there were no blacks in the area."

"Exactly. You heard me right."

"But are you saying you did see racism there?"

"Certainly did."

Hal started, "But how …"

Walt interrupted, "Are you telling me that you have gotten to your senior year in high school, and still think that only black people suffer from racism?"

"Uh, I thought that was what we were talking about," Joey said defensively.

Walt shook his head, "Well, I wasn't. I was thinking of the racism I did see. And it did not involve black people at all. It was aimed at the Indians."

"Indians?" All three students seemed puzzled.

"Yes, the Indians. I think you've been misled into thinking that racism is a white versus black thing. I hear that stuff on the news, and I see it in some of the newspapers I read. But that's a very shallow and truncated view of racism. Sure, America had its problem with black-white racism, and I do not doubt there is some lingering animosity. But, let me tell you, I have traveled around this globe, and everywhere I've been there was always a minority group despised by the majority - usually, for no good reason other than that I think everybody wants to think of themselves as superior to somebody."

Joey nodded and said, "That's very believable, but the Indians?"

Walt asked, "What do you read, son? Are you reading some fanciful utopian literature about the Noble Savage?"

"Well, I guess I just don't see any …"

"Well, of course not. First, you are powerfully under read. Second, you are far too young, and Third, there are no large reservations nearby, and you have virtually no contact."

Hal said, "Tell us about Montana, then."

Walt nodded and said, "First, you need to learn about the geographic history of Montana and the major events that brought the Indians and white people together. And that started more than 200 years ago when settlers, white people, began moving west across the Mississippi River. Understand the culture of the Indian tribes of the area was mostly nomadic, they made temporary camps, ate off the land, and moved when necessary. The settlers wanted to put up fences, plow the ground, plant crops, and raise cattle."

"Oh," said the students.

"I can't believe you don't know all this," Walt said, shaking his head. "Indians poaching cattle from farmers started some regular confrontations which worsened when more settlers pushed into Indian territory. Conflicts became aggravated up and down the Plains and involved U.S. Army units trying to prevent Indian attacks on civilian settlements from Texas to Canada."

"The Indians recognized large areas of the West as their land for hunting. And the farmers knew nothing of that and trespassed right and left. After the Civil War, many veterans were sent to the West to 'pacify' the area. I'm sure you know about the battle at Little Big Horn."

"Custer," said Hal quickly.

"And there were many other such battles, like Wood Lake, Rosebud Creek, and Big Mound. Sand Creek, was a massacre and led to decades of fighting, peace talks, negotiated treaties, and broken treaties that finally resulted in all the tribes being given land reserved for them …"

"Reservations," Joey said. Walt nodded and continued, "For eighty years or more before I was in high school, the Indians of Montana lived in reservations. Montana has seven of these reservations; one of them is the Fort Peck Reservation, right close to Whealton. The people of Montana remember the Indians as fierce, uncivilized pillagers. And, after nearly a century of being treated poorly by the U.S. Government, these tribes are anything but fearful. They are poor, repressed, and looked down upon by every 'right-thinking' person in the state. Even though their treaties with the U.S. Government label them as independent nations, they are totally dependent on the U.S. government. I'm afraid the next generation will only remember them as owners and operators of casinos."

Walt stopped talking and looked at his audience. They were following his every word. He continued, "And the descendants of the white settlers have come to look down on the Indians as dirty, alcoholic, and unreliable. They shun the Indians that come to town for any reason, they won't hire one to work on a job, judging them as 'lazy'. The whites in Whealton looked down on the Indians with scorn, at the same time they were hearing of racially tense situations in the South and criticizing the white people there for being 'racist'. I frequently heard some of these discussions involving adults in Whealton with the ending, "I'm glad we don't have that kind of trouble up here."

The three students were still and quiet; each probably rummaging in their memories for comparable stories.

Walt said, "I know I'm not supposed to give you homework but I think your knowledge about conflict between white settlers and native Indians needs some brushing up."

"What are you suggesting," Bella asked.

"Reading," Walt paused as Hal flinched. "There are two excellent books that portray both sides of the history in good detail."

"And they are…?" Bella asked with her pen poised. Walt spoke directly to her, "The first is *Bury My Heart at Wounded Knee*. And the second, which is in some way a sequel, is "*Empire of the Summer Moon.*"

Finally, after completing her notes on Walt's recommendations, Bella asked, "So, you really did see racism when you were in high school?"

"Yes, dear, I certainly did. And since my family was not native to the area, stories of why we should look down on the Indians as a tribe, as a nation, or as individuals had no traction with my parents. So, I didn't learn to look down on them either."

"Did you know any Indians?" Joey asked, noting that Bella was closing her notebook.

"Yes, I did. He was a friend for a while, and then moved back to the reservation."

Hal pushed, "Can you tell us about him?"

"Perhaps someday, Hal. But not today. Bella is packing to leave and you haven't yet told me about what you got for Christmas."

So, time spent rebundling them for the cold weather was occupied with stories of their Christmas gifts without any obvious angst among them about forgetting to gift Walt. And he did not mention it.

# CHAPTER 28

## 01/7/2020 TUESDAY

Walt's memories that evening centered mostly on Christmases remembered. And the most memorable Christmases in the Dell household in Whealton, Montana were the early ones. Walt and his father would tramp in the woods north of town to seek the perfect tree. Looking back on that experience with more mature and experienced eyes, Walt could recognize that the characteristics of such a perfect tree became more subjective as the air became colder, and the snow became deeper. But, they always found the right one, sawed it off, and transported it back to the house as if they were bringing home food for the next month from their hunt.

The tree always was positioned in the front corner of the living room, in front of the large window. In that place, the tree was visible to passersby and in the dining room through the open doorway. Walt's mother enjoyed decorating the tree, creating a new set of decorations each year. Walt especially remembered the year all the decorations involved pinecones painted different colors and adorned with sprinkles of gold, red, and silver. Walt's last year at home, his mother had the tree flocked, in pink. She decorated the tree that year with blue ornaments only. Walt thought the whole enterprise was goofy that year and did not invite his friends over to see the tree.

Another tradition in the Dell home involved Christmas Eve, sitting with friends and singing carols while drinking spiced apple cider. Walt's father was the cider master; he spent most of the afternoon in the kitchen, stirring, sampling, and making additions to the brew. The Dells' neighbors would drop by for small ham sandwiches and a piece of the famous Irish plum pudding. Walt's mother made the pudding at least a week in advance and kept it away from prying hands until Christmas Eve. When the first guests arrived, they would help Walt's father with the critical step; his dad would pour about a half-cup of Irish whiskey on the pudding and light it with a match. Such a pretty and pleasant smell filled the room.

After the fire died, Walt's mother served the pudding with a dollop of freshly prepared whipped cream. Then everyone sang four or five favorite carols and more guests arrived. Neighbors always wanted to enjoy his mother's plum pudding, Walt recalled, and he suspected that some of the men also got a dab of Irish whiskey in their spiced cider, too.

Walt sipped on his coffee sitting at the kitchen table. He let the fire in the living room die out while preparing his drink and felt no need to restart it. He thought for a moment about trying his hand at making a plum pudding as his mother did, but the idea faded quickly. He certainly did not know all the ingredients, but his memory of his mother making the pudding involved her covering the available counter space in the kitchen with various items. That represented more work than Walt was willing to invest.

Walt took another of the oatmeal cookies he had made for the students and made a personal vow to stick to the chocolate chip and peanut butter ones in the future. He wondered why he had even made oatmeal cookies in the first place. For some reason the oatmeal cookie question caused him to remember the Indian boy he had befriended in the 5th or 6th grade. David Gray Wolf, that was his name. David and Walt were about the same size and ended up on the same side in recess games. They became friends when Walt stayed after school one day to talk to a teacher about something. When Walt left the building, David was sitting out front, under a tree.

David was a half-breed. He and his Indian mother lived at the edge of town with his father, who worked construction on the dam project. That day David's mother told him to wait at the school for her to pick him up instead of walking home. So, Walt sat with him, and they shared thoughts and experiences until David's mother arrived. After that, the boys would often go to one or the other's home after school and play until time for the visitor to go home for supper. Walt remembered that David was an exceptional marble player, whether shooting for keeps at each other's marbles in the two-foot circle or lagging their agates at a hole in the ground eight feet away to play 'poison'.

Even though David won most of their games and took possession of many of his marbles, Walt was saddened when David told him they were moving to the Reservation. He left Whealton a day later, and Walt never saw him again. Walt finished his coffee but didn't get up from the kitchen table. He wondered why David had to move to the Reservation. He had no idea, then or later. As he thought about David Grey Wolf, Walt also remembered when Reservation Indians would come into town wearing full-feathered regalia to perform some ritual dances in front of the school building for tourists. These were members of the great Sioux Nation who lived on the reservation at Fort Peck. Once or twice a year this group would come during tourist season and entertain people who had come to see and tour the Dam.

Walt remembered going to these dances and looking for David for several years until his father told him that David was of the Crow Nation and was on a reservation on the other side of the state. He also recalled the sadness that news caused him; the recognition that he would never see his friend again had given him an intense gripping pain in his abdomen; he went to bed early without supper.

Sitting at his kitchen table almost seventy years later, Walt still felt that twinge in his gut as he thought about his friend. He thought about his similar feelings when recalling Jan.

*Why do I do this?* he asked himself. *What is the value of recreating these mental images that cause me so much separation pain?*

He got no answer.

So, Walt decided he should have a drink before bed. He went back into the living room, opened his liquor cabinet, grabbed a bottle of gin, and returned to the kitchen. He quickly found a small glass, poured himself three fingers of the clear liquid, and went upstairs to his bedroom.

# CHAPTER 29

## 01/21/2020 TUESDAY

They arrived at different times; Hal was on time, but Bella and Joey were almost fifteen minutes late. Walt met Hal at the door and asked, "Is it only you today, Hal?"

"Ah, no, sir. Joey and Bella were meeting with someone about their SAT scores."

"Come in. Do your scores not merit discussion then, Hal?"

They entered the living room with its cozy fire, and Hal took his usual seat. "Well, sir, it seems my score was not interesting to the recruiters from the Ivy League."

"I see. That's who's here today, is it?"

"Hmm. Are those chocolate chip?"

"Absolutely. And I promise no more of the oatmeal cookies."

"Joey seemed to like them."

"Well, perhaps I could make some just for him."

"He's like your favorite, then?"

"What? Not really, no. I don't play favorites, Hal. But I think I prefer talking to you."

"Me? Why?"

"Well, you don't seem to have an agenda. Bella is completely centered on this project you're working on, and Joey only pays attention to things he is already interested in. So, you're my favorite to talk to."

"Wow. Okay. What are we gonna talk about today?"

"Last week I believe you showed some interest in my friend, David."

"Who's he?"

"David Grey Wolf. My Indian friend."

"Oh, yeah. What about him?"

Walt introduced Hal to David at the 5th-grade level, describing his height, black hair, and light skin coloring. He was about to tell about their friendship after school when Hal asked, "Did he know an Indian language?"

Walt thought about that question before answering, "I don't know. I never asked him; we always talked in English. Why do you want to know, Hal?"

"Well, if he did and you learned it from him, maybe you could teach it to me."

"I see. I am sorry to disappoint you, but that never came up in discussion."

"How long did you know him?"

"Two years. Then he had to move to the reservation for some reason, and I never saw him again."

"That's tough. Did you feel really close to him?"

"Yes, I guess I did. Plus, I had lost most of my marbles, and I never got a chance to win them back."

"What do you mean, lost your marbles?"

Walt laughed and tried to school Hal about the value of glass marbles to young teenagers in the early 1950s. He described the various sizes and colors, and the two were in deep discussion about the strategy of playing 'poison' when Joey and Bella arrived.

They burst through the door wearing satisfied smiles, quickly shed their winter clothes, and hurried into the living room. Bella immediately picked up on the camaraderie and asked, "What are you guys talking about?"

"Marbles," Hal said, smiling and leaning back. "And Indians."

Joey grabbed a cookie and said, "I thought we heard all about that last week."

"Oh yes, Joey," Walt said. "We did. What's on your agenda this week?"

Joey hesitated to swallow his cookie, then said, "See, I was puzzled about the people in Montana having all those negative ideas about the Indians but not about the African-Americans."

"You mean, how could they be prejudiced against one group and not the other? Or, all others?"

"Yeah, maybe that's what I'm saying."

Walt looked at Bella, who had her notebook open and pen in hand, ready to record the answer to this question. But, instead of answering, Walt asked her opinion of the people in Montana regarding their obvious prejudice.

Bella scratched her nose and then said, "Well, in a way, it made some sense for them to hate the Indians because of their past …" Her reasoning dropped off, and she looked at Walt to get a clue about how to proceed.

He asked, "And they didn't understand the Southern racist attitude looking down on the blacks?"

She nodded quickly in agreement, "Yes, right."

Walt looked at her and asked, "Why couldn't they recognize the pattern? They were prejudiced against a racial minority they knew and had lived with for centuries. Wasn't that much like what the people in the South were exhibiting?"

Walt said, "Some have postulated the difference lies in the previous relationships. Southerners had thought Blacks were inferior and were being forced to treat them as equals. Northerners saw the Indians as opponents in a Range War and hated them but now were expected to put all those thoughts aside.

Bella squinted at Walt and looked down in her lap. Joey said, "I think that's what they both were doing, and probably both groups thought there was ample reason to think as they did."

Hal said, "That's pretty smart, Joey. Where'd you learn that?"

Joey started to react negatively to Hal's comment but stopped and said, "Probably learned that in this room. Didn't we all?"

Bella spoke, "Oh, I see. Yeah. Right, Joey. People are more likely to look down on folks they know about and are nearby. Is that it, Mr. Dell?"

Walt smiled and said, "That is the way of the world, of course. How many black students in your school?"

All three students nodded. Hal said, "There's ten of us in our grade."

"And how many of them do you count as friends?"

The White students shrugged and shook their heads. Then Joey pointed at Hal and said, "This guy is a friend."

"So, then are you racist?"

"No!" they said at once.

"Uh-huh. You just don't 'happen' to know these black kids, so they don't get included. What if you invited one of them to your study group and found them disruptive, and so didn't invite them back? Would that make you racist?"

"No, of course not," Joey said quickly. The Bella frowned at the suggestion and shook her head to agree with Joey. Hal made no response, Walt looked at him and asked, "Hal, what about it?"

He said, "Look, I don't feel like a token here, but I've been in classes with these two before and I have not seen 'racist' attitudes from them. Snobbish, maybe but not frank racism."

Joey started to say, "Wait, I'm not …" when Walt stopped him and asked Hal why he thought that about them. Bella leaned forward.

Hal's answer was simple. "I believe it's basic 'groupism', you know, a tendency to identify with a group. I've been in their classes for three years and that kinda makes me in the group. I don't know for sure what they would do if one of my Black friends that they don't know came in here and was disruptive."

Walt pressed Hal, "Hal, would you agree with not asking him back?"

Hal smiled and said, "Not until we had explained the 'rules' of the group and he, or she, chose not to comply."

Joey said, "That's right. We should tell them why."

Walt smiled and went on, "But if someone outside your group heard about it, or even the Black person brought it up, could you understand that they might think your decision was based on racism?"

"But it wasn't!" Bella said. And then all three looked at each other and slowly began to nod their heads.

Walt explained, "This is a thorny issue for everyone, my good friends. And there does not seem to be a clear way out of the forest when others are making charges of racism without factual information."

"I guess so," Bella agreed.

Walt said, "And then there are others who act out of real racist beliefs and make things even tougher for everyone. Racism is not an easy problem to solve. Mankind has a long history of looking down on some group - and it varies all over the world. The trick is you can't let your personal discomfort with any one person become a reason for judging a whole group."

"Okay," Hal said, and the others nodded.

Walt looked at each of them and said, "My own theory is we have fallen into a trap of thinking that diversity is a visual construct. We have been pushed into believing a diverse group must have colors of the rainbow. My own experience in the Army is that real, workable diversity that leads to improvement is diversity of ideas and thoughts - not skin color."

Slowly, each of the students nodded their head as they mentally wrestled with this concept.

Walt waited a minute, allowing the students to bring up another topic. When they didn't, he said, "Let me tell you a story. It's a real event. You know my wife was a teacher. One day, back in the mid-1960s, she brought home a postcard that one of her students said her mother got from someone in Germany back in 1957. The picture showed the front steps of the Central High School in Little Rock, Arkansas and focused on armed National Guard soldiers standing at the front door. Coming up the steps were some black students. And the banner across the postcard read, in German, "American Troops block black students from attending school."

Hal, Joey, and Bella exchanged glances but did not speak.

Walt asked, "Do you know what was going on there?"

"Not really," Hal said. Walt waited until both Joey and Bella shrugged their shoulders. Then he shook his head and said, "My wife had a friend teaching in Little Rock Central that year. She told us that the Governor of Arkansas sent the National Guard to block the students' entry, but President Eisenhower then federalized the Guard to prevent them from doing so in the future. He mobilized a guard unit from Kentucky to face down any mob and escort the black kids into the school. The picture on the postcard shows the Kentucky Guard assuring the entry of the black kids to the school, not the opposite."

"Wow," said Hal. "Did not know all that. I just heard the Army was called out to prevent integration."

"Something that was only partially true. But that's what stuck in many people's minds. Even now, there are some who claim the country is totally racist, and this is one of the examples they use. I tell you, I've seen a lot of racism in the world. This thing on the school steps was bad enough, but I don't see anything like that around today."

"Do you think there's no racism in America?" asked Joey.

"Not what I said, Joey. Of course, there's some racism in America. Just like the rest of the world. Always has been and always probably will."

"That's depressing," said Bella.

"Well," Walt said, "you're the generation to wipe it out."

Belle slumped back against the couch cushion, "I can't see any way to do that." Joey nodded and Hal avoided everyone's eyes.

Walt said, "John Roberts, Chief Justice of the Supreme Court told us all exactly how to do it several years ago."

The students expressed their curiosity. "What?" "What did he say?

Walt held up his hand and said, "Roberts said, 'The way to stop discrimination on the basis of race is to stop discriminating on the basis of race.' …That's pretty straight-forward then, isn't it?"

Belle opined, "I don't know …", Joey said "Simplistic."

Hal said, "Functional, and personal. And that will take generations."

# CHAPTER 30

01/21/2020 TUESDAY

After the students left, Walt stood in front of the fire and thought about their reaction to his comment about their responsibility for ending racism. At first, they seemed seriously awed by the prospect and then, as they redressed for the outside, they had begun to comment on reasons why the task was too large. Oddly, Bella seemed the most resistant to taking on the mission.

Walt watched them navigate the slick sidewalk to the street, then closed the door and returned to the fire. He wondered if they would return when the Tuesday for their next scheduled meeting appeared. They had gathered all the information they would need for their project. Walt remembered they had said so, back in December.

*But,* Walt thought, *they did come back after that. For more … what did Bella say? "A deeper understanding", that's what it was.* Walt worried that the deeper understanding they may have gained might make them hesitant to learn any more about their role in growing up.

Walt shook his head, and asked himself, *'What are you thinking, old man? Do you believe you were so much smarter than they are when you were that age? You ran off and joined the Army. Didn't have any idea what that was all about, did you?'*

He wasn't about to answer himself. Walt didn't want to get into the can of worms behind his sudden decision to leave Whealton. And, of course, he knew that signing up for the military was the only place he had to go if he left town.

Walt thought to himself, *Cut it out, old man. You don't want those memories.* He went into the kitchen and started the ritual of making his evening coffee. While the kettle was heating, he located the leftover cookies from the last few weeks and put them on a plate. Later, while the coffee was brewing in the French Press, he sorted the oatmeal cookies from the others and threw them away.

The fire was a long way from being burned out, so Walt sat in his chair and stared into the flames, sipping the coffee. He wondered why he had gone all 'Sergeant-at-arms' on the students. He had no place giving them a life-long assignment, especially one so all-encompassing as the elimination of racism. Thankfully, they had already begun extracting themselves from the obligation before they got out the door. Walt determined he would not be that directive with them again - if they returned.

He got up, moved to the liquor cabinet and found the bottle of Kahlua. He poured a shot into his coffee and replaced the bottle. Sipping his fortified drink, Walt wondered why he wasn't racist. Was it because he had been raised away from Blacks, and even Indians? That was certainly true, except for David. Or maybe it was because he knew David and didn't believe all Indians were inferior. David was certainly not inferior when it came to winning at marbles.

Walt was certain that he was not racist when he left Whealton. In fact, he remembered right after he arrived in Boot Camp, the guy in the next bunk was Black, from St. Louis. And he was funny. A great sense of humor kept the whole barracks laughing. What was that guy's name? Walt closed his eyes to help visualize the man in the next bunk. Big guy, probably six foot two, very muscular, incredibly white teeth. *Tim? Tom? Tom, no ... Thomas.*

Walt opened his eyes, pleased that he could bring back that memory of Thomas' name. *Not going to try to remember his last name. Only the Sergeant called anybody by a last name.* Walt remembered Thomas's strength and stamina during boot camp. He remembered Thomas finishing the five-mile run comfortably in third or fourth place and explaining later that he could have finished first, but he didn't want 'to attract attention'.

Walt also remembered exchanging stories of high school with Thomas at meals. Thomas had also played football, but his team won most of their games.

He played basketball, too, and that team was district champion in his junior year. So, not so similar, but whatever, they both were athletes. Walt took a deep draught of his coffee and puzzled over whatever happened to Thomas. They were separated after boot camp and did not maintain contact. Walt didn't know what happened to anybody in the barracks after they left boot camp. *Huh.*

Walt wondered if he had any other Black friends while in service. There were some Black guys and women that he worked with; friends, not so much. He did recollect this one guy, a Sergeant, who was known for pushing people and nit-picking their work. Walt certainly didn't like that Black man. He sipped his coffee again and wondered, *'Did I dislike him because he was Black?'* He told himself that skin color wasn't the cause of the dislike - even the Black guys hated that Sergeant.

Then Walt remembered Leo. Another Black Sergeant that Walt had encountered in Gordon. By then, Walt was also a Sergeant, and Leo was not pulling rank. Leo was just the most foul-mouthed individual Walt had encountered. Leo could not complete a sentence without including a swear word or a reference to some smutty activity. Walt recalled that Leo wanted the two of them to go for drinks after work, and Walt had trouble keeping that from happening. And, he remembered, he also knew some White guys with very foul mouths. *Apparently foul language is not race-restricted.*

Walt's coffee was gone. Walt snuggled back in his chair and contemplated the fire. So, he thought, I met a lot of Blacks, men and women, in the service. Most of them were bright, adventurous, and motivated. And they were all disciplined. The Army will do that for you. But Walt could not decide if he had ever treated those Blacks differently from the way he treated others. He decided he had probably not. Because he couldn't remember, except for Leo, any reason to act differently or to avoid them. But they were all different, Walt remembered. Some were funny, like Thomas, others were stiff and withdrawn, even somewhat defensive.

Well, Walt concluded, those differences were not at variance from his observations about everybody in the military. In boot camp, the Sergeants kept telling them they were no longer individuals; they were part of a team. The drill Sergeant yelled at Walt many times about not trying to understand an order. If he was told to jump, Sergeant said the only response was 'how high?' Walt remembered those encounters with a grim smile and wondering *I guess drill sergeant never met Sergeant Miles or learned about HUA.* He continued thinking about the differences between each man in the platoon and his neighbor.

One thing he remembered was how all the Irish guys talked about how they were knew they were going to die. Not the manner of their death so much, as the conviction that the next activity they were forced to complete would end with them dead in the dust. When he first heard this, Walt had been alarmed but by the end of boot camp, he understood this fatalism was a trait of the Irish. And that trait made Walt think about the few Italians he had met and how they could cuss you up one side and down the other and take you cussing them back with what appeared to be a pleasure. But nobody could insult that man's mother without getting punched in the face and thrown to the ground for kicking.

And, Walt remembered, thinking about mothers and sons, how nearly everyone thought their mother was the best cook in world history, but those southern boys took that belief to an astronomical level. Walt also remembered that many of the guys were willing to concede the 'best cook' title to a mother whose reported best dishes involved things like okra, fried green tomatoes, chitlins, a dish called hoppin' john, collard greens, and fried pickles. Or that involved oysters in the dressing on Thanksgiving.

The fire was dying as Walt thought about his time on the target range. He knew right away that anybody from one of Midwestern states was going to be better with a rifle than anybody from back East big cities. People who had hunted and brought home their dinner for several years before joining the Army were happy that they were finally going to shoot the 'big guns'.

Walt stood up and stretched. He carried his cup and the cookie plate into the kitchen and put them in the sink. The liquor was making him sleepy, but he remembered his question for the evening. Was he or had he ever been racist? He blinked hard a few times, but the answer escaped him. All he could be certain of, after his experiences in the Army and hearing from his wife about students and their parents, was that people are people. Some are likable, others are not. And to the best of his mind at that moment, Walt couldn't think of those differences related to where you're from or how you were raised, or what your skin color was. People were just people. Walt knew he liked most people he had met, but there were a few he avoided - and, come to think of it - probably because they were acting like racists.

Walt went upstairs thinking perhaps he had solved one of the great mysteries of the world.He decided he would write it down the next morning.

# CHAPTER 31



The students did come back to see Walt. He had made some fudge hoping that they would arrive to share it. Walt was a little embarrassed that the fudge had not properly set and was somewhat runny; he supplied small bowls and spoons along with a pitcher of milk.

The students burst through the door, talking to each other and shouting questions at Walt. They were clearly not inhibited by the last discussion they had with him.

Bella wanted to know if his wife had any experience as a social worker. Walt was puzzled about the question but couldn't give his negative answer quickly enough to prevent Joey from interrupting to ask whether Walt knew anything about the LSAT test. These questions, along with some pushing and inter-group comments, supplemented their move from the doorway into the living room.

After they had taken their usual seat, Walt explained the bowls and spoons for the fudge, and Joey made the distribution of several spoonsful in each bowl while Bella addressed the dispersal of milk in glasses. That operation took several minutes, also accompanied by joking and ad-libs.

Walt sat quietly in his chair and thought about how differently they acted during those first few sessions. Back then, they were quiet, relatively still, seemingly serious students. That first impression contrasted greatly with the happy, active, talkative young people they had become. He was pleased and determined not to bring up the serious topic that closed their last meeting.

Satisfied with the allotment of fudge, Joey took a small bite and asked, "So, what do you know about the LSAT, Mr. Dell?"

Walt smiled at him and answered, "You know, Joey, I do believe we have known each other long enough and well enough that we could use our first names. You may call me Walt. At least in this house."

"Yes, sir. I'd like that. I think we all feel like we know you pretty well."

"All right, then Walt it is. And your question is rather easily answered. I don't know much at all about the LSAT. Are you thinking of choosing law as a profession?"

"A little, yeah. One of my father's friends was talking about it with me last week and he encouraged me to consider the law."

"Do you know what Shakespeare thought of lawyers, Joey"

"Uh, I guess I don't."

Bella started to laugh.

Walt noted this and said, "I believe Bella knows what I'm talking about."

"What?" Hal asked.

Bella explained, "Shakespeare wrote, 'First, let's kill all the lawyers.' That's what you mean, isn't it, Mr., er, Walt?"

"Yes, Bella, that is the quote most often used to support Shakespeare's disdain for the profession. But that's not what everyone thinks is the meaning of what Shakespeare wrote."

"Eh?" said Hal.

"What do you mean?" asked Bella while Joey spread upturned palms.

"Well, the speaker of those lines was encouraging revolution and the removal of restrictions on society, saying basically, 'for our plan to succeed, there must be chaos and lawlessness.' At least that's how lawyers always interpret the line."

"Huh. I never heard that before."

"Probably haven't discussed it with a lawyer. Truth is, however, Shakespearean experts have no question that he was showing disdain for the profession. The men involved in that scene go on to mock the parchment on which a law degree is printed, and then they murder someone for not meeting their definition of a man of honor."

"So, what's the real meaning?"

Walt smiled and leaned back in his chair. "Oh, I'm pretty certain the old Bard meant the comment as a slam against lawyers. Didn't like them at all."

After a brief silence and a good deal of fudge eating, Joey asked, "What does all that have to do with the LSAT?"

Walt nodded and put down his bowl of fudge. "Next to nothing, Joey. I don't know about the LSAT. I have known some guys who took the test and said it was difficult, but that's it."

"Difficult how?"

"Mostly, I believe, because it made them think. These guys were smart enough, but they were a little lazy in thinking things through. So, I'm guessing the test made them think, and that was too hard for some."

"Oh."

Hal butted in to ask, "Why didn't you go to college? I mean, why did you go directly into the Army and then stay there?"

Walt picked at the last bit of fudge in his bowl before answering. "See, Hal, when I graduated from high school, going to college was not always an option for everyone. It cost money that many of us in high school didn't have. And our parents didn't have that kind of money in savings either."

"But why the Army?"

"I promised you I'd tell you about the G.I. Bill some time, didn't I? Well, this is going to be the time."

"Okay."

Walt settled back into his chair and said, "At the end of the war, 1944 or 45, the United States government realized it had some issues with all the veterans coming home. Congress passed this bill that spent money on hospitals for vets, and provided low-interest loans to buy a house. But they also put something in the bill to pay for tuition and expenses for veterans who wanted to attend school and learn a trade or get a degree."

"I didn't know that." Hal's comment was reflected in the blank look on the faces of both Bella and Joey.

"It was possibly the greatest government program ever. And, even today, it is not a well-advertised feature of military service."

Hal scratched his head and asked, "If you had that opportunity to go to school, why didn't you?"

Walt shrugged and answered, "I don't reckon college is for everyone, Hal. Didn't seem like it was for me. I don't mind learning, but I wasn't keen on being in a classroom. After all, there was a library on every base where the Army sent me. I could go there for information on any topic. I came out of high school in 1957 and by the time I was eligible to leave the Army and get the GI Bill, I had a good job and liked what I was doing. I didn't want to do something else at the moment, and I never developed a wish to do other than what the Army had me doing."

"What was that, Walt? I mean, what all did you do in the military?" Joey wanted to know.

"Well, I was in Communications, and back then, that meant radio mostly. I guess I had a unit commander who thought I could do more than that; he's responsible for getting me assigned to keyboarding, and that got me into the computer business. I told you I was involved with card punch input into the early computers."

"Yeah, that was fascinating."

"Well, what I didn't tell you was that the military was definitely in the lead on the development of computer science. Our enemies were working on it, and so we were, too. I learned different computer programming skills, and when I retired from the Army in 1980, I came here and went to work for a little company called RPG."

"Little? You know that RPG is one of the biggest military and industrial contractors!" Bella said, impressed.

"Well, they weren't then. And I was just a young CWO."

Bella wanted to know, "What's a CWO?"

"Chief Warrant Officer, Bella. It's neither fish nor fowl in the military. It is a rank between the enlisted ranks and the officer corps."

"Why did you do that?" Hal wanted to know as he reached to see if any fudge remained in the pan.

"You mean, why did I become a Warrant Officer?"

"Yes."

"For the money. I got paid like an officer, and I got to keep my regular job and not boss a bunch of other guys around."

Hal asked, "How long does it take to get promoted like that in the Army?"

Walt looked at Hal for a long time before answering, "It varies, Hal. Certain areas require more highly skilled and capable persons, like fixed-wing aircraft or helicopter pilots, or nuclear energy experts. They like to start with college graduates but not always. Other fields with a lot of demand include anything that requires intelligence and where the civilian job market offers a high salary."

"Huh."

"It's kinda wide open, Hal."

"I don't know what I want to do."

Walt gestured at Bella and Joey, "Even those who think they know what path they want to be on, change their minds. I've told kids for years that unless you have a fire in your belly for something, don't go to college to figure things out. Instead, take some time and spend two years in the military. You'll be a better person for it and whatever decision you make at that point is more likely to be right for you than the one you would have made coming out of high school."

"Really?"

"Yes. You probably don't know this, but most Master's degree programs will not consider taking a person right out of college. They insist their applicants have at least two years of work experience before the program will consider them for an advanced degree."

Bella said, "I didn't know that. Why?"

"Experience, I presume. Another level of maturity, maybe."

Joey asked, "Is that true of Law Schools, too?"

Walt smiled, "I don't think so, Joey. I don't think so. I knew some guys that went to Law School from college. They were in a Guard Unit, and I met them on weekends."

After a moment's pause in the conversation, Bella changed the subject, "We were thinking about what you said last time we were here."

Walt swallowed heavily and said nothing.

She went on, "We think it's too big for any one of us to make the necessary changes, but maybe we can make little ones. Like maybe Social Work or Legal Aid." She smiled at Joey, who shrugged.

Then they all started talking at once and ran over their scheduled time to leave. Bella noticed about thirty minutes later and said, "Oh gosh, we're going to be late!"

They grabbed their coats and left in a hurry, but each one said to Walt, "We'll finish this when we get back."

Walt stood at the door and watched them hustle toward the school.

*"Kids today,"* he thought to himself as he headed for the kitchen.

# CHAPTER 32

## 02/04/2020 TUESDAY

Walt sat in the kitchen with his coffee. He tried scraping the fudge pan for a little treat, but found that Hal had taken care of any residual. He put the pan in the sink to soak and sat down, thinking about what a protected life he had experienced. Walt had thought about this topic before and this time the litany of personal successes came quickly to mind.

First, there was the escape from Whealton. He preferred not to think about the events that led up to that departure and moved quickly on.

The Army assigned him to the Communications Branch right out of Boot Camp. He learned the classroom lessons easily and did well enough as a lineman that he was promoted on time. Walt suddenly realized there were other reasons he had been so happy in the Army, especially in those early years. He recalled telling Madeline many years later that he actually enjoyed the freedom from having to decide what to wear each morning. Walt admitted that he had no memory of being clothes conscious in high school, but knowing what he was going to wear every day was 'freedom' for him. Plus, he might tell the students, your name is sewed on all your clothes so you can't lose them in the laundry. Just like kindergarten. Walt believed that. In some degree, the 'freedom' he had from wardrobe choice allowed him to be successful at his work. Then, when Command came looking for someone to move into the keycarding position, his unit commander recommended him.

Once he was oriented and started work in the computer group, Walt was again promoted and moved into the air-conditioned room with the big computer boxes with the whirling discs. After that, he never faced the possibility of being assigned to a mission that would require him to fire a weapon. Walt thought how much he appreciated that shelter. He had done well on the target range, even earning a Marksman badge. But, thinking back to Whealton, he wanted to never again hold a weapon in a conflict with another person.

Walt thought again that he might help Hal and the others understand his attraction to the military if he could explain his own satisfaction with having a responsibility to and for a power greater than himself and a job that carried a satisfaction of doing it for something other than money. He remembered one programmer saying, "As little as we get paid, you can be sure we ain't working for the money."

His move from keypunch operator to programmer was slower in coming but was only made possible by Walt taking some programming courses. He also received some personal tutoring from one of the programmers. Not everyone in the unit had those experiences. Because of those sessions and classes, Walt was the obvious choice as commander of the unit a couple of years later. That move put him in Army leadership courses and led directly to him accepting a Warrant Officer position.

Walt had been proud of the WO designation. It allowed him and his wife to eat at the Officers Club, for one thing. He remembered that he had previously bragged about his service time as compensated by 'free food and lodging.' After he attended one of the Beef and Burgundy galas at the Officers Club, however, he developed a new, even higher, opinion of military meals. The most important part of that promotion, Walt recalled, was that he was no longer subject to mobilization alerts. That reminded him of another major benefit of military service: free medical care. He had his pelvic fracture treated and carried a classification of 20% disabled because of it.

The timing of his appointment to the Warrant Officer ranks abetted by the speed at which the computing science advanced, Walt made Chief quickly. His first commanding officer after that appointment recommended that he enter Officer Candidate School. Walt and his relatively new wife, Madeline, sat down for a detailed talk about this opportunity. They decided to turn it down, have Walt remain at his rank for the next few years and retire to Madeline's hometown. Walt remembers thinking he wouldn't make rank to field grade before retiring and likely would have less income if he went to OCS.

Madeline was happy with their retirement in Springfield. She quickly found a job teaching seventh grade science in the local school system and Walt found a job in the senior management of RPG overseeing the computerization of their operations. Walt sipped on his coffee thinking about their relocation to Springfield and their indecision about where to live. They initially thought about a mobile home in a park but Walt found the home where he now sat before they left Gordon. He smiled thinking that some of their belongings didn't arrive until they were in the new house, almost as if the trunks and boxes had been purposefully waiting in a military warehouse until the Dells settled on their new home.

It had been an exciting time, Walt thought. Many mentors and teachers had been involved in his career. Even after he got to RPG, he found one of the owners was a former programmer for the Army with some significant skills. The man didn't want to manage, he just wanted to program, so he put Walt in a senior position and backed him with the other owners. That man lived only six years after Walt joined the company and Walt was chosen by the partners to gain a partnership position when his mentor died.

The decision to make Walt a partner settled his retirement security, although he and Madeline had no difficulty living on her salary, his military retirement, and access to the Exchange. When Madeline became ill with multiple sclerosis and took a drastic downhill course, Walt was glad to have the medical care from Tricare available locally since getting to a military medical facility was at least 90 minutes away. But, after Madeline died, Walt realized he had no driving interest in his work any longer. He wanted only to sit on his porch and read Great Books.

Sitting in the kitchen and recalling these major milestones of his life, Walt realized he had no memories of success or mentoring in Whealton. He had told the students a smattering of memories from his childhood, most of which were bare of significant detail. He knew the memory blank he experienced had more to do with the events and the people surrounding his leaving. Perhaps he could bring back good memories of his high school time, now that he had started peeling back that onion with these students.

But, as he sat there with his coffee getting cold, Walt found it difficult to recall anything about that long ago time without Jan being in the picture as well. He thought of the school or classes and there she was. If he tried to focus on athletic events, Jan the cheerleader always appeared. Most painful was Walt's inability to recall the Philosophy Group sessions without Jan's presence.

Walt rinsed his cup and started upstairs. Then, he changed course, went back to the liquor cabinet to get the bottle of gin and to pour himself three fingers.

# CHAPTER 33

## 02/14/2020 FRIDAY

"You're kidding, right?" Hal asked.

"Really?" echoed Bella.

"I can show it all to you, right here on Google Earth. More accurately, I can show you where it was."

"How can it be gone?" Hal wondered. "I mean, aren't there some streets and buildings and stuff?"

"Well, yeah," Joey admitted, "There are buildings and some remaining streets, but it's nothing like Walt was telling us."

"So, you think he was making it all up?" Bella asked.

"That's not what I said and not what I meant. Let me show you."

Joey opened his laptop, quickly moved to Google Earth, and situated the camera to show a plat in Northern Montana, just off U.S Rt. 2. The circle road that moved west of Rt.2, then rejoined the highway was still present. Near the apex of the circle formed by that road were three branching roads internal to the circle. Each of these roads swung into the circle and then back to rejoin it. On the second road was a two-story building labeled 'Whealton Hotel'. There appeared to be no store, gas station, or other commercial activity in the area. Within the circle were ten to twelve structures that might be dwellings. These were near the internal roads, and some appeared near the few scattered trees.

Unmarked roads in the area ran between squares and rectangles of property. South of Rt.2 was a large curve in the Missouri River, coming up from the Fort Peck area and then curving southeasterly towards the Dakotas. Two large sandbars were clearly visible in the river south of the curve. A sloping riverside nearby provided access.

"Yipes," Hal said. "It's like a ghost town."

"Without the saloon and sheriff's office," Bella noted.

Joey moved the screen to the south and showed them the better-preserved town of Fort Peck with several streets, a hundred houses, and a post office. "If you compare these two towns, it's obvious which one the government keeps up, isn't it?"

"Is that the difference?" Bella asked.

"Oh, yeah. Fort Peck was a government town during construction, and Whealton just grew up to support the men working there. Once the job was over and those men and their families moved away, there was no real need for the town."

"Fort Peck doesn't look all that big itself," Hal noted. "I don't even see a building called a school."

Joey said, "I looked it up. They're less than 250 people living there now. Almost all are government employees with jobs at the dam itself."

Bella asked, "What do they do, watch the waterfall?"

Joey grinned at her, "You know the dam is hydroelectric, right? The employees are there for maintenance of the dam and road and powerhouses, and even the spillway. Some are engineers running the care of the turbines, and the powerhouses, and the others have to keep up the facility for visitors and keep dredge out of the spill. There are also some people who work for the Indian Reservations, both civilians and Bureau of Indian Affairs."

"But Whealton?" Hal pursued.

"According to what I read, several shanty towns sprang up in the area to handle the construction workers. Whealton had been there before and was the first to grow in population. Maybe because it had a school, a post office, and stuff like that."

"And the lack of construction made that all collapse?" Bella was skeptical.

"It appears so. I mean, Whealton had a C-class high school and competed in the local athletic league, so they were different from the other shantytowns that were basically just housing with some eating places and maybe a grocery store. But, when they all died, that also shut down Whealton."

"Huh," Hal said. "That makes us talking to Walt sorta like opening a time capsule."

Bella nodded, noting, "That's what Ms. Postella was after."

Joey asked, "What do you mean?"

"I mean, her intent with this project is for us, and every team, to 'open up a time capsule' by interviewing people like Walt."

"How'd you come to that conclusion?"

"Well, look at her instructions. The project can't be based primarily on reading, and it's not something our parents can help with either. She wants stuff that's not written down. Stuff that only folks like Walt know and can tell us."

Joey said, "That may make my idea about how to present this package even better."

Hal asked, "How's that, Joey?"

"Well, you remember how I was talking about using the computer to game up a virtual world? Given this information from Bella, we can make the history around the Hungarian Revolution interpreted by the people Walt has told us about."

"That's not a lot of characters," Bella noted.

"So, we talk to him some more and get him talking about the people in the town."

Bella looked at joey with an amused grin, "You know, K.I.A., I think that sounds like you're enjoying talking to the old man."

Joey sheepishly grinned back. "I am. He's interesting. I kinda thought all old people were hunkered down to their schedules and early bedtimes. Walt doesn't seem like that at all."

Hal agreed, "Right. He sounds like a lot of common sense to me."

"So, let's all listen carefully to what he says and get him talking more about the people there in Whealton. We don't have to get wrapped up in their later history. We need some individuals to populate our virtual town."

# CHAPTER 34

## 02/18/2020 TUESDAY

Walt was not at the door to greet them as he usually was. They knocked and heard a distant voice, "Come on in!"

The students entered the hallway and noted the empty living room. Bella loudly announced, "We're here."

Walt's voice came from the kitchen, "I'm in the kitchen. Come back here."

They followed his advice and found him sitting at the table with a large cup of coffee and several thick catalogs opened in front of him. He was making detailed notes on a legal paper pad. The students stood quietly observing for a moment, and then Hal asked, "What's going on?"

"My favorite activity in February. Going through all this year's seed catalogs."

"What for?" Joey asked, sitting down across the table from Walt.

"Two purposes, really, I guess. One is to see what's new in breeding of some varieties. These geneticists in agriculture have made great improvements over the last couple of decades, you know."

Hal and Bella took seats across from each other, and Bella wanted to know, "What kinds of improvements?"

Walt detected some skepticism in the girl's question. He replied, "Let's take tomatoes, for instance. Maybe you aren't aware, but tomatoes have been grown in American gardens for two centuries, even though they were initially considered poisonous."

"What?"

"Oh, yes. When tomatoes first were taken to Europe from Central America, they were a small fruit, larger than berries but not by much. The plants were used ornamentally for decades - even in Italy and the Mediterranean area."

"Huh, I didn't know that," Hal said.

"Even in America, when people started eating them, they weren't large and mostly ended up in sauces."

"So, what happened," Joey asked.

Walt took a sip of his coffee and replied, "There was a man named Alexander Livingston who started cross-fertilizing plants for different characteristics. At first, his interest was to create a uniform shape and size of the fruit for canning. Of course, his work also produced bigger fruit, different colored fruit, consistent odd-shaped fruit and some with thick flesh, others with more seeds."

"When was all this?"

"Oh, late 19th century and early 20th."

"And that made everyone want tomatoes?"

"Well, there were a lot of recipes using tomatoes brought here by immigrants from Europe, especially Mediterranean countries. Plus, Livingston showed that almost anyone could raise their own tomatoes; the plants are hardy. So, people started growing them in home gardens. The tomato is today the most common home garden plant in America. Everybody loves them, and every gardener has personal secrets about growing them."

"Do you/?" asked Hal.

"Of course, I do."

"Will you show us?"

"Perhaps. But that day is far off."

"Why?"

Walt stopped and looked at each student before asking, "Do your parents have a home vegetable garden?"

Bella and Joey shook their heads as if acknowledging an obvious trait of the Upper Class. Hal nodded briskly, however, and said, "Yeah, my Mom grows tomatoes and peppers."

Walt turned to him and asked, "Does she do well?"

"I guess so. I mean, we have plenty of tomatoes in the fall. I don't care for the peppers and I don't know about them."

"How does she plant?"

"She gets some plants from the hardware store."

"Yes, many people do that. I prefer to start the plants myself. So I get seeds."

Joey was intrigued. "When do you plant seeds? It seems like you would be way behind the guys that put plants in the ground."

"That's true, Joey. But I don't plant seeds in the ground. I put them in little potting containers and grow my own seedlings. And I try to time things, so I plant my seedlings about the same time the commercial ones are ready to go in the ground."

"When is that?" Bella asked, rejoining the conversation after a period of thinking about the genetic modification of tomato plants.

Walt said, "At this latitude, early to mid-May is best. Usually have some fruit around the fourth of July."

"So, what seeds are you looking to get from these catalogs?"

"My little garden is getting hard to keep, and I have cut down on the plants I get compared to several years ago. I've tried growing some odd things in that garden."

"Like what?"

"Bok Choy, for one. Chinese vegetable. But I tried Broccoli, Cauliflower, Brussels sprouts, and several types of lettuce."

"All from seeds?"

"Yes, of course. But the last few years, I've only grown tomatoes, peppers and cucumbers."

The students were silent for several moments, so Walt closed his catalogs and said, "I don't believe, for a minute, you came here today to get my gardening secrets. What is the topic for today, Bella?"

She smiled at him and answered, "We would like more detail about some of the people in Whealton. You know, background to their attitude and comments about the Revolution."

"Anybody in particular?"

"How about the barber?" Hal stuck in.

Walt finished his coffee and looked at Hal. He said, "I don't remember the guy's name for certain, but I think it was Joe. Probably about five foot ten or so, a little overweight. He had very short-cut hair, what I have come to think of as a military cut. And he had a little bald spot starting at the top in the back."

"Was he for America going into Hungary?"

"You know, I don't recall. And that's probably because he was such a good barber."

Joey scoffed, "What's cutting hair got to do with political beliefs?"

"Absolutely nothing, of course. And a good barber would never risk alienating a customer by arguing a different side of a political question."

"What?"

"Barbers are a lot like bartenders, you know. Except I'll bet you don't know a lot of bartenders."

"What do you mean?"

"Both types of jobs are face-to-face customer service positions. To some degree, their income may depend on repeat business, right?"

"I suppose …"

"So, they don't want to drive away customers by arguing with them - unless that's what the customer wants."

"They want an argument?"

"Well, they may want to have a vigorous and detailed discussion with someone from the other side and not risk alienating their brother-in-law, or somebody like that."

"Oh."

"Most every barber I've seen will ask questions, not answer them. They will give very central opinions when pushed, and they spend a lot of time with their mouth shut. And the good bartenders do the same. To do either job well, a person should be a good listener. And I mean hearing what is being said and keeping the customer talking. One should never get into that kind of conversation and try to play Can You Top This? Or give advice. The worst thing in the world is to give advice. No, I take that back. The worst thing for either of those positions would be to break a confidence."

"So, was this 'Joe' a good barber?"

"Best I could tell, he was. But, remember, I was in high school, and he wasn't about to talk politics with me anyway. I never heard anyone mentioning Joe's position on anything other than the weather."

"How about your neighbors or your friends' parents?"

"Yeah, we did have some conversations with them. Charlie's Dad was an engineer on the dam construction, and didn't want any distractions. He argued with me about the need for America to intervene, but the discussion was always moderately paced and muted volume. His calmness prevented me from becoming more vigorous in arguing. He was the first adult to tell me he understood how I would come to the decision to intervene, but he predicted I would understand why that was wrong in 10 years."

Walt paused, looked up at the ceiling, calculated dates, and then said, "And, that's just about how long it took."

"Was he a veteran?"

"No. He wasn't. But one of our neighbors was. I cut this man's lawn for several years, and I had asked his opinion, because he was retired military. He was very strong in his position that we should not stick our noses into 'that mess in Europe' as he called it. He did not want to see war again and was convinced the Soviets would see our involvement as cause for war."

Bella scribbled as fast as she could to keep up with Walt. Joey asked, "Do you remember anyone specifically who was in favor of American intervention?"

"Oh yes. One of the Mingo brothers. He had graduated a couple of years before but didn't go to college. He was a bag boy at the grocery store, and he and I agreed about the need for our Army to get into Hungary to support the Revolution. If I remember right, he went and enlisted."

"Wow. That's really following your principles," Hal noted.

"Yes, it is," Walt noted, "That may have played a part in my decision, too. But that was more than a year later."

Bella nudged, "Anyone else?"

"Oh. I remember the couple in the drug store. He was the pharmacist, and she ran the soda fountain. Coach used to give us quarters to get a milkshake at the fountain after games where he judged that we had played well and tried hard. Thankfully, he didn't reward wins only. We'd never have been in that store."

Joey noted the tendency to get off the path, and asked, "Did they agree with you about the Revolution?"

"Well, that was a split decision. The pharmacist had a medical deferment from military service, and thought the Army should invade and 'shoot them all'. His wife was a complete pacifist and opposed any involvement at all. I remember because Charlie used to try to get them to argue when he ordered a strawberry shake. He thought the wife might get distracted and put an excess of strawberries in his drink. Never happened. She was a professional."

Walt paused and thought of something else. "Speaking of professionals, let me tell you about the Sheriff in Whealton. He was about fifty, and had mostly white hair. I think he had retired from some city police job. The deputy was not a lot older than us. He was from one of the ranches around. For some reason, about this same time, they were spending part of their day showing kids around the jail, locking them in the cells for a few minutes to show them what a life of crime would get them."

"Anyway, when they showed us around, they argued different positions. Deputy wanted to go over there, personally. The Sheriff said he couldn't imagine a good outcome if America went in. And, no, Bella, Neither one of them was a veteran."

"Did you know any veterans in favor of intervention?"

Walt made a little smile and said, "Actually, there was one. I almost forgot about him. Funny guy. I mean weird, not humorous. He was the guy at the front desk of the small hotel in town we had for visitors. He looked too thin for height, always had a scraggly beard, and often had a bandana tied around his head. He usually wore blue jeans and a large buckle on the belt. No matter the outside temperature, he only wore a T-shirt and a vest. This guy had tattoos on both arms and always had a lit cigarette in his mouth. Sometimes our

Philosophy Group would go to the hotel lobby where we could get 32-ounce bottles of our favorite soda. And Andy Steward would always go talk to this guy whose name was also Andy."

"And Andy, the desk man, was all for intervention. He was a veteran and would explain to us how the U.S. Army had such powerful weapons that the Soviets would run and hide if we went into Hungary. None of us believed he knew what he was talking about, but he was fun to listen to."

"There was another guy down the block from our house with a flagpole in his front yard. He had a yard sign that supported going into Hungary, but I never talked to him about it.

"Veteran?" Bella asked.

"Don't know. Or can't remember. Sorry."

Bella looked up from her notes and smiled, "That's very helpful, Walt. We needed that kind of information. It's a big help."

Walt smiled knowingly at her. She blushed and said, "Well, our time is up. See you soon."

She and the boys returned to the front door, got their coats, and were gone in a few seconds. Walt didn't move from his seat at the table. He thought about that day's talk briefly, and then decided it was time for another cup of coffee to finish his plan for seed orders.

# CHAPTER 35

02/18/2020 TUESDAY

Walt let his thoughts ramble as he leafed through the catalogs. He browsed the identical ones and considered similar seeds every year, but he only ordered tomato and pepper seeds for the backyard. But, he enjoyed looking at the fruit and vegetables and imagining that his garden was big enough for them all. He sipped his coffee and recalled how his father would go through similar catalogs each winter to discuss with Walt's mother the options of one new vegetable to order for that year. His father tried something new every year; if it grew in Northern Montana, he would decide about future plantings by the reception it got at the dinner table.

His father's willingness to try new things each year provided Walt with an introduction to bok choy. The funny-looking Chinese cabbage did well in the cool spring and in the fall leading up to the first snow. Walt's mother was unsure about the best way to cook bok choy, so she prepared it the same way she did cabbage - she boiled it. When she brought it to the table, steaming and well garnished with butter, it was an instant favorite; Walt's father added it to the list of seeds he ordered from Burpee every spring. That attitude was why Mr. Dell was the first in the area to try the soon-to-be-famous Big Boy tomato.

Walt had many pleasant memories of the garden. He and his father would go early in the spring when there was still snow on the ground to break up the dirt and turn the clover under. Mr. Dell used a two-handled push plow to break up the topsoil; Walt's job was to follow behind, turn the top layer over and use a hoe to break up any large clods. When they returned to the area several weeks later to begin preparation for planting, the growth of weeds was minimal and easily handled. Then, they would work the soil with a hoe and rake until it was loose and contained no large clods. Mr. Dell organized planting in mid-May using a map of the plot he had drawn rotating crops. Corn was planted in five to six close rows across one edge of the garden to increase the likelihood of fertilization; pole beans were planted in between the cornrows. Mr. Dell had made some large cages of wire fencing to hold tomatoes; these were in a different part of the garden each year but always easily accessible from the outside. Mr. Dell cautioned Walt not to walk in the garden space; he warned that doing so would pack the earth and limit growth.

Walt remembered his father's cages for peppers and cucumbers and the large plot of ground given over to potato plants. His father always put a couple of long rows of lettuce at the very edge of the garden, usually two or three types, such as Buttercrunch, loose leaf Simpson and Romaine. Walt remembered that no matter what they tried, the lettuce always bolted before they had a satisfactory crop.

Walt smiled to himself as he thought about the potato crop. Every year, right after the first frost, he and his father would dig the potato mounds by using a pitchfork to turn the soil and vegetables up. Walt's mother followed them and further turned the broken soil with her hands to find the potatoes. She tossed them into large baskets that they took home and spread on the kitchen floor on top of sheets of newspaper. His mother sorted the potatoes by size and put several in a basket under the sink. The remainder went into a root cellar under the front porch. Walt's job during the winter was to clear a path into the root cellar and get potatoes for dinner.

As he considered the Walden-like memory of the family garden, Walt had to admit it wasn't exactly as idyllic as that mental picture. He knew how angry his father got when the raccoons got into the corn; one year the Dell's had only one meal from their corn crop. He also knew how the birds would hit the tomatoes as soon as they began to change color. Mr. Dell used to say, "I know the tomatoes are ripe when the birds start eating them!"

And there was no forgetting the rapidity in which the weeds tried to regain their foothold on the garden plot. Walt spent far too many summer days in the plot, pulling weeds and loosening the topsoil. Those days were miserable in several ways, he reminded himself. First, he had to either crouch uncomfortably to get at the weeds or lie on the ground to gain access under the leafy vegetable plants. Second, he always got dirt all over himself. Third, Northern Montana was hot in the summer, and the usual dry humidity was not present in the garden where Walt's father watered regularly. So, with a high ambient humidity and his own sweating, most of the dirt quickly became mud on his head, brow, and arms. Walt became so dirty after weeding, that he required a lengthy shower to get clean and cool off.

As he thought about those weeding adventures, Walt remembered how Billy and Charlie would come by the garden plot on their bicycles to see if he wanted to go swimming with them. And, he recalled, they would always comment on how hot the weather was, how the river would be cool, and, of course, how they would think of him while they bathed and cooled off. Walt grinned a little to himself; those guys really laid it on. He also remembered that they would remind him that Jan would be at the sandbar, too. And they would talk about the skimpy little swimsuit she wore and mention that they might have a meeting of the Philosophy Group while they were out on the sandbar.

All those memories made Walt anxious again. He thought about Jan in the two-piece bathing suit. Such contemplation made him nervous, and he got up and went into the living room to the liquor cabinet. Walt noted that the gin bottle was nearly empty and momentarily wondered who had been getting into his stock. Then, he remembered where the gin had gone and switched to grabbing one of the whiskey bottles. He took the bottle to the kitchen and poured four fingers of Johnny Walker Black Label into a glass.

Then he sat at the table, sipping the whiskey and allowing his memory to focus and expand on Jan, the lithe and curvy Jan, in her blue two-piece bathing suit. His mind's eye watched her walking to and from the river, getting into the water and coming out to towel off. After a few minutes of those visions, Walt got disgusted with himself. He tossed down the remainder of the drink and went off to the bedroom.

# CHAPTER 36



Joey was not in a mood to explain either his actions or his motives. He had brought a quart of strawberry ice cream to the meeting and made no excuses, and would brook no discussion. He went up the porch stairs two at a time and handed the ice cream to Walt when he opened the door.

Walt looked at the cold container and raised an eyebrow at Joey.

"I like strawberry," Joey said by way of explanation.

"I think most everyone does," Walt replied and headed for the kitchen. Bella joined him there and asked, "Where are the spoons?"

Walt indicated the drawer with silverware, fetched four bowls from the cabinet, and opened the ice cream container. He started scooping the ice cream into the bowls using one of the large serving spoons. Bella put a spoon in each bowl and waited for him to complete his task.

After Walt put the remaining ice cream in the freezer and rinsed off the large spoon, they each carried two bowls into the living room and distributed them. The next few minutes were quiet except for the clink of spoon against bowl.

Hal broke the silence, "Thanks, Joey. Good choice and all that."

"Hmm," Joey responded, waving his spoon.

Bella put her bowl down and asked Walt, "Could we get some more descriptions and personal feelings about people in your high school? You said last time we talked that some of the folks in town didn't talk to you much, but that was different in school, right?"

Walt put his bowl down on the table and thoughtfully said, "I guess that's mostly true. I sure saw those people every day."

Bella's notebook appeared, and she asked, "Would you tell us about the teachers you remember?"

"Sure. One of the most memorable was our principal, Mr. Arnold. Roger Arnold, but everybody called him Arnie. Well, not us kids, of course. To us, he was Mr. Arnold. His office was at the end of the main hall on the second floor of the school building, and when his door was open, he could see all the way down the hall. No one ever seriously considered making trouble in the hallway between classes because that door was open."

"Was he a frightening person?"

"Not exactly. Mr. Arnold wasn't big. Actually, he wasn't tall, but he was thick and muscular. I didn't mean to suggest we were afraid of him physically. Although, if he came walking toward you and staring at you with those fierce black eyes, you might think things would get physical."

"Did it ever?"

"Oh, no. That was never an option. Mr. Arnold was the principal, and so he was the authority. If he called you down, you were doing something wrong. No question about it. Same for all the teachers. Nobody was a rebel."

"What else did Mr. Arnold do besides hall monitor?"

"Well, he taught the Civics class where we got into the discussion about the Hungarian Revolution. He also taught history. I think he called it something else, like 'Western Civilization, I think. Anyway, he taught European history to us as juniors and American history to us as seniors. And he was the monitor in the last period study hall. You know, kids on the athletic teams went to gym class and started practice on their sport, everyone else got a forty-five-minute study period to get most of their homework completed. Mr. Arnold didn't tolerate any goofing around, so most homework was finished."

Hal asked, "Did you have any women teachers?"

"Only two, Miss Wayle the civics teacher and Miss Drew. She taught two classes, English and Literature. She taught me how to diagram a sentence."

Joey sat up straight to ask, "What's that?"

"Do you not know how to diagram a sentence?" Walt asked.

"Never heard of any such thing."

"I am not surprised. Education has changed a great deal since I was in the system."

"So, what's this diagramming stuff?"

Walt pursed his lips a bit and responded, "It is a standardized way of graphically putting the words in a sentence in relation to each other. Done properly, diagramming helps one to learn the parts of speech and their relationship to each other in properly crafted sentences. One is unlikely to become a competent, comfortable communicator if one can't write well. Diagramming is a skill that helps everyone to understand good communication is not just about words, but also how they are assembled."

"Huh," Joey said, "sounds like make-work to me. I write just fine."

"If you say so," Walt smiled at him.

Hal still had questions. He asked, "What did this Miss Drew look like?"

"Attractive. She was about five and a half feet tall and had brown hair in a pageboy cut. She probably wasn't more than five years older than us. She acted stiff around us, but was patient and very fair in grading."

"What did she think about the Revolution?"

"It's funny that you should ask about her opinion. We spent one class period right after Civics still talking about it. Her input during that class was correcting the language of students speaking their opinion."

"What do you mean?"

"I mean, when Andy said something like, "I'm thinking we've got to do something, or it's going make something bad happen to us", then she would interrupt and make him defend his sentence and word choice. He worked at it until he would say, "I believe we need to take action to prevent something worse happening in the future.""

"Really?"

"Oh, yes. Miss Drew was a stickler for proper use of the English language. I do believe that I have enjoyed reading some of the classics in literature because she made me appreciate the written word."

"Huh."

"Any other teachers?"

"Oh, certainly. Thinking of Miss Drew reminds me of John Howard Estes. He was sweet on Miss Drew. They ate lunch together, and I think they had dates like going to the movies."

"What did he teach?"

"He was the head of our Science Department."

"How many people were in that department?"

"Two. Mr. Estes and Cooper Young. Cooper was the junior varsity basketball coach. He also taught Shop and Chemistry. Cooper probably only had a bachelor's degree, but Estes had a Master's degree. Cooper wasn't very good at teaching Chemistry; he always seemed to be barely one page ahead of us when we were juniors. But he was a whiz in Shop, and the junior varsity guys loved him."

"Did he have an opinion about the Revolution?"

"Yes, I believe he did. Cooper also taught our Driving Training course each year to rising drivers. The rumor was he told somebody during their time on the driving course that he thought the United States should drop 'one of them Japanese bombs' on Russia and take care of the problem."

"Wow," Joey said. "Did anyone say anything to anyone about that?"

Walt smiled at Joey, "Now there's a sentence that needs diagramming and complete reconstruction."

Joey frowned and sat back, trying to remember what he had said.

"What did Estes teach?" Bella pressed.

"Well, he taught Physics to seniors, a math class at each level, and was responsible for the Typing Class for sophomores."

"Why do you say 'responsible for'?" Bella asked.

"It was obvious that he did not know how to type himself, and the girls in the class said he would simply tell them what to practice that day and then read a book for the rest of the class period."

"What did he think about the Revolution?"

"Well, first of all, Estes was also less than a decade older than the guys in my class, and he was not a veteran. Too young for the war or had a deferment for education, I guess. And, he was a complete stuffed shirt."

"What does that mean?"

"He was the only teacher to wear a suit all the time. Other than Mr. Arnold, that is. Everyone else wore a shirt and or a sweater. Miss Drew always dressed like she was going to a party, and we thought Estes was dressing up to that standard to impress her. Anyway, he always wore a three-piece suit with a matching tie and had his blondish hair swept back, looking more like a fop than he realized."

"What's a fop?" Hal queried.

"That's a word for a man overly concerned about his clothes and appearance. Also, known as a 'dandy'," Walt said.

Hal nodded, "Not the kind of guy looked up to by high school boys, I bet."

"Absolutely not. Someone said he overheard Estes talking with Mr. Arnold about the discussion and ridiculed anyone thinking another war was appropriate."

"So, he was in favor of just leaving Hungary alone?"

"Yes, I'd say so."

"That's not a very big faculty."

"Well, we were a very small school, Class 'C', I believe, meaning we had less than 100 students in the four-year high school. But wait, I forgot one guy, the coach. Shorty Vann."

"Is that all he did, coach?"

"I think he also taught remedial math, but mostly, he was the coach."

"For which sport?"

"All of them. At least, all of the sports where Whealton fielded a team."

"And those were what?"

"We had a football team, basketball, and track. We didn't do hockey, and we didn't do baseball."

"Any girl's sports?"

"There were none. I don't think there were any in the state at the time. Maybe at the college level but not in any of the districts I knew."

"Why those three?"

"They occurred during the school year. We had no rink for skating, and baseball was a summer sport."

"Tell us about Coach Vann."

"He was about five foot two inches and a little sensitive about his height. He tried to teach us better rebounding in basketball, but he couldn't show us how, because anyone under the basket could swat the ball away from him."

"Was he a good coach?"

"I don't know. Shorty showed us a few things that were better than what we did at pickup games, but our teams were not very good."

 "How so?"

"We lost every football game we played the last two years I was there. We often lost by four or more touchdowns. And our basketball team was pretty average. One of my friends, Charlie Tatum, was six foot one and the tallest guy on our team. Charlie was a fair shooter, especially from his place under the basket. And he was a good rebounder. But he couldn't defend worth a plugged nickel. We had only three substitutes, and we got run to death in every game."

"What was your record?"

'I don't remember exactly. But I do know that we only won three games in my senior year. And one of those was the first game of the season; we beat the pre-season favorite. They were on the road, playing at our school, and it was wonderful. Of course, when we played at their school, they won by thirty points."

"Did Coach Vann have an opinion about Hungary and the Revolution?"

"I doubt anybody had a clue. Shorty never talked to us about anything but sports. He told us how to exercise to get better on our own time, during practice his favorite comment was 'run it again', and after a game or a meet, he usually gave a little critique on our performance and then gave us quarters to get a milkshake at the counter at the drug store."

Bella closed her notebook and said, "Thanks, Walt. And thank you, Joey, for the ice cream. We've got to go, but maybe you could tell us something about your track team next time Walt."

"If you wish. I can do that."

Hal picked up the empty bowls, took them to the kitchen, and ran water in them to rinse out the ice cream. When he returned, the three students made a quick exit and went down the walk, chatting among themselves.

Walt watched from the doorway until they turned toward the school. He closed the door and leaned back against it. He had been surprised how easily those memories returned to him, how clearly he could see his teachers, and how detailed the recollections were of long-ago conversations. He hoped that such detail would help distract him from thinking about other things and people from those days that caused him so much anxiety and grief.

Still hoping for that emotional cover, Walt went to the kitchen and turned on the kettle for his coffee.

# CHAPTER 37



Walt did not find any escape from his memories, good and bad, in his coffee that evening. Finishing his second cup sitting in the living room and staring at the dying fire, he realized he was replaying the memories he had brought out of hiding to discuss with the students. Once again, Walt was in the study hall between seasons, staring at his trigonometry homework without comprehension. As he had back then, Walt's thoughts were focused on Jan and not on the math assignment. It seemed that he spent his study hall time conjuring up mental images of her walking down the hall by his locker, smiling at him in recognition as she talked with some other girl.

And there was Mr. Arnold, standing beside his desk, asking, "Are you having trouble with the sine and cosine, Walter?"

To Walt's best estimation, everyone in the class had 'trouble' with the sine and the cosine. He was not unique in that regard. He once told Andy that he intended to pursue an occupation where he would never have to deal with the sine and the cosine. Andy pointed out that almost all jobs and every occupation fit that criterion. Walt remembered denying to Mr. Arnold that he was having any difficulty with his mathematics homework and gave up his daydream about Jan for the moment.

Thinking about his difficulty with trigonometry, Walt's thoughts turned to his mathematics teacher, Mr. Estes. With some insight gained over the years, Walt believed that Estes' snooty attitude and distance from his students were signs of poor self-confidence. Walt could remember one instance in class where a student corrected a mistake of Estes' and was ignored for the rest of the class period. Walt wondered what ever happened to Estes. Did he stay in Whealton? Did he marry Miss Drew? Then, as he pondered those questions, Walt realized he didn't care. He had managed to earn a living without ever having to calculate or utilize a sine or a cosine. But he was happy that he had learned how to diagram a sentence.

Walt looked at his empty coffee cup, then went to the liquor cabinet, poured four fingers of whiskey into his cup, and returned to his chair. One sip, and Walt was thinking about Jan again. For some reason, the whiskey led him to recall the several times he tried to dance with her at the Canteen. She was always willing to be his partner, but her attention on the floor was watching the door for Billy Parks to arrive. If Billy Parks was in the building, Walt had no chance of holding her attention; she would break off the dance to stand beside Billy, or he would come and break into their dance. Either way, Walt was obviously a distant second choice. Walt could feel the hurt and the anxiety behind his breastbone as these memories floated up. He felt embarrassed all over again.

Walt shook his head and went to poke the dying fire into the last few flames. He turned and warmed himself before returning to the chair. He determined not to keep allowing those painful memories to surface and thought back over the afternoon discussion to pick a different topic for reminiscence. The most prominent thoughts were those involving Shorty Vann. The man had some of the most memorable critiques Walt had ever heard, including those of his drill Sergeant. One came immediately to mind, Walt thought, because it involved someone other than himself.

At halftime of one football game the Whealton Bison were losing by several touchdowns, Shorty was particularly upset by the play of the left defensive end. The opponents had effected several long gains by running directly at this hapless individual. Shorty's criticism in the locker room was, as always, heavily spiced with swear words. But the nut of Shorty's criticism was "Johnny, you're standing out there like the quarter post on a mile race, watching the runners go by you. Jump in and tackle somebody!"

Walt grinned to himself, recalling the energy and volume of Shorty's halftime talks. Walt finally understood that Shorty never expected the Whealton team to win, but he would not be satisfied if they didn't play the game right. To Shorty, playing the game right meant giving the maximum effort on every play. If you couldn't do that, you likely would spend most of your time on the bench.

That made Walt think of a basketball game where Shorty put him on the bench for most of the first half. Shorty became convinced that Walt was not giving a maximum effort and sat him down. Walt's memory of the occasion was not as embarrassing as the game where he fouled out. Remembering those occasions, Walt also realized that he was remembering that Jan was a cheerleader and was bouncing around in front of him in her little short cheerleader skirt as he sat on the bench. There he was, thinking about Jan again. Particularly thinking about her long legs and that short skirt.

Walt got back up from the chair, angry with himself for his inability to control his thoughts. He wondered why Jan and their interactions were so prominent now in his mind. Walt had not thought about her for years, decades even. Why was Jan intruding at this time, when he and Madeline had shared many happier and comforting memories? Walt had an inkling of why but didn't want to allow that particular memory to surface. Nonetheless, trying to keep those specific memories out of his mind only brought them closer to the surface.

Walt sat back down, leaned back and closed his eyes. He allowed the mental image of the wilderness north of Whealton to play on his vision. The vast, empty, rolling plain stretched out to the horizon; Walt began to relax in that restful vista. He had walked that countryside many times, hunting and fishing, walking for miles without seeing anyone. Walt took a shuddering, deep breath and began to relax.

Then, in the distance of the vista, he perceived a shadow that grew to show a man. The man was facing away from him, holding a shotgun on his right shoulder. Although the man was standing perfectly still, the inner eye vista Walt was viewing centered on the man and drew his image closer. As it did, the man put the shotgun down, butt first, at his side and turned to face Walt.

Walt snapped his eyes open and realized he had fallen asleep, warmed by the dying fire and the alcohol. His heart was beating rapidly, and he was having trouble getting his breath. What was happening? Then he remembered the dream, the vista, and the man. He noticed he was still holding his coffee cup and tried to put it on the glass-top coffee table. It rattled against the glass as his hand shook. He put his face in his hands, forced himself to take slow, deep breaths, and thought about his grocery list to calm down.

When he had no further trouble breathing, Walt took his pulse and continued to sit quietly, thinking about picking up some cereal and vegetables at the store. Finally, his pulse was back to baseline and steady. Walt allowed himself to take the cup into the kitchen for rinsing. He noticed the bowls in the sink and decided against washing them. Walt felt uneasy about his ability to shut out memories associated with the day's discussion right then. He turned and went upstairs and tried reading in his favorite chair. He found he couldn't concentrate and after reading a particular section twice and realizing he didn't know what it said, he gave up and went to bed.

His sleep was fitful that night.

# CHAPTER 38

## 03/17/2020 TUESDAY

Walt had prepared for the next visit by the students. He baked some cookies, prepared hot chocolate and had them on the living room table. He had set a low fire earlier in the day, and the room was comfortable. When he saw them coming up the walk, he opened the door and went to his chair in the living room to await their entrance.

Bella came through the door, telling Joey some facts, but he didn't appear interested. Hal pulled his boots off and quickly hung up his coat to beat the other two into the living room.

"Hey, Walt," Hal said in greeting, although his eyes were on the cookies.

"Good afternoon," Walt said. He waited while they poured some drinks and grabbed a cookie or two before saying, "Bella asked me to discuss my experiences on the track team in high school, and I agreed. But before I do so, I should like to hear from each of you some of your own experiences."

Bella said, "But we are doing the interviewing, aren't we?"

"Yes, of course. However, I have given some thought to this topic since you were last here, and I doubt there are any new insights into the people involved. I can give you a little more history on some of my friends, but the track experiences only bring to mind more stories about Shorty Vann."

"Well, we'd like to hear those, anyway."

"And you shall. But first, didn't you boys participate in your school's football team last fall? I recall you leaving after a short visit because of practice."

Joey quickly looked at Hal and said, "Yes, sir, we were both on the team, but neither of us played very much. There are several players on the team that are bigger and faster than either Hal or me."

"Size and speed are always an advantage in athletics. But skill can compensate for those absences. May I interpret from your statement that the two of you were lacking in that department?"

Hal answered, "That's the truth. We ended up on the Scout Team. Those are the guys who wear yellow T-shirts in practice and try to run the opponent's offense. Our defense knocked us around pretty good."

Walt nodded, "And, did that enable your team to succeed on Friday night?"

"Sometimes," Joey noted. "But since we weren't very good to start with, we didn't always give the best representation of the opponent for our guys to practice against. Some of the guys we played were just faster than anybody on our team."

"How did the season end up?"

"We were fourth in the league. Didn't make the playoffs, but one of our running backs was voted first-team backfield."

"Nice."

"Yeah, but he's the only one that will play in college."

Walt shifted in his seat and asked, "Well, then, how about basketball? Did either of you play?"

Both boys looked down at their feet and Hal said, "Uh, no. We both got cut."

"Size and speed again?"

"And skill. We have a couple of guys that can hit the basket from way downtown. I'm pretty good shooting free throws, but can't hit the backboard if somebody has their hand in my face."

Joey picked up on the story, "And our boy's basketball team did quite well this year. They went into the tournament ranked third in the league and took second place."

Bella interrupted, "Which is exactly what our girl's team did, too. And I did play on that team."

Walt smiled at her, encouraging her to continue. Hal jumped into the conversation before Bella could elaborate, however. He said, "They were really good, Walt. I think they had more people come to their games than the boys did to theirs."

Walt nodded at Bella, who commented, "We have had a good girl's team for a couple of years, and everything just worked well this year."

"It's like they say on the A-Team, 'I love it when a plan comes together'," Walt said, grinning widely.

"What's the A-Team?" Hal asked. Joey also had a puzzled look on his face. Walt realized his reference to a television program from the 1980s had gone over their heads.

"Just an old reference to things that go well," Walt explained and changed the subject. "Now, how about track?"

Bella said, "I'm going to try out for the girl's soccer team."

Hal said, "There's the issue of size and speed, again."

Joey laughed and turned to Walt, "Are you going to tell us about your track experiences now?"

Walt nodded gently and allowed them to refresh their cookie supply before saying, "We didn't have soccer in Montana in the 1950s. Our only spring sport was track and field. Being a small school, we didn't have somebody competing in every event. Mostly the field events got left out."

"What are those?" Joey asked.

"Pretty much if you're not running against other people, it's a field event," Walt explained. "There's shot put, discus, javelin, high jump, long jump, and pole vault. We had a guy who threw the javelin, and I tried the high jump my last year. But I think that was it for Whealton in field events."

"What did you do in track?" Bella pushed.

"I ran the half-mile."

"Is that an official race?" Joey asked. "I don't remember hearing that race when I watched the Olympics."

Walt smiled tolerantly and explained, "In the 1950s, we in America didn't pay much attention to the metric system. The mile race was 1760 yards long, four times around the track. You may not know this but the four-minute mile was only broken in 1954. The mile race was a big thing. The next biggest was the half-mile, two trips around the track, followed by the quarter-mile, also known as the 440. Because it was 440 yards in a quarter mile."

"Isn't that what is now the 400?" asked Hal.

"Yes. Of course. Four hundred meters is 437.5 yards."

Joey said, "Wait, then the half-mile is the 800!"

"That's right, Joey. But when I was running it back then, we referred to it as the 880. That's for the number of yards. But it's a half a mile."

"That's a good distance," Bella said. "But it's considered a distance run, right?"

Walt almost laughed out loud, then said, "Yes. It is. But you just reminded me of how Shorty used to tell me how to run the 880. He would say, "Listen, kid. This is an easy race to run. All you gotta do is start out running as fast as you can and then speed up all the way around." And he was dead serious."

Bella started to disagree, "But …"

Joey stopped her, saying "It's a joke, Bella."

Walt said, "It was never my joke. Shorty said that to me every meet. And the 880 was one of the last races of the day, so I had to sit around and watch everything else before I got to run."

"How'd you do?" Hal asked.

"Overall, probably so-so. I won a couple of races in dual meets, and I lost a few. Never ran better than fourth up against the bigger schools, though."

Joey was about to ask 'why' when Walt continued, "Size and speed were not on my side," he said, and everyone chuckled.

Bella asked, "Was that your whole track experience?"

Walt answered, "Yes, pretty much. There are the bus rides to get there, the sitting around waiting, the tension for the last hour, then finally running as hard as you can for about two minutes straight, then there's the falling on the ground, sometimes there's some puking, and then there's the bus ride home. Six or eight times a year. That's what it was."

Bella closed her book and looked at him. "What other things did you do during the summer then?" she asked.

"I told you I mowed several lawns. That had to be done every week or so. My friends and I rode our bikes around town, sometimes we'd put a playing card in the spokes and hold it there with a clothes pin."

"Why?"

"Because it made a lot of noise, I guess."

"Who were your friends?"

"Well, a small group of us hung together starting in the seventh grade. Charlie Tatum was a year ahead of Andy and me. He was tall, over six feet, and real skinny. He played on our basketball team his last two years. He could score under the basket and do all right with rebounds, but he couldn't play defense at all. Smart guy, his dad was an engineer in construction. He had an older brother. Harry, I think. They both went to the University of Montana.

"And my closest friend was Andy Steward. What a guy. An only child. Funny thing about him was he lived next door to the Mingos, and they had a daughter a couple of years older than us. Barbara, I think, and she was a beauty. She would go into her backyard and sunbathe. Rumor was she did it in the nude. But she always put up some cardboard shield, and Andy couldn't see over it because he was so short. Andy had daydreams about Barbara Mingo even after she graduated and left town.

"We had a girl in our group, too. Jay Berryman. Sorta like a pixie with lots of energy. The family owned a farm worked by her father and two older brothers. The best thing about her was her laugh, it actually tinkled."

Joey was obviously bored at this recitation, staring off in space. Hal asked, "What did you guys do?"

"I said, we rode our bikes a lot. But we also formed a Philosophy Group. We would find a good place to lie in the grass and stare at the sky and we would discuss issues of great importance."

"What kind of issues?"

"Oh, you know, things of great importance to teenagers of that day and time. Issues like the possibility of time travel or whether cheeseburgers were better than hamburgers."

"You're kidding."

"Nope. One long-running question dealt with the far edge of the universe."

"What?"

The question was a two-part one. First, 'what is at the edge of the universe?' meaning, when you got there, how could you recognize that it was the edge of the universe?"

"What's the answer?"

"Well, we never actually determined that. But, for the sake of argument, we postulated there was a brick wall. When we got to the edge of the universe, there would be a brick wall."

"So what?"

"Well, that led to the second question. Which was 'what's on the other side of the brick wall?' We never answered that question either."

"And that was your Philosophy Group?"

"Yes. And we met several times a week during the summer. Usually about dark so we could see the stars as we lay in the grass, talked, and philosophized. But many days, we went to the sandbar.

Hal asked, "You could actually see stars?"

"Oh yeah, sky was very clear at night. Not like today. We also got to see the Northern Lights sometimes."

"What was that?"

The Northern Lights are a magnificent display of electricity and color in the sky near the magnetic poles. Scientists say they are related to sun spots causing energy particles from the sun to ignite molecules in the atmosphere."

Hal was astounded, "How long has this been going on?"

"Probably millions of years. But they are usually only seen on dark nights in the higher latitudes, like Montana, Yukon, Alaska, Norway and Siberia."

"Are they still there?"

"Sure. Probably seen less because industry has lightened the sky, though."

Joey jumped into the conversation, asking, "Tell me about the sandbar, Walt. Where was it?"

"Just a couple of miles away, the Missouri river made a big turn and left a couple of sandbars in the curve. The riverbank had washed away, and we could get close in a car and walk less than a hundred yards to the sand bar. Lots of bonfires and picnics on the sandbar. We'd go swimming in the river, which wasn't very deep or fast, play touch football and eat hotdogs we burned in the bonfire."

"That's more fun than anything we do," Hal said.

Walt nodded, "Another day, different times." He stared into the fire and became silent. Joey looked at his fellow students and they all nodded, remembering what Joey had shown them about the river near Whealton on Google Maps. Bella took Walt's silence and reverie as a cue to close her notebook and motion for the students to leave.

They each said goodbye to Walt, receiving a nod or a mumble, and they made their way outside.

"Joey said, "That was spooky."

Bella said, "I hope he was having pleasant memories."

# CHAPTER 39



Walt's memories were not unpleasant, but they did cause him anxiety. His hands were sweating, and he could feel his heart beating in his chest. His breath became short, and he finally got up from his chair and walked around the room to help with his growing feeling of dread.

Why did he let the students get him talking about his friends? Walt wondered. He had planned to keep the discussion on the sports activities, but they asked, and he just opened up and told them everything. Well, he admitted, not everything. There were a couple of things that he had never told anyone. He kept the memories of those events carefully sealed off; had there been a door in his mind, Walt would have locked it.

As he calmed a little, Walt told himself that he didn't mind talking about his friends and their biking adventures or even the Philosophy Group meetings. Those memories were pleasant, even the ones including Jan. He could remember her as the young pixie, sitting cross-legged and picking at the dandelions as they talked. That memory was okay, neutral. That mental picture of Jan was before she blossomed into an attractive young woman and took his breath away whenever they were close. Those later memories fought to gain supremacy in Walt's mind, and came with accompanying dread, anxiety, and personal dismay. Walt had learned over the years not to let his mind wander down the paths in the garden of senior year memories, and he pulled himself back from them now.

He and the students had talked of sports, he thought. I can stick to that. He directed his walk into the kitchen and used a little trick on himself that he had learned many years before. He forced himself to think about each step of the coffee preparation, from filling the kettle for water to the length of time he allowed for brewing before pushing down the plunger on the French Press. He studied the possible snack options and decided on some vanilla wafers, taking the whole box out of the cupboard. He took his tray with coffee and wafers back into the living room and decided to sit in a different chair. Perhaps that will disrupt the pathways he didn't want to travel.

The first sip of the strong coffee brought him new memories. He smiled tenuously at remembering taking Madeline to Florence shortly after they married. They joined a small walking group tour and spent an afternoon seeing a few blocks of the old city. Those few blocks, however, led them to the famous marketplace where they rubbed the shiny nose of the bronze boar and bought shirts to take home. Walt remembered how they marveled at the Palazzo Vecchio, home of the famous de' Medici family at one time. And Walt recalled how he and Madeline stared at the clock on the top of the Arnolfo Tower, thinking it was broken. The guide explained that a single-handed clock was typical in the Middle Ages, and the one in Arnolfo Tower was the first public clock in Florence.

Walt was relaxing with these memories of Madeline and Italy. They had differed over what was most impressive, the Ponte Vecchio or the statuary in the passage outside the Uffizi Gallery. They both agreed that the David statue by Michelangelo was the most stunning of all. Over the years, Walt had told friends about their tour and mentioned that their guide had a drinking problem. When asked what he meant, Walt explained that the guide stopped every thirty minutes, and the whole group sat and drank espresso before resuming their walk. He and Madeline were so caffeinated by the end of the tour that they did not sleep at all that night.

Walt felt a warm glow at these memories flooding over him and extruding the high school thoughts out of his mind. He drank deeply of his coffee. Then, something triggered his mind to think about basketball. The thoughts that came to his mind, however, did not take place on the court, but rather involved activities on the team bus on a return trip from an away game. On the trip to the game, the team sat in the front rows of seats, and Coach Vann was in the front row. He would occasionally stand and give some reminders about play and public behavior. The cheerleaders, dressed in school clothes, sat in the back of the bus.

On the way home after the game, however, seating was different. Coach Vann was up front again, but the team scattered throughout the bus, one or two of the boys paired up with a cheerleader. Walt ended up sitting toward the front of the bus and was acutely aware of Jan, in her short skirt outfit, sitting near the back with Billy Parks. More accurately, Jan was sitting on Billy Parks and they nuzzled each other all the way home.

Walt was starting to feel anxious again as he thought about Jan and Billy. How did he let those memories get into this reverie anyway? He got up, downed the last of his coffee, and went into the kitchen. Walt tried busying himself, cleaning up the dishes, straightening the cupboards, and adjusting the chairs at the kitchen table, but that didn't bring the calmness he desired.

Walt tried to change the subject in his mind. What else did those kids talk about? Running? I don't want to think about that. He started to make another small pot of coffee when he stopped and realized, he would not be able to sleep if he did that. And that understanding reminded him of the Florence tour and the espresso drinking. Walt smiled and thought, well, if I'm not having any more coffee tonight, maybe I need something else.

Returning to the front room, Walt opened the liquor cabinet and drew out the whiskey bottle. He looked at it carefully because of its light weight and realized that it, like the gin bottle, was nearly empty. Walt hesitated but decided that he would go to the liquor store the following day, and there was no good reason to delay drinking what whiskey was left. He poured it into a glass and headed off upstairs to his bedroom.

# CHAPTER 40



Springfield had not finished with snow that winter. The day before the students' visit, the city was gifted an eight-inch blanket. The snow was light, and was steady for several hours but unaccompanied by any wind. Walt's front yard and environs resembled one of the snow globes at the airport gift shop, a steady white as far as the eye could see and measurable depth slowly accumulating on the porch steps.

Walt watched the snow several times during the day, always with a cup of coffee. The accumulation on his walk and steps did not concern him; he had made arrangements years before with several boys in the neighborhood. They agreed to clean his walk, porch steps, and driveway within twenty-four hours of the snow stopping; he agreed to pay them $25. Walt knew that some of the boys he made the original agreement with had grown older and left the business but had introduced their younger brothers to the arrangement.

Walt sipped his coffee and assumed that the students would not be coming for a visit that day, even though the walks were clear. He expected they might have snow-shoveling responsibilities at their own homes or at least little interest in getting out in the wintery weather. He chided himself for not checking the school closures on television that morning.

The arrival of Bella and the guys, then, was a surprise. To increase the unexpected factor of the day, Bella brought something her mother had made for the occasion. The students were loud on entry and were stomping snow off their boots and hanging up coats when Walt came into the vestibule to greet them.

"Hello! I was not expecting you to come today. It seemed to me we had met your needs, and this weather …, well, welcome."

Bella handed him the warm loaf of bread, wrapped in aluminum foil, and said, "Mother thought it was time she contributed to our eating your food. It's banana nut bread."

"How delightful! It's heavy," Walt said, weighing the loaf in his hand. "I think it has plentiful nuts."

The boys went into the living room and busied themselves with lighting the already laid fire. Bella followed Walt into the kitchen and helped gather some small plates, a knife, and glasses for milk. Walt brought the plate with the unwrapped banana nut bread and a half-gallon of milk to the coffee table. Bella divided the loaf and distributed the pieces while Joey assumed the role of pouring everyone a glass of milk.

But Hal was not to be silent with his piece of bread. He asked, "Did you get out there and clean off that walk, Walt?"

"No, of course not. I have a deal with some of the neighbor's boys. They are quite prompt. And, they do a good job, don't they?"

"Yeah," Joey added. "Better than what I do at home. It's all going to melt anyway."

"True, Joey. But these boys are taking some pride in their work. They make sure they clean the walk to the edge. And that has impressed others in the neighborhood to hire them for their walks. I believe it has become a local business and a source of income for the young men."

Bella almost spoke with her mouth full. "No girls involved?"

"Actually, Bella, I am not certain. My original arrangement several years ago was with three young boys up the street. They are no longer involved, and I have always assumed the current shovelers were their younger brothers. But all I can say for sure is the one who collects the money is male. There may well be a girl under all the heavy garments."

"Should be," Bella opined and took another piece of bread.

Walt said, "I didn't think you'd be coming today."

"Not gonna let a little snow stop us," Hal said.

Bella said, "There was no school today. The roads are too slick or something. We talked about it and decided we would like to hear more about small town living a half-century ago."

Walt smiled and nodded. "I'm glad you came. There's certainly more that I can talk about, but not everything will be interesting or helpful with your project …"

Joey waved his hand. "Oh, the project is almost done." Bella waved at him, and he quit talking and looked down at his plate, embarrassed.

Bella explained, "We're doing a little fine-tuning and could use the input."

"That's perfectly fine." Walt smiled at the inadvertent admission. " I am enjoying our afternoons together, also. What would you like to talk about today?"

Hal raised his hand and replied, "Well, there is the topic of snow. What was it like 50 years ago?"

Walt put his chin on his chest and thought a moment. He looked at Hal and said, "Unlike here, the plains of northern Montana are wide open spaces, and there is nothing between the small towns there and the North Pole but the Canadian border and a barbed wire fence. And when I was growing up, one of the strands on that fence was down."

Joey looked sideways at Walt and asked, "What do you mean?"

"I mean, the north wind would blow straight down the plain, carrying snow all winter and dirt all summer. There was nothing to break the wind. So, whatever snowfall was measured was interesting, but the drifting from the wind-blown snow was something else. The North side of buildings might have drifted up to the second-floor level; hardly anyone had their front door facing north. And snowfall didn't stop after a few hours; it sometimes went on for days."

Joey laughed, "I bet that messed up the shoveling,"

"Oh, it did. I remember some snow plow drivers saying they might be on the road for two or three days, constantly plowing to keep the streets and highways passable."

Hal asked, "Were you one of the boys making money shoveling sidewalks?"

"Sometimes. I worked for a couple of older couples doing yard work and cleaning the snow off their walks in the winter. But timing was everything."

Bella didn't grasp Walt's meaning. She asked, "What about timing? I mean, I know you didn't shovel when it was coming down."

"No, Bella, the timing was between the road snow plows and the sidewalk shoveling. If you wait too late, the plows would come down the street and throw the roadway snow off to the side and onto the sidewalk. And you would have six feet deep drifts to get through where there had been only two-foot drifts before."

"Oh, man," Hal could immediately empathize.

Bella objected, "But if you cleaned the walks off first, wouldn't the plows cover up your work/"

"Absolutely. That's the timing. You had to get there first to get the walks cleaned, then rest and get loaded with hot chocolate before going out and removing the pile dumped on the end of the walk by the plows."

"That's double shovel," Hal noted.

"Had to be done, my young friend. And it usually had to be done once or twice a week for five or six months. That was the snow of the fifties in Montana."

"I don't think I would like that," Joey affirmed. Hal nodded his vigorous agreement.

Walt eyed them both and asked, "Do you not enjoy winter sports?"

Joey thought about the question and answered, "I do like to ski."

"Ah, downhill or cross country?"

"Uh, downhill."

"Well, Montana would not be the place for you, then. Too flat. At least around Whealton and places in the East. We only did cross country."

"That's just walking on snow," Bella offered.

"Right," said Walt. "But kids our age didn't have any other way to get around. We walked or rode our bikes everywhere, rain or shine, winter or summer."

"You make it all sound like A Christmas Story," Joey noted.

"Well, I would imagine that nearly every boy and girl who grew up in the Midwest Plains of the Fifties thinks they lived parts of that story. I know I did."

"What parts?" Bella had her notebook ready.

"Well, I witnessed the boy licking a metal post like in the movie, and I know two other men who told me they had seen it, too."

"Really?"

"Yes. It took the firemen over an hour to get him off the post. He was a fifth-grader taking a dare and trying to impress some girl."

`"That wasn't in the movie. That part about a girl," Bella said.

"I guess not. But that's what happened in Whealton."

They stayed another hour since there was no school and no sports practices. The four of them ate all of the banana bread and drank all of the milk. Bella had planned not to leave Walt alone this time unless he was in a good mood, so she kept up the chatter about winter issues such as radiators, floor furnaces, and the smell of wet clothes in the entryway.

Hal and Joey told tales of their snowball fights, some won and others lost, with serious criticism from everyone about the boys who put rocks in the snowballs. They made Walt laugh with a story about building a snowman one year when the snow wasn't wet enough to stick together, and they tried to spray it with a hose. Then he made some hot chocolate, and they sipped their drinks and watched the fire die down.

Finally, they left with many good feelings expressed and promises to return in two weeks for more stories.

Walt returned to his chair after seeing them out. He sat quietly for several minutes. Bella and Hal had taken the cups and glasses into the kitchen and rinsed them out; all the cleaning up was done.

Finally, with a small effort, Walt got out of the chair, went to the replenished liquor cabinet, and opened a new bottle of gin. He carried it into the kitchen and poured four fingers into one of the rinsed glasses. Walt replaced the cap, sat the bottle on the counter, and smelled the alcohol in his glass. He took a sip and headed for the living room.

# CHAPTER 41

03/31/2020 TUESDAY

The fire had almost died out, and Walt left it alone. The room was warm and comfortable, so he sat in his favorite chair and mused, sipping on the gin. The first thought that formed in his mind was his break from tradition, drinking gin instead of coffee as he wound down at the end of the day. After a brief thought, Walt gave himself permission to break the cycle, noting that he was only shortening his activities because the students stayed later than usual; he would be getting into the gin by this time anyway. Walt accepted his argument even knowing that his drinking before bedtime was a recent change in his long-standing habits.

Walt stared into the embers, and thought about his days shoveling the snow at his home. His Whealton home had a short sidewalk from the porch to the driveway and in most instances was easily cleared. The driveway was an entirely different challenge, however. It was necessarily wide since cars of that day were also wide, and the location at the side of the house favored drifting of snow to heights of six or more feet. Walt's memory of clearing that driveway included remembering times he might shovel for an hour and have little cleared driveway to show for it. He also remembered the bitterly cold wind that seemed a constant companion whenever he was outdoors. It had the capability to penetrate even several layers of woolen clothing, biting any unprotected skin as if it objected to any rearrangement of the snow it had blown.

Walt had many misgivings about the climate change movement; best he could tell, any likely change would be very modest and tolerable. Similar changes had clearly occurred in past ages and the planet survived. Walt had a high level of skepticism for the climate change warriors; undoubtedly believing their motives were not solely pure. But he did agree that the recent winters of the Northern Plains, as reported on television, seemed milder than those in his memories.

Another sip of the gin, and Walt wondered if his memory recall was of the type mocked by others. "Had to walk to school in snow three feet deep, uphill both ways," immediately came to mind. Walt had a little chuckle at that; he had never claimed it was uphill either way. At the same time he had knowledge the temperature had actually been more than twenty degrees below zero at times; he remembered the local weatherman mentioning that figure. *Maybe the world is getting a little warmer,* he considered. *But it's still darned cold at times.*

Another sip, and he thought about some grassy areas around the Whealton High School where he and the Philosophy Group often held impromptu meetings. Those areas in winter commonly had drifts several feet high. The Group sometimes commented on the pleasure they experienced in mid-Summer thinking how lucky they were to not be lying in the snow to discuss philosophy. At one time or another, either Charlie or Andy brought up the bliss of their grassy meeting place, comparing it to the way it would look in five or six months.

Then Walt found he was thinking of summertime gatherings again. He, Charlie, Jan, and Andy, lying side by side, hands behind heads, staring into the darkening sky past dusk. Walt tried to recall what they had talked about during those sessions, but all he could recall of their topics other than the absence of snow were the debates over hamburgers versus cheeseburgers. On the other hand, he could recall with clarity what Jan was wearing at various times.

Walt knew his memories of the Group meetings seemed entirely bent on watching Jan. This was particularly true as they all aged and Jan developed toward womanhood. Watching her movements, her dancer's grace and balance, watching when she hitched up her skirt to sit cross-legged to face the others during some part of a debate, and, of course, watching the front of her shirt move up and down with her emphatic arguments. It seemed to Walt, sipping his gin, that all he could recall doing in Group meetings was staring at Jan.

Walt noted he could specifically recall some of her summer-wear shirts. Jan was one of the first girls in Whealton to wear sleeveless tops. Walt would not forget her browned shoulders and her thin but strong arms. And, he discovered, he could recall some of the shirts' designs - the striped ones, others solid-colored with small images imprinted, maybe checkered …

Walt jerked himself upright and almost spilled his gin. What in the world was he doing, fantasizing about the form and dress of a long-ago high school girl? Walt felt he must not think on these things, yet they remained central in his memory. Talking with these students every couple of weeks was bringing these thoughts and images back into his forebrain, Walt realized. But he didn't want to stop meeting with the students, and he didn't want to stop thinking about Jan.

Walt looked at his glass and considered the final swallow. After that, he would go to bed and sleep, he hoped. Recently, he had difficulty sleeping through the night because of dreams. He had awakened a few times sweating and panicky, believing he had heard a gunshot that awakened him.

Walt had been trying to convince himself that he slept better if he skipped the late evening coffee and substituted the gin - or the whiskey. But, he didn't keep track of 'good' nights and was not remembering many of those recently, anyway. The truth was, Walt knew he was making excuses for his drinking and was determined not to examine his actions closely.

Walt decided the argument of Hamburger v. Cheeseburger was not a winnable one because, like many discussions held by the Philosophy Group, there was insufficient data to resolve. Walt was an ardent cheeseburger fan, but that totally depended on the cheese in his opinion. There had been a move to emphasize American cheese but Walt was a confirmed Sharp Cheddar fan. He often said if cheddar cheese were unavailable for his cheeseburger, he would go without - and eat a plain hamburger. Walt smiled at that memory, swallowed the remainder of the gin, leaned back in the chair, and decided to indulge in one more Jan fantasy before retiring.

He closed his eyes and allowed himself to return to that basketball game where he spent so much time on the bench, within inches of the cheerleaders.

He easily pulled up a mental image of Jan, bouncing and twirling just a few feet away. He focused on her and watched as her cheerleader skirt, already short, twirled away from her body and revealed her legs. Long, tapered, and tanned, those legs moved with a rhythm that Walt found hypnotic. He stared and admired the shape of her legs, the texture of the skin, and the muscular movement that allowed a circumferential view.

Walt could feel his heart beating rapidly, but this time he recognized the absence of anxiety or fear. He was only enjoying the view.

But the view was short, just as it had been back in high school. The cheerleaders moved away from the players on the bench to do their encouragement of the student body where more students were sitting. Walt tried to get the mental movie to run again, but the image that appeared was the ball game that was right in front of him. Whealton was down by six points, it was late in the game, and the team could not overcome the point gap.

Walt already knew the game's outcome, and did not need a replay. No good feelings would result from dwelling on that experience. In no small way, Walt felt his fouling out had removed the last chance his team had to win that game. He shook his head, stood up, and went into the kitchen where he put his glass in the sink and headed for the bedroom.

# CHAPTER 42

## 04/14/2020 TUESDAY

Springfield was enjoying a few days of early spring. With bright sunny skies and temperate breeze, the soil had warmed a bit, and Walt was in his backyard digging when the students arrived. When they found no one in the house, Joey led them through the kitchen and onto the back porch.

Walt was sitting on a garden stool on an old brick walkway, leaning into the beds to pull out the early clumps of grass and transient weeds. He was dragging a medium-sized black plastic sack to carry the debris he created and was energetically working the soil, loosening weeds. The students stood for a moment, watching him work before announcing their presence.

"Walt," Bella called, "would you like some help with that?"

Walt slowly turned on the stool and smiled when he saw them. He waved and indicated they could join him. They went to stand around him, but Hal bent over and took up a handful of dirt from the area where Walt had loosened it.

"Hey, this is good topsoil," he exclaimed. "Look at this!" He held up a fistful of dirt, squeezed it into a ball, and opened his hand. Half the dirt pulled away from the ball and fell to the ground; Hal then lightly massaged the remaining ball, and it crumbled, broke up and fell apart. "How'd you get such good dirt, Walt?"

" It takes some time, Hal. I've used several tricks I learned on travels around the world."

"Such as?"

"Well, the first is to build the soil with organic material, manure, and compost. I've composted and dug it into these beds for the last twenty years."

"That's impressive, but my Dad also composts, and he doesn't get anything this dark or fluffy."

"That may be due to the dishwater."

" What's that about?"

"I learned this from some housewives in England. Apparently, they started discarding their used dishwater into their flower garden and noted how that helped loosen the soil. It got fluffy, as you say."

"I never heard that."

"I don't think it's a secret, but most folks don't know it or find the practice a little hard."

Bella nodded, "I can see that. I'm not eager to wander through the house with a pan full of dishwater. Besides, we have a machine."

Joey made a short laughing sound, "Another 'improvement' from modern science, right, Walt?"

"I guess so, at least as far as the flower beds go. But I have a dishwasher, too. I just bring some water out regularly with a little dishwashing soap in it. I just pour it around and after several years of that and the compost, this is what I got," he held up a handful of dirt and let it trickle through his fingers.

"So, this is where you're going to plant those vegetables we saw you starting from seeds?" Bella asked.

"Yes, Bella. Those little seedlings will go in this part of the garden. From here to the fence and back toward the corner. Plus I'll put the tomato plans over on the other side."

"Why?" Hal asked, "Soil or sun?"

"Sun. That big Oak over the fence there brings shadows to this side of my yard in the mid to late afternoon. The other side is sunny all day."

Joey wondered, "How are those seeds doing? Are they up?"

Walt struggled to regain his feet and said, "Let's go see." He led the way back to the porch and up into the house. In the kitchen, Walt paused to wash his hands before showing them where he was raising the seeds. It was in a small pantry area; Walt had placed two tables in the room, almost covering the available floor space. Four aquariums were sitting on the tabletops. Each contained two, small egg crate-like plastic cup trays. Each cup was filled almost to the top with a mixture of peat moss and soil, and every cup contained a single, inch-high seedling protruding upward.

The secret to the success was the top of each aquarium covered by an electric grow light. Walt turned some of the lights off and allowed the students to reach into the aquarium and touch the small green wisps.

Joey said, "I don't see any labels. How do you know which one is what?"

"Another crystal clear question, Joey," Walt said patting him on the back. "I'd wager that members of your family do not wear name tags when they get together, do they?"

"What? Of course not."

"Why not?"

"Because we know who everybody is."

"And I know who everybody is in these aquariums. I've seen tomato plants for fifty or more years, I know what they look like."

"That's just crazy cool. You can recognize plants from their seedlings."

"Neither crazy nor especially cool. Any gardener can do it. Experience teaches many things, and pattern recognition is a key one. Doctors recognize certain features that reveal an internal abnormality, lawyers can see patterns in cases, and accountants can recognize patterns in deposits and withdrawals. It's all pattern recognition. But it only comes with experience. And paying attention."

Joey changed the subject. "I talked to my Dad about going to law school and he thought that might be a good fit for me."

Walt replied, "Just remember, that's choosing a path at a crossroads. And that particular crossroads is far down the road for you. Don't get so stuck on one idea that you can't change if something else develops that you might like better."

"Hmm. Like what?"

"I don't know, Joey. Keep your eyes open."

Hal said, "I talked to my Dad, too. He said me going in the military seemed like a right thing, too."

"When did you make that decision, Hal?" Bella asked.

Walt steered them from the pantry and into the living room, where they took their usual seats. "Yes, Hal," Walt asked, "when did that idea become a choice for you?"

"I don't know. I mean, we talked about it, and I didn't see anything appealing about going to college, you know. So, it seemed like the thing to do."

Walt nodded and said, "Which branch?"

"Uh, well, I was thinking the Army. What do you think?"

"You know I was in the Army."

"Yeah, but you know about the others, too, don't you?"

"I don't know much about them except for jokes they tell on each other."

Joey asked, "Like what?"

Walt said, "There's a story about a politician who wanted the military to secure a particular building. He asked a friend in the Pentagon who would do the best job. The friend said, "If you tell the Air Force to secure the building, they will put a lock on the door; if you ask the Navy to secure it, they will put a fence around the building, and the Army will secure the building with guard towers on every corner of the fence and twenty-four-hour guards at all gates. But if you ask the Marines to secure the building, they'll blow it up!"

Joey couldn't stop laughing for the next two minutes. Bella and Hal thought that was funny but not hilarious.

Walt said, "Each branch has its place in defense and security. And they have their little quirks like the Air Force guys have much longer haircuts than the others. Just know what you think the service branch can do for you."

Then he turned to Bella and asked, "Since we're questioning you guys today instead of me, what's your future plan, Bella?"

She blushed and tightened her lips. But Joey said, "Oh no, you don't. Hal and I talked about plans, and you can, too. Come on, girl. Spill."

Bella looked at each one of them and said, "You know I like music, right? Do you know I play the guitar?"

Everyone looked surprised and she hurriedly went on, "Yes, I play the bass guitar in a small all-girl band." She hesitated and then said, "And I'm the lead singer, too."

Hal and Joey both applauded this statement and patted her on the back. Walt said, "I was not aware of this interest or aptitude. How long have you been involved to this degree?"

"More than two years now with the band. We've only done a couple performances, like for each other's birthdays and such. But I've been singing in the church choir and even had some solos since I was ten."

"And you have plans for this interest to become a career?"

"Yes, I do. I want to study music and performing arts in college and try my hand at making it career, but I'm also interested in teaching."

Hal said, "Wow. I am impressed. I didn't know you could do that. Would you sing at my birthday party?" Bella lightly hit him on the shoulder but grinned and nodded.

Walt chuckled lightly, and the students looked at him. "You know," he said, "if you really love whatever you are doing, you will end up not working a day in your whole life."

Joey said, "You know, you told us about things you have grown in your gardens over the years, but when do you plan to plant? Are there any tricks we should know?"

"There are tricks to everything, Joey. Here in Springfield I won't put plants in the ground before early to mid-May, always following the Almanac. And by that time, I hope to have five to six-inch stalks on the tomatoes, peppers, and cucumbers. Then, I plant them deep in a hole, and leave only the top two leaves sticking out. The stem then turns into a deep taproot and helps the plants during any dry spell. I keep them watered and feed them some bone meal after about a month."

"What's that for?" Hal asked.

"Bone meal has a form of phosphorus that is slowly released into the soil all summer. Phosphorus increases a plant's ability to form blooms, and you can't get fruit or vegetables without blooms."

"Does that work for flowers, too?"

"Blooms, Hal. Flowers come from blooms."

"Right."

Walt saw Bella checking her watch and asked, "So, what did we learn today?"

Joey said, "A lot about gardening and some about growing up into the right job or career."

Walt smiled, "Who would have thought those topics would come up while talking about the Hungarian Revolution?"

Bella smiled at him as she packed up her notes, "Well, the Revolution was started by students, wasn't it?"

# CHAPTER 43

## 04/14/2020 TUESDAY

After the students left, Walt went into the kitchen and started the kettle for his coffee. He realized that he had not provided the students with cookies or drinks, yet they stayed and talked anyway. He remembered a senior Sergeant he had served with who commented on the difficulty of getting enlisted men to attend mandatory training sessions. Walt had suggested they have some food to attract them, and the Sergeant said, "Dell, I tell you, if you bring 'em in with sandwiches, you'll have to keep 'em with sandwiches." Walt was now surprised that the students did seem to expect him to feed them anymore and that they came anyway, and they seemed to want to talk to an old man.

He prepared his coffee and went into the living room to get the bottle of Bailey's Irish Cream he had purchased a few days before. After he poured his coffee, he added a generous portion of Bailey's to his cup and carried it on the tray back to the living room. He had not laid a fire for the past two weeks, but the room was not cold. He sat in his chair and envisioned each of the students sitting in their usual places around the coffee table.

Hal always chose one of the wingback chairs, sitting on the front of the cushion, upright or leaning both elbows on his knees. The chair was across the table from the small couch placing Hal facing Joey and Bella. Walt noted that Hal paid attention to whoever was speaking by facing them directly and engaging them with his eyes. Hal's face was a barometer of his feelings about any subject, and often displayed small frowns, smiles, or grimaces and often accompanied by squinting or rolling his eyes. Walt had learned he did not need to prod Hal for his opinion, it was written on his face.

Joey always sat on the far end of the couch from Walt's chair, slouched against the back unless sampling whatever food was on the table. Joey commonly rested his head on the back of the couch, and looked upward while others were speaking. Many of his comments were aimed at the ceiling. Walt could see Joey's interest in a topic during a discussion because he would sit up and start watching speakers. Walt thought only Joey's training in courtesy and polite conversation kept him from interrupting the discussion at times. Walt also was not fooled by the appearance of a distance between Joey and the talk at the table; Joey was carefully listening and noting everything.

But the person who was recording everything was Bella. She usually occupied the other end of the couch, cross-legged with her notebook in her lap. She held a ballpoint pen lightly; her hand appeared never to stop moving. Walt became aware of her note taking on the students' second visit. What struck him first was her tendency to continue to write notes when asking a question or making a reply. Walt had become convinced that she was using some form of shorthand; he felt that his words and messaging were being captured but was uncertain that the capture was exactly what he said.

Walt lifted his cup in silent salute to each of them in the empty seats and took a sip of his coffee. The Bailey's was a nice touch, he thought; no need for sugar or cream, and it provided a little warmth of its own. He decided to have another cup. But as he started to pour the coffee, he remembered his difficulty falling asleep if he drank too much coffee in the early evening. He paused, then filled his cup with Bailey's and returned to his chair to ponder.

*Why are these kids coming back? We have talked about whatever they said they wanted to know. I told them about the people in town, teachers, the Sheriff, everybody. I even told them about Andy and Charlie and even Jan. What more do they want?*

Walt drank deeply from the cup of Bailey's, closed his eyes, and leaned back. He didn't want to talk about Andy, Charlie and Jan. He didn't even want to think about them. At that time in his life, everything about Whealton was over and done. He wanted it to fade away. His memories of good times and events back then always led to thoughts about painful, or embarrassing times, or frightening times. In Walt's mind's eye, he was standing in an old, dusty attic. Around him were several ancient boxes and trunks, each tightly bound with strong rope except for a single trunk near the window under the eave.

Walt did not want to touch the unbound trunk. He wanted to find the stairs and leave the attic. But what Walt actually did in his mind's eye was walk over to the trunk and stare at it. While staring, Walt felt like he wanted to close his eyes, but instead knelt beside the trunk to be closer to it. He could feel his heart beating strong and quick in his chest; he began to feel smothered, his breath sticking in his throat. The last thing Walt wanted at that moment was to put out his hand and open that trunk.

So he did. He reached out and lifted the trunk lid. And in his mind's eye, intensified with ample Bailey's, Walt could see the contents of the trunk - it was a brilliantly lit image of Whealton from high in the air. As he watched, Walt felt pulled into the image: he alighted near the front of the school building. Standing there, he watched his friends walk by, Andy and Charlie, arguing about some arcane aspect of scoring a baseball game. Then, Jan ran past him to catch up with them. He strained and could hear her ask. "Where's Billy? Have you seen Billy Parks?" And he felt an aching in his chest like an icy hand had grabbed his heart.

"Put down the trunk lid!" Walt heard himself say. "Close the trunk and leave this attic!" But instead, he stayed and watched as Jan ran off to find Billy Parks, and the sensation in his chest fell into his belly. His friends continued walking, getting further away; Walt felt abandoned, lonely, and incredibly sad.

Using all the effort he could muster, Walt sat upright in his chair and opened his eyes. The attic, the trunk, and Whealton vanished. He took a deep breath but noted that he didn't feel like it was deep enough. The discomfort in his chest began to subside but still left him feeling like a weight rested on his chest. He also felt the sadness and realized it had not changed or receded. Walt looked in his cup and swallowed the remaining contents; the warmth of the alcohol seemed to soothe his chest a little, and he decided he should try to sleep.

As he went into the kitchen to rinse his glass, Walt felt his chest discomfort lightening but seeming to move to his left shoulder. He moved his arm in circles to make the shoulder discomfort go away. As he did so, Walt remembered how his recent sleep pattern, maybe since the students began coming to his house, had been disturbed by dreams. Dreams that were somewhat like the vision inside the trunk. Dreams that made him ache for Jan and acutely miss his other companions.

After a few moments of indecision, Walt decided he would use one of the sleeping pills Dr. Ingraham had given him after Madeline died. One should be enough, he thought and headed for the bedroom.

# CHAPTER 44

## 04/28/2020 TUESDAY

Walt had recovered from his emotional funk when the students arrived the next time. Only the two boys arrived, however. Their ebullient mood lifted his spirits more as they burst into the house, chattering about their recent experiences. Walt met them at the door and noted that they quickly moved from the entry hall into the living room without any urging from him. And, of course, they took their routine, familiar seats, still talking amongst themselves.

Walt sat in his chair and discerned they were discussing experiences in Drivers Training. He smiled at their eagerness and their recounting of errors made through inexperience. Joey turned to him to explain, "We just watched the sophomores' first class in Drivers Education, Walt. It was fun!"

"Where's Bella?" Walt asked.

"She's sick or something," Hal said. "She wasn't in school at all today."

Walt nodded and asked, "Is there still any ice on the road?"

Hal asked, "What's that about?"

"Oh," Walt replied, "driving education should take place partially on ice, don't you think?"

"No, I don't think," Joey said, quickly. "That sounds tricky and difficult, and we didn't have to do it."

Walt fixed him with a gaze and asked, "But you will still drive on icy roads someday, wouldn't you?"

Joey frowned, "Someday, I imagine. Why are you bringing this up, Walt?"

"Just remembering that my driver's education course in high school took place on our skating rink in the dead of winter."

"Wow. What was that about?"

"Well, think about it. Almost half of the driving time in Northern Montana was on snow or ice. A driver needed to know not only how to navigate the surfaces, but also how to care for his car."

"What do you mean?"

"Well, we needed to know how to put chains on the tires for driving on snow-packed or icy roads. We needed to know when to change the thermometer to let the engine run hotter than in the summer. And you had to know your engine and radiator volume to calculate the amount of antifreeze needed to protect your engine down to minus ten or twenty degrees."

Hal said, "There was nothing about any of that in our class."

"I'm not surprised. The cars of today are far better engineered. And, if you take the car in for regular service checks, the dealer will do what winterizing is needed."

"Huh."

"But none of that takes the place of understanding how to drive on slippery roads."

"How's that different?'

"In my day," Walt went on like he had not heard Hal's question, "the driving part of our education took place on ice and dry pavement. We learned that when you are going too fast, and your rear end starts to slide one way, the proper way to get out of the spin is to turn your front end in the same direction. Sorta let your front end catch up with the rear."

"We did mostly classroom stuff.. Studying the signs and stuff. It's all stuff we already knew from riding around. The driving part came when we tested for our license."

"What shape is a stop sign?" Walt asked.

"Octagonal," Joey said quickly.

"And what color is it?"

"Red," Hal beat Joey to the answer.

"Yep," Walt said, "And, I even remember when those signs were yellow."

"What?"

"Yes. The earliest stop signs at intersections were yellow. I think when stoplights were installed, someone thought that red for a stop at one intersection and yellow for a stop at another was confusing. So they all became red."

"I didn't know that!"

Walt sat back in his chair and said, "If you're interested in other differences between then and now, think about these things: cars didn't have air conditioning back then. Most people were content to roll the windows down. Or get on the road and turn the little triangular window at the front of the door so it would blow air on passengers. And the starter was a big button on the floor by the driver's right foot."

"What?"

"Yes. You started the car by stomping on that starter button on the floor and then moving your foot to the gas pedal and simultaneously pulling out a throttle control on the dashboard."

Hal said, "That sounds tricky."

Walt agreed, "A little, yeah."

Joey asked, "What was your first car?"

"I had a used 1947 Chevy coupe."

"What kind of mileage did you get?"

"You know, we didn't pay much attention to that. Gasoline was twenty-five to thirty cents a gallon then. Those old cars used a lot of oil, though. I had to add oil every third time I filled the gas tank."

"I've got to ask my dad about those things," Joey said. "He's fascinated about your stories. He said he remembers some of the stuff you talk about from his father's stories."

"Ask him what cars he remembers from his childhood. Most American cars were on their way out even then, I think. I remember one of my friend's family had a Nash Rambler."

"Never heard of it."

"How about a Packard?"

"Nope."

"Sometime in the fifties, the Packard sedan had a side light at the bottom of the post between front and back doors. How about Studebaker?"

"I've heard of them."

"Hudson?"

"Nope."

"Willys?"

"You're kidding. Nobody named a car Willis."

"How about the DeSoto?"

"No."

"Ever heard of the push button gear selector?"

"You're making that up."

"Nope. Charlie's dad had a late 50s Chrysler with push buttons on the dash. I was never in the car when it was on the road, so I don't know how well it worked."

"What was your next car after the 1947 Chevy?"

"Walt grinned and said, "My next car was one made by that manufacturer you thought was a joke."

"Who?"

"Willys."

Joey spread his hands in a silent question, and Hal's eyebrows went up.

"Willys was the manufacturer of the Jeep. My second car was a U.S. Army jeep. And I didn't get to drive that until I'd been in for over a year."

"Huh," Joey said. "If we were to put something in our project about the vehicles in your high school career, what would you think we need to mention?"

Walt thought a moment, then said, "The things I notice that are different are little things, like that cars no longer have running boards, and some of them are hard to get into. I haven't been to your school in years, but even back when Maddy was alive, and I'd be there to pick her up, I would see some really nice, clean, and shiny trucks in the parking lot."

When Walt paused at that, Joey ventured "And what's so different about that from Whealton?"

"Well, for one thing, the trucks in our parking lot were dirty. They were working trucks and might get hosed off, now and then, but they spent more time dirty than not. And second, every truck had a gun rack. And most every gun rack had at least one gun, rifle, shotgun, whatever."

"That really is different," Hal noted.

"Something else different today," Walt noted, "is that Bella's not here to take notes. Which of you is going to remember what we talked about?"

Joey spoke confidently, "Oh, we will, Walt. Both of us. We like cars and stuff, and this was fascinating."

"I suggest you each write down what you can recall and give it to Bella tomorrow."

"If she's there."

# CHAPTER 45

## 04/28/2020 TUESDAY

Walt stood in the doorway and watched the boys head back toward the school. He had enjoyed their session together, remembering old cars and odd things like running boards and yellow stop signs. He closed the door and returned to the kitchen to put on the kettle for his coffee.

While the kettle was heating, Walt rummaged through cabinets and the refrigerator looking for cookies but found none. *How did that happen?* he wondered. *I should have had some cookies here for the students.*

He changed his mind about sweets, and retrieved a block of Muenster cheese from the refrigerator and placed that on his tray with a slicing knife. Then the careful pouring, stirring, waiting, and decanting occupied his thoughts. With his carafe, cup, cream, and cheese, Walt decided to put on a jacket and try sitting on the porch.

The weather wasn't cold, but Walt was glad to have the warm jacket and the hot coffee. He leaned back in the chair and stared toward the sunset, thinking about his recent conversation with the boys. He hadn't told them that his memories of old cars went somewhat farther than he had recounted.

As a sophomore in high school, he and Charles had gone rabbit hunting with two seniors. One of the older boys owned an old Model A Ford coupe, and he loaded the car with six boys to hunt. Walt, one of the smallest, was positioned in the middle in the front seat. His job was to aim the beam from a hand-held industrial flashlight into the dark ahead of the reach of the headlights. The flashlight beam would pick up the red reflection from a rabbit's eyes, and the driver would speed in that direction, the three boys in the back seat whooping and hollering. Cruising at twenty miles an hour over rough terrain, lurching from side to side in a vain attempt to catch a running rabbit, was considered fun for an hour or so.

Walt's memories of those 'hunting trips' were two: first, they never caught a rabbit. Second, Walt often was criticized for his handling of the flashlight because he was more focused on shifting his legs to keep from being hit on the knee by the constant movement of the floor gearshift. Walt never told his parents about those excursions into the farmland around Whealton; it was one of several secrets kept only with Charlie and Andy.

The cheese was good, cold, but still good. It would probably be better if left to warm up some, Walt thought. He sliced off two extra pieces and set them where the setting sun might strike them for a few minutes. As he poured his second cup from the carafe, Walt thought about those 'hunting trips' and the fact that Jan was never included. And, of course, he immediately began thinking more about Jan and even wondering where she was on those nights; probably hanging with Billy Parks.

Walt and Charlie had often spent evenings driving around town after Charlie got a car. He was a year older than Walt and Andy, and that came with certain privileges. That year Charlie was a senior, and the three of them would ride around town, drinking soda and eating candy bars from after supper till ten o'clock. Sometimes Andy was absent, off with that girl he was dating, what was her name? Dark hair, I think. Anyway, the driving discussion concerned the philosophy of life, their grand plans for the future, and whether grapefruit soda was better than orange crush.

Sometimes Charlie would drive down to the sandbar and park; on summer and fall nights, there often was a small fire, and they could see shadows of the people there. Walt knew Jan was probably down there with Billy Parks, so he didn't want to stay long.

Those memories made Walt think about the philosophic talks when Jan was present for their sessions on the grass in front of the school. Walt sipped the cooling coffee and tried to remember what his friends had said about their life goals and aspirations. Charlie had talked about college, worrying whether his grades were sufficient for admission. Andy was interested in what Charlie could tell him about college, but neither of them expressed a life interest beyond that level of education, at least Walt couldn't remember if they had. What had Jan wanted beyond high school? Walt could easily recall her lying beside him on the grass, rolled on her side, head propped in one hand, talking about something.

But all Walt could remember, sitting on his porch decades later, was how her hair looked, rimming her face. Her face caught the glow from her bright red blouse and seemed to light her like a sunset. Her eyes, dark and yet sparkling, held Walt's gaze even all this time later. And, just as in yesteryear, Walt could not remember the subject of that discussion. For him, it was play-acting, seeming to be interested in her topic while only wanting to prolong their time together. Walt's coffee now was definitely cold. He considered that perhaps Billy Parks was a better listener than he was at the time. Huh. Walt thought, *maybe so, but I bet he can't remember what she was wearing like I still can, to this day.*

Walt shook his head and picked up the last piece of cheese. He caught the flash of color in the street and looked up just in time to see a boy on a bike rounding the corner. He thought about the times he and his friends spent on their bikes in the years before they discovered cars. Walt estimated that he had ridden between four and five miles a day, five or six days a week for at least twenty weeks a year, three years in a row. Those weren't training miles, however; many were at slow speed and hardly ever uphill.

Walt remembered how taken he had been with the English racing bike that David Swain had when they were in the seventh grade. Skinny little tires, cables over the handlebars, gearshift on the right hand, gleaming red and yellow. Walt asked David if he could ride it, and David let him. Walt remembered playing with the gears and pumping up the one small hill at the edge of town. With his friends watching, he turned and headed back down. As he gathered speed, Walt tried to slow his descent by applying the pedal brakes - and learned there were no pedal brakes.

Then, with his feet furiously backpedaling to no avail, Walt thought, "I'm going to crash, and David will kill me for harming his bike." The thought of that confrontation made Walt grip the handlebars tightly - which applied the brakes and brought the bike to a complete stop. Walt didn't stop, though. He went smartly over the handlebars and landed at the roadside, barely missing a windmill landing directly on a fire hydrant. The bike toppled softly on its side, unscratched, while Walt would carry a nasty scrape on his cheek for weeks before it completely healed. And, of course, David told everyone at school about the event, complete with wildly waving his arms.

Walt chuckled to himself and cut off another chunk of cheese. His first encounter with international commerce was a hard lesson but well learned in the end. He was especially pleased that Jan had not been present to watch his 'Jack fell down' act, but he remembered that Andy and Charlie were only too pleased to recount all the details, especially the part where Walt went flying in the air over the handlebars and landed like a duffel bag full of old shoes. Jan did show some concern for Walt's well-being after that, however. But not until she had laughed so hard at him that snot ran out her nose. *What a marvelous memory,* Walt thought.

Try as he might, Walt could not remember what Jan was wearing that day. Maybe that's a good sign, he thought. He gathered up his tray and returned to the kitchen. He rinsed off the dishes, got a glass for whiskey, and went into the living room. As he poured himself four fingers, Walt thought about alcohol and sleeping pills; he had been taking a sleeping pill every night now, for weeks. But he had only been drinking once or twice during that time. Walt knew he had trouble sleeping whenever he thought too much about Jan, the way he left town, and wondering whatever happened to her. And that was going to be his worries tonight, he knew. *But,* he thought, *I want this drink, too.*

He rubbed his left shoulder, where he began to note some aching and determined to try sleeping without the pill that night. He took a swallow of whiskey and started off upstairs.

# CHAPTER 46

## 05/12/2020 TUESDAY

Bella came with them this time. The boys were somewhat more subdued in her presence but still enthusiastic in their discussion. Walt opened the door for them and stood by as they hung up coats on the newel post and moved into the living room. Bella commented to Walt about missing the last session and went to join the boys.

Walt asked as he entered the room, "How is your project going? Aren't you pushing the deadline and still collecting information?"

Bella, notebook open on her lap, responded, "We can never have too much information, Walt."

Her answer ran over Hal's response, which had started, " Oh, we're all finished …" but he quit talking when Bella answered.

Walt smiled at them and said, "Well then, what area of further information do you want to discuss today?"

Bella was ready for this question and said, "Walt, we have noticed that you have given us a great insight into facts of the times and the opinion of several different individuals about our historical event, the Hungarian Revolution. What we would like, at this point, is to have more information about the personal interactions of people. Particularly interactions between people with different views. I guess we are asking for some perception about the emotional culture of the time."

Walt looked at her and debated whether to mention how her statement seemed practiced and pre-prepared. He decided to treat it as if she had answered spontaneously.

"Well," he said, "my impression of those days is that the public discourse was mostly shallow, even when people disagreed. I certainly never heard adults yelling at each other in public about someone's opinion of another person's stupid viewpoints. I'm not sure what went on in bars and other locations, but out in public, disagreement led to someone walking away."

Joey was fascinated by this revelation. "You mean there were no debates?"

"Not exactly. I mean one just didn't see ugly public confrontations over differences of opinion. And certainly not over differences of political opinion."

"Were people not interested in politics back then?" Hal asked.

"Oh my, of course, they were. And there were public debates to hear from candidates around election time. But the rest of the time, people simply criticized whoever was in office and usually got no resistance." He paused for effect. "You see, the unwritten rule at that time was polite conversation avoided two topics specifically: politics and religion. That allowed criticism of the current president and minimal defense, but no heated discussion.

Bella wrote furiously in her notebook.

Joey asked, "What about in your classes? Did you ever have arguments there?"

"Well, yes, I guess we did. But much of that was artificial. The teachers would take a position and push us to argue with it. That was usually kinda fun. Sometimes they could get us arguing among ourselves but not with facts, just opinion."

"What do you mean?"

"The principal, Mr. Arnold once told us that schools in his day had a course called Rhetoric, which really meant Debate. He said learning to defend a position was part of classical education. We were to use our wits to defeat opponents, but as someone said, we engaged in a battle of wits, and both sides were unarmed."

"That's funny," Joey said.

Walt said, "And it was largely true. In class, most of us only parroted the viewpoints we had heard at home. We didn't have talk radio to listen to, and television news was straight facts."

Bella looked up and asked, "And the Revolution? Did you ever discuss that?"

Walt sat quietly for a moment and then quietly asked Bella, "Are you asking whether we ever discussed the Hungarian Revolution in our classes back then?"

Bella blushed and seemed to get a little smaller in her seat, but she bravely said, "Yes."

Walt nodded and said, "As I explained several months ago, our discussions in Civics class did occur, and emotional feelings were expressed. But we had no pitched arguments because everyone's heated feelings were aimed at the President and the government, not someone in the class."

Bella said, "I remember you mentioning those discussions."

Walt responded, "I thought so."

Hal said, "Maybe we should have picked a different event. Something like Pearl Harbor."

Walt recognized Hal's attempt to defuse a tense situation and said, "That would have had entirely different discussions in a classroom, I'm sure. But I could not have spoken to it because I was only four years old, and my family was more Irish than American at that time."

Hal shrugged, "Oh, well."

Walt asked, "What else is going on in your lives?"

Bella was glad to see the conversation change and responded, "We're coming up to Prom pretty soon."

"Ah, and have you driven your family car yet?" Walt asked.

Joey and Hal nodded, but Bella said, "My dad said I have to show him I can drive before I can get behind the wheel by myself."

Joey said, "Yeah, Dad didn't let me drive the car until I had a license and passed all the tests. But I'll be driving to the Prom."

"Me, too," Hal offered.

Walt asked, "Should I assume you young men know all the acceptable social skills for such an evening?"

"What are you talking about?"

"Do you know the proper etiquette for a formal evening with your date?"

"Uh, what?"

"For instance, you drive to your date's home and park out front. Then, you get out of the car, walk to the front door and knock."

"Yeah, yeah."

"The door will be answered by one of her parents, and you greet them and ask if their daughter is ready?"

"Really? Come on. They know why I'm there."

"And, when your date comes into the room, you express appreciation of her dress, and hand her the corsage you have carefully picked out and obtained that afternoon."

Bella clapped her hands silently.

"Then you offer her your arm and escort her to the waiting car. You open her door and confirm she is seated and the dress is inside before closing the door and going to the driver's side."

Bella said, "Right on, Walt."

"Are dance cards still being used?" Walt asked.

Joey looked puzzled and said, "My Dad asked the same thing."

Hal said, "What is this dance card thing?"

Walt said, "For many years, when formal dances were a regular event in society, women had a dance card, a small booklet they carried that allowed them to accept an invitation to dance with someone other than their date for a particular song or dance. She would use a small, attached pencil to write the gentleman's name in the book for that particular dance. It became a nice keepsake and memory of the dance."

"Never heard of it."

Walt nodded, "Ever heard someone say 'I'll pencil you in,' whenever someone asks for a meeting?"

"Yeah …"

"Well, that phrase comes from the dance card era. So does the idea 'my dance card is full' indicating that the person is too busy to take on a new project."

"Cool," Hal said. "I've heard my mother say that."

Bella joined, "Walt, your ideas are very proper but completely out of touch with today's Prom expectations. I imagine during your day, the dance was the major event of the evening. School gym all decorated up and like that, right?"

"Yes, of course."

"Today, the dance is almost a side event. People are more interested in getting the right reservation for dinner before the dance and having the right people at your party after the dance. I appreciate your instruction to the boys, here, but you've covered about six minutes of their planned evening, right Hal?"

"Yeah, but that's okay."

Walt said, "Whatever the venue, you should be a gentleman through the evening. It is a formal event, is it not?"

"Of course," Joey said. Hal nodded.

Bella changed the topic again, "Walt have you put those seedlings out in the garden yet?"

"Last Saturday," he answered, rising from his chair and asking, "Want to see?"

The students all followed him through the kitchen and out into the backyard. Joey used his phone to take pictures of the small plants to show his parents. They left after another fifteen minutes and made no comment about returning.

# CHAPTER 47

05/12/2020 TUESDAY

Later, Walt sat on the porch with his coffee laced with a generous dollop of Bailey's. His chest was aching again, and he felt somewhat short of breath. He could no longer stop himself from thinking about his own senior Prom. His mind went racing over the events from the few days before the dance, to that evening itself including events at the sandbar, and crucially to an isolated field north of town weeks later. The events of Prom night, unexpected as they were, had set in motion his last days in Whealton and provided his reason for joining the Army, and his separation from the only life he had known. Walt's memories of those few weeks pressed on his conscience and created an aching in his chest, shortness of breath, and tearfulness.

The tears rolled softly down his cheeks; and he made no attempt to stop them. Walt thought perhaps he could let the painful memories out of his head with the tears. So, he sat straight in the chair, tearfully sipping his Bailey's laced coffee and pulling memories from deep in his background, examining them in detail.

Walt had kept these memories hidden from his conscious thoughts for nearly sixty years; a thought crossed his mind that they might now be dim or imperceptible. But, when he opened the gate, the remembrances were vivid and plush and complete in such detail that Walt could smell the fresh air and flowers of those spring days in northern Montana.

He had never understood Billy Parks. One year behind Walt and Andy, and Jan in school, Billy was the drummer in the small band at school. The music teacher must have liked Billy because she always featured a drum solo at some part of every band performance. *Billy was pretty good with the drums,* Walt had to admit. Not good enough to be a recording artist, of course, but entertaining in his own way.

Walt knew the event that, in retrospect, he understood to be the first in the cascade. It was the day that Spring when Elin Ericsdottir moved to Whealton and came to school. Elin was from Iceland; she was a pale girl, about five and a half feet tall, with long blondish white hair and a pair of knockers that had to be forty inches. Walt imagined that Elin was pretty enough in the face to attract attention from all the boys in the school; her chest, however, was her most prominent feature and seemed to be the only thing the boys noticed.

Elin turned out to be a shy person, and she turned down requests for dates in the first few months she was in Whealton. Her lack of interest in dating earned her the title of Ice Queen. The question of who would get the first date became a common topic of conversation among the boys.

Enter Billy Parks. In spite of seeming to have a monopoly on all of Jan's time, Billy showed up around Elin often. He occasionally walked her home from school and often sat with her at lunch. In a normal situation, other boys might have taken these events as an indication of Elin defrosting, and trying to talk with her themselves. But no one did, not as long as Billy Parks was around.

Billy Parks was a bit of a bully. He played offensive guard on the football team and, although the team did poorly, talked openly about wanting to be recruited to play for the University of Oklahoma. Billy was only five foot nine inches and weighed less than 170 pounds, but he acted taller and heavier. His mouth was always picking on those he believed his lesser, and that was almost everyone. Billy particularly liked to say things to embarrass Walt, knowing Walt's fondness for Jan.

So, it was not a complete surprise when Billy Parks asked Elin to be his date for the Prom. Not a surprise, but it was a shock to both Walt and Jan. The arrangement was known publicly several weeks before the Prom, and Jan was visibly at a loss. She avoided the Philosophy Group, and Walt had to chase after her at school to walk her home. She lived on the family farm just outside of town, and they walked most of the way without her speaking.

Walt finally broke her silence by asking her to be his date for the Prom. It was a long-time dream of his to have Jan as his Prom date, and he let her know. She smiled at him and said, 'sure' without much enthusiasm, but Walt's memory was how his heart skipped in his chest when she agreed.

In the intervening weeks before the Prom, Billy paid less attention to Jan and seemed smitten with Elin. Jan did not rejoin the Group or show any interest in dating, Walt or anyone. So Walt was determined to make her Prom night memorable. He carefully selected a corsage for the evening, had his black suit cleaned and pressed, learned how to tie a bowtie, and talked his father into allowing him use of the family car.

When Walt picked her up that evening, she was wearing a blue-green tea-length gown with multiple taffeta underskirts. In his opinion, she would be the prettiest girl at the Prom. He let her mother pin on the corsage to the strapless top, helped her into a shawl, and escorted her to the car, feeling like the happiest man on earth.

Walt had controlled the dance card for the evening and had carefully omitted Billy Parks from having even one dance with Jan. He expected that she would be upset by that and was hesitant about sharing the card with her when they arrived at the dance. But Jan seemed pleased with his choices, especially that he had saved the last two dances for himself. Walt remembered how pleasantly surprised he was that Jan acted as if she was having the date of her life. She smiled at everything, laughed at Walt's jokes, and never obviously looked across the dance floor at the table where Billy Parks sat with his arm around Elin Ericsdottir.

Walt drew deeply on his coffee and tried to remember every dance from that evening, but all he could recall clearly were the last two. Jan hung tightly to him for the slow dances, and he remembered trying to will the DJ to play those songs for hours. But, as he recalled, at the beginning of the last song, he caught a glimpse of Billy and Elin slipping out a side door. Shortly, Jan whispered in his ear, 'Let's get out of here, okay?' so they, too, left the Prom before the lights went up

As soon as they were in the car, Jan suggested they change into their swimsuits and go to the sand bar. Walt remembered how his heart sank at that suggestion, thinking she was planning on finding Billy there. But, he went along with the idea. His suit and towels were already in the car, and Jan said she had put hers in bushes at the front of her driveway where they could be easily retrieved.

They found only a few couples at the sandbar, Billy and Elin not among them. Walt knew that he had expected Jan to spend time looking for Billy, but that was not what happened. Surprisingly, Jan spent all the time with him, and made Walt feel like the man of her dreams that night. As he drank the last of his Baileys-coffee mix, Walt felt the aching in his chest again, surfacing with the memory of him and Jan wrapped in each other's arms.

Walt poured the second cup of coffee from the carafe and thought about the weeks following the Prom. He thought about how Jan seemed to disappear. She always worked in the family truck garden in the spring, along with her two brothers, but her absence this time seemed more deliberate and more complete. Even at graduation, Jan seemed distant but polite and disappeared from the class party early.

Walt looked in his cup as if he expected to find answers. He knew and remembered what occurred soon after graduation, but those events only raised persistent questions, questions that had lingered with him for decades. Walt wanted no part of those memories, so he stood up and walked around the porch, trying to shed the ache in his chest and the hurt in his mind from the details he had brought out of the dark recesses in his memory.

The position change did not completely drive the painful memories out of Walt's mind, however. Standing at the steps, he stared toward the setting sun and recalled the post-graduation encounter outside town, his lonely trip back, and his decision overnight to join the Army. With the last of the coffee, Walt tried to turn his thoughts to the happy times in the Army, meeting and marrying Maddy, and his retirement.

But he couldn't hold those thoughts; they were consistently pushed out by the events in the grassland. When the mental image of the bloodstained shirt appeared, Walt threw out his remaining coffee and headed for the bedroom, intent on taking two sleeping pills that night.

# CHAPTER 48

## 05/20/2020 WEDNESDAY

Walt was having trouble getting out of bed. He was waking at his usual hour of 6:00 AM, even without the alarm, but he had no interest in getting out of bed. For several days, Walt had looked at the clock, thought about things he intended to do that day, and rolled over and pulled the covers over his head to block the light. Walt had a little prostate problem and usually had to get up at least once a night to urinate. Recently he learned that if he didn't drink anything while he was up for that purpose, he did not need to urinate at 6:00 AM and could stay in his bed.

Even if he tried, however, Walt could not go back to sleep. His army training throughout his formative years had been to hit the floor with both feet at the first sound of the morning bugle. Being a kid from a small town with no nightlife, Walt was a sound sleeper. When the bugle sounded, Walt became instantly awake and found himself refreshed. The previous day's weariness and aches were replaced with strength and eagerness. So, Walt was one of the first in the shower and usually the first dressed, out the door, and in formation.

After boot camp, Walt maintained this discipline and gained some admiration from Madeline, who was herself a bit of a night owl and late sleeper. During his Army career, Walt took responsibility for their breakfast. He became inventive with scrambled eggs when they moved to Springfield, adding cheese, onions, green peppers, or mushrooms to the mix at various times. He also became a fan of French toast and tried various toppings. His favorite was bananas and peanut butter, but he fixed Madeline's favorite, strawberries and clotted cream, at least twice a week for her.

After Madeline died, Walt's interest in breakfast slowly ebbed, his intake decreased to a soft-boiled egg and an English muffin on most days. Recently, he noted a lack of interest in eating anything. He usually rolled out of bed by 10 AM and sometimes did not eat anything for several hours. Walt noticed how the presence of the students had affected his sleeping pattern and his eating habits. As he anticipated their interview, he would spend several days thinking about a snack for them, which seemed to increase his interest in food. But, in the days after their visits, Walt often found himself disinterested and lackadaisical about cooking or shopping for food. He continued to go for his walks in the neighborhood and seemed to find himself at the small liquor store far more often than at the grocery store.

Walt had not been a daily drinker until Madeline got sick. Her prognosis with multiple sclerosis was so poor, that he had turned to whiskey to help him relax and sleep. After her death, he became less discriminating, drinking gin, whiskey, scotch, or vodka almost all day for several months. Walt did his drinking sitting on his porch, waving to his neighbors as if his glass was plain iced tea. Then, one day Patrick, the postman, stopped to talk with Walt and said, "You know, Walt, You're going to end up in an early grave if you keep drinking like you are."

Walt had wanted to argue but found he couldn't get his thoughts straight, and Patrick went on, "I been watching you since the Missus died, and it is not a pretty sight, my friend."

Walt was not aware until that very moment that Patrick was a friend. He was speechless.

"I'm going to be retiring from the Service here next week. There'll be some new person bringing your mail around from now on. I doubt that person will say anything to you about the drinking, so I knew it would have to be me."

Walt finally knew what to say. "What?" he asked.

"You gotta stop drinking. That's what. Do it now before your liver falls down and dies."

Walt found himself saying, "Okay." Then Patrick patted him on the shoulder and left. Walt had only a vague memory of sitting on the porch until well after sundown that day. He had no idea what, if anything, he was thinking about during that time. But Walt did remember that when he realized how dark it was and got up to go inside, he found his drink glass was still mostly full. He recalled going to the edge of the porch and pouring the drink into the bushes before going inside. He stopped drinking that day and had not had any further alcohol until he began having the aching in his chest when thinking about Jan and Whealton and his high school antics.

Walt lay in bed and wondered, *"Why am I drinking again?"* He thought he knew the answer but did not want to put it into words. Thoughts ran through his head of Jan in her swimsuit, Charlie driving his car around town, Andy reporting his epic failures at getting a peek at Barbara Mingo sunbathing; each thought caused additional pain and aching.

*"What's today?"* he thought, remembering that he was supposed to get up early for some reason.

So, at 10 AM, Walt did get out of bed and went into the bathroom. He cleaned up but decided not to shave, dressed in the same clothes he had worn the day before, and went downstairs to the kitchen. He sat at the kitchen table and thought about making some coffee, but the effort seemed more than he could handle at that moment. He laid his head on his arms and considered whether to go back to bed, as he thought about it, he realized he was feeling sorry for himself, and about then, the specialness of the day dawned on him.

*"It's my birthday!"* Walt mumbled to himself. *And nobody remembered,* he thought. Well, who is there to remember? Not anyone in his family, nor Madeline's. Not anyone from work. That's the way it had been for the past several years. No one else thought the day was special.

Walt almost cried, then he sniffed it all back and thought, *I need to put on my big boy pants and eat some breakfast! Then maybe I'll sit in the backyard and tell the plants about my birthday.'*

Every action Walt took in preparing for his big day made him feel better about himself and the whole world. After a quick shower and shave, he dressed in a clean shirt, khakis, and comfortable sandals. Back in the kitchen, he put on the kettle for coffee and rummaged through the refrigerator to find eggs. He chopped some green peppers into the eggs as he scrambled them and toasted an English muffin. When the coffee was ready, he anointed the cup with cream and sat down for breakfast.

No longer feeling sorry for himself, Walt cleaned up the kitchen and went into the backyard to check on his plantings. He spent a little while pulling an occasional weed and loosening the earth around the plants so water would soak in. Then he stubbed back into the house to find the last book he had been reading. The book was in the living room. It was Manchester's *A World Lit Only by Fire,* a historical recollection of the Middle Ages. Walt had become interested in history since retiring and wondered how long it had been since he held this book in his hand.

So that is why Walt Dell was sitting in his favorite chair on his front porch, reading about the Borgia family and the Papacy, when the three students turned in at his walk and raced up the stairs to the porch. Hal was carrying a cardboard cube very carefully, and Bella and Joey had small sacks in their hands. Walt watched them ascend the stairs and burst into song, "Happy Birthday to You. Happy Birthday to you, Happy Birthday, dear Walter, Happy Birthday to you!"

The song took Walt aback and more so when Joey and Bella pulled handfuls of confetti from the stuffed sacks and threw them into the air around his head. He was shocked by the singing, recognizing Bella's pleasing voice leading. And Walt was able to laugh with them at the confetti in his hair. Hal flipped open the cube he was carrying to reveal a tall, round chocolate frosted cake. "It's chocolate cake!" Hal explained. They indicated they should continue the celebration inside, and Walt opened the door.

Joey ushered Walt to a seat while Hal and Bella went into the kitchen to fetch saucers and forks. Bella remembered to get glasses and snag a half-gallon of milk from the refrigerator. Walt saw that and had a secret thought wondering, *When did I go to the grocery store and buy milk?*

When the cake was cut, and everyone had their piece, Joey led another round of 'Happy Birthday' before everyone turned their attention to the cake and milk.

"Who gave this away?" Walt asked after several bites.

"Who do you think?" Bella countered. "Ms. Postella told us the day and emphasized that chocolate cake with chocolate icing was your favorite."

"Mmm," Walt replied, taking another large bite.

Hal wanted Walt to know their attention was not just for his birthday. "You know, coming over to see you this year has been one of the highlights for us. We enjoyed it, learned some things, you know."

Walt nodded at him and smiled.

Joey added, "I even got to know these two, and it turns out, they are actually friendly people."

Walt asked, "Didn't you know each other?"

"Not exactly," Bella said. "Ms. Postella puts people who don't know each other together in teams. She says the idea is to foster how to learn from someone you don't already know and trust."

Walt nodded. He had heard this theory from Madeline years before.

Bella continued, "I had a little experience with Joey, but I didn't know Hal other than by his face."

Hal interrupted her, "Wait a minute. You knew Joey well enough to refer to him as K.I.A."

"Well, yeah. But that was from years ago."

Walt stopped her and asked, "What's K.I.A?"

Joey jumped in to explain, "It means Know It All. Bella and I went to camp together one summer, and I was trying to help kids get settled, and somebody tagged me as the Know It All."

"Somebody? It was everybody at camp that year," Bella said.

"No, it wasn't."

"Joey, it was almost everyone. Even the counselors referred to you that way."

"I didn't know that."

"That was perhaps the only thing you didn't know all summer."

Joey sat back, and his face fell.

Bella put down her bowl and hugged him. "Don't worry, I have been calling everyone from camp to tell them what a good guy you are."

"What? How do you know all those people?"

"Cut it out, Bella," Hal said.

She smiled at Joey and said, "I don't have to tell people, silly. They already know you're a good guy and only trying to help."

Walt looked at the three of them and tried to remember the shy trio that first came to interview him months before. He noted a more secure Hal, a more relaxed Joey, and a less serious Bella. He wondered if they were aware of these changes in themselves.

Walt insisted they take the remainder of the cake with them; he knew he would make himself sick eating it. Hal insisted they leave him one piece for a later snack. They all wanted to hug him and say again how much they appreciated his time and insight in helping them with their project.

As they were leaving but still on the porch, Walt asked if he could see their project, and Joey said, "Certainly. It's got a little bit of touching up needed. Ms. Postella said she would want your opinion, anyway."

And then they were gone, down the sidewalk and around the corner. And Walt's birthday felt happy and complete.

# CHAPTER 49

05/20/2020 TUESDAY

Walt returned to the living room and sat down in his chair. Bella had cleaned the dishes and glasses from the table and rinsed them in the sink. She also put the piece of cake they insisted he have for later on the kitchen table. Walt sat quietly in the chair and let the memory of the last hour or so sink into his brain.

Three lively high school students had taken the time from their day to help celebrate his birthday. What a surprise. Tears began to form in Walt's eyes, and he allowed them to gather. Sandra told them that his birthday was this day. She told them what cake he loved. Why would she have remembered any of those facts? What wonderful things to remember - young people with their life in front of them planning to spend a birthday celebration with an old man. *Who would have ever thought such a thing?* Not Walter Dell.

Walter Dell had been a self-centered high school student, and so were his friends. He struggled to remember his parents' birthdays, usually reminded by the other that one of those days was approaching. Walt realized he had no idea what either parent would have described as their favorite cake for celebrations.

As he continued to sit in the living room, the sun began to set, and the light started to fade. Walt could feel a darkness settling on his shoulders like a heavy cloak. He thought the darkness would make his feelings of happiness and the good memories of the day disappear, and he fought the growing weight by standing and returning to the porch where he could watch the sunset.

Later, Walt cleaned up the kitchen and put the piece of cake in the refrigerator. That would be his ticket to enjoying this day again, perhaps tomorrow. When he realized he had missed his evening coffee watching the sunset, Walt decided he needed stronger sustenance and went to the liquor cabinet.

Armed with a stiff whiskey, he returned to his chair and relaxed. Sipping his drink, and marveling at the warmth it induced, Walt thought again of his youth and times in Whealton, Montana. His first thought was a birthday cake made for him by Charlie's mother, chocolate with chocolate icing. Charlie's family and Andy sang Happy Birthday, and everyone had cake and ice cream.

He thought of the many days his father spent trying to teach him how to ride a bicycle. Walt had received a bike on his seventh birthday; he and his father spent hours in the street in front of the house learning control. The effort made clear from the outset that Walt Dell was not a natural for the bicycle, wavering his front tire more like a flag than a wheel. His father had run himself ragged trying to keep Walt upright, but as soon as he let go of the bike, Walt made an abrupt move with the handlebars and took the bike down.

Walt remembered several days of scuffed knees and elbows and his father doubting that Walt would ever be able to ride. But, then the magic happened, and balance was restored, Walt rode all around the block without falling, and for the remainder of the summer, he rode farther every day. By the summer he was ten, Walt and his friends were bicycling all over town and gone from home most of a summer day. Walt sipped his whiskey and fondly recalled those days of pedaling hard to get up speed and then coasting while eating ice cream and steering with his knees.

The memories were happy ones at first: bicycling with friends, swimming off the sandbar, harvesting potatoes, and even basketball games. Each memory had bright spots where Walt could almost bring the conversation to mind, but there were larger parts where the picture was fuzzy or running too fast to appreciate. Then there were moments like remembering how it felt to dance with Jan, Walt had to change the memory to amplify the time the two of them talked during the dance, and minimizing the time she looked around the room trying to find Billy Parks.

Oddly, one of the prominent memories Walt experienced involved a week at a Summer Camp. He found he remembered each boy in his cabin and could recall many of his shared adventures. Canoeing the river was an exciting time; Walt had to learn the various paddle strokes and imagined himself as an explorer with Lewis and Clark. Likewise, Walt's experience at the archery range was his first exposure to the craft, but he was a good student and became proficient before the end of Camp. Walt also recalled how he had regaled his father about all the events during the ride home at the end of the week.

Slowly, Walt began to remember events and circumstances that were not as comfortable as the previous ones. He somehow found himself in situations where the memory was uncomfortable rather than happy. He found himself in an angry discussion with Mr. Arnold, the principal, about whether Walt had allowed another boy to copy his answers on a test. Walt was unaware of the cheating at the time, but the other boy admitted to it and implicated Walt as a co-conspirator. On another occasion, Miss Drew scolded Walt for being unprepared in class.

Walt took larger sips of his whiskey as these events unfolded in his forebrain. The memories of Jan began to push others out of his mind and Walt felt his chest ache with each of her appearances. Initially, Jan was part of the Philosophy Group, lying in the grass with Charlie and Andy. Once again, the memory was indistinct, and he couldn't make out the conversation, but what Jan was wearing was in vivid color. He closed his eyes and tried to find a happy memory.

As Walt took the last swallow of his whiskey, he thought about the last time he had seen each of his friends. Charlie had driven by Walt's house to shake his hand as he headed out of town for the University of Montana. Charlie's father was a senior engineer on the construction project at the dam; he and the family moved somewhere the next spring, and Walt never heard from Charlie again. He, Andy, and Jan continued the Philosophy Group Meetings, but less frequently as seniors. Andy started seriously dating that dark-haired girl; what was her name? And Jan spent more time with Billy Parks. Walt remembered that Andy had indicated he was applying to Montana State Teachers College and wanted to be a teacher. Walt thought about Andy's involvement in the Theatre Group and agreed that Andy had the moxie to stand in front of an audience. They had spoken to each other for the last time two days before Walt left town to join the Army. Walt couldn't remember what they talked about, but it wasn't about leaving because Walt made that decision later. He had no idea what happened to Andy.

As Walt thought about these last meetings, the ache in his chest recurred as he recalled his last time to see Jan. He had snuck into her backyard and saw her through the window. She had a black eye, and the discussion he overheard indicated who had hit her. Walt realized his presence would not improve things for Jan, and he slipped away. A few days later, he left for Boot Camp and never found out what happened to Jan. As he sat there looking at his empty whiskey glass, Walt imagined his life was now as empty as that glass. His wife had died, they had no children, and the only childhood friends he had known had disappeared from his life decades ago.

Walt went into the kitchen, rinsed out his glass, heated a single-serve tomato soup container, and sat at the table slowly eating the soup and considering his barren life. He had been lifted out of doldrums and limited horizons by the students this past year, but now they, too, were not likely to be around anymore. As he cleaned up his dishes, Walt thought he should be depressed from all the negative thoughts and memories, but he realized he was not. Sad, certainly, but not depressed. He headed to bed.

Sleep was not coming easily or quickly for Walt most nights. He would turn and toss in the bed for over an hour before falling asleep. His slumber was not restful, and he often awoke in mid-morning, tired and disinterested in getting up or dressed. This night, Walt did get to sleep but awakened in the early hours of the morning from a bad dream. He was suddenly awake, heart pounding, chest aching, and short of breath. Walt remembered the dream: Jan and Charlie calling to him for help from some far-off location and running toward the sound of their voice but tripping and falling on uneven ground.

Walt sat upright in the bed. He knew he could not get back to sleep for some time and decided to get up and try again later. He sat in the chair in his bedroom and opened up his smartphone. He had purchased the phone more than a year before but still did not understand many of its functions. He did know two uses: using a browser to search the Internet and looking at the national news on a dedicated website.

First, Walt opened the news website and scrolled through several stories without much interest. He opened the browser and typed Jan's name into the search bar. Walt hesitated for a moment before finally pushing Enter. The search engine rapidly gave him information on several individuals with the same name but not the Janice Berryton of his age. Nor did he find an obituary for her. She was not findable. Jan was gone.

Walt felt the loss of any information about Jan more acutely than he had expected. His breath became short, and he felt the growing ache in his chest and shoulder.

Lying back down in his bed seemed unreasonable, as he knew he would not be able to sleep, so Walt pulled on his pants, slipped on some sandals, and went back downstairs. In the kitchen, he carefully made a carafe of French press coffee and took it to the porch where he sat in the dark, sipping his coffee and wondering why he had allowed all his friends to fade into the mist of time. Walt knew the answer was not disinterest on his part, but the result of a decision he had made all those years before. A decision to break any attachment to Whealton, - not having anyone in Whealton know where he was. He had been successful in the separation, but now it had come back to cause him discomfort.

Walt decided his present discomfort was a penance for his past actions responsible for having to leave Whealton. He thoughtfully accepted the price. Until the sun came up that morning, Walt Dell sat on his porch, sipping coffee and having regrets.

# CHAPTER 50

## 06/8/2020 TUESDAY

Walt was in the backyard when Sandra came so he didn't hear her knock. Sandra was not going to leave without seeing him, so she tried the door and found it unlocked. She opened the door and called Walt's name. After getting no response, she went through the kitchen to the back door and found Walt pulling weeds in the tomato patch.

Sandra opened the screen door and moved onto the back stoop. "How is the garden this year, Walt?"

He looked up at her and waved in recognition but continued weeding. Sandra understood and waited for him to finish working the small area he was weeding. A few minutes later, Walt said, "There's lemonade in the fridge. I'll be through in a minute."

Sandra nodded, said, "Okay," and went back into the kitchen. She opened the cabinets, found two similar glasses, put them on the table, and located the lemonade pitcher in the refrigerator. She poured both glasses and put the pitcher between them. She took her laptop out of the purse and was opening a program when Walt came through the back door.

He greeted her saying, "Those kids you sent were certainly serious about your assignment."

She said, "I agree. They were deep into the process, and they loved their time with you."

"Well, I have to say, I enjoyed it, too."

"I thought you would. Especially since you've done this before for me."

"Several years ago."

"Still …like riding a bike."

Walt laughed and said, "You have no idea how hard it was for me to learn to ride a bike."

"Well, once done, not forgotten."

"Did you bring the project for me to see?"

"I did. You know, those kids continued to play with it until the last day of school. And they begged me not to show it to you until they "got it right" as Joey would say.

"And now it is, right?"

"Well, Walt, it's done as far as I'm concerned. They've shown it to others, and won a prize at the Fair, so I declare it finished."

Sandra turned to her laptop and brought up an animated program. Before turning on the program, she said, "Now, understand that what they did here was to answer my question with a set of scenes from a fictional small town in mid-America set in 1957."

"Huh."

"They named the town, Smallville initially."

"You mean like Superman?"

"Exactly, and I made them change the name to Tinytown."

"Okay."

Sandra started the program and sat back in her chair, sipping the lemonade and closely watching Walt's reaction to the program.

What unfolded was an animated video written by Joey depicting a virtual small Midwestern town, populated by many faceless figures in the background and several titled individuals in the foreground. Those in the foreground were avatars interviewed by a local television station about the recent Hungarian Revolution.

The opening was a wide shot of the town with a voiceover (Joey) introducing the footage. "Good evening. I'm Bobby Blatant from Channel Zero, covering the Hungarian Revolution from here in Tinytown, America."

The camera shot then allowed 'Bobby Blatant' to enter from the side. The avatar Joey had chosen was a wide-shouldered blond man wearing a white sports coat.

As the camera then moved for a closer view of the town's major streets, Joey's voiceover explained that the recent Hungarian Revolution had created some controversy over an appropriate American response, and Washington was interested in the opinions of the populace, and "this is their story."

For background, the voiceover explained the population of TinyTown and described its main streets and buildings. The camera panned down the main street and showed the barbershop, the hardware store, a tobacco shop, and the drug store. Other cuts showed where the school was in relation to the town square and the Mayor's office and the location of the movie theatre and the small hotel. Walt noted the similarity of these fictitious buildings and their locations to what he had described as Whealton's 'downtown' during the sessions with the students.

'Bobby Blatant' then began interviewing individuals on the street, asking if they knew about the Hungarian Revolution, whether they approved of the Revolution, what they had expected the U.S. Government to do in response and how they felt about what the Government actually did. Each of these interviews began with a short sketch and bio of the interviewee. The first 'person' interviewed was the 'mayor' with a voiceover belonging to Hal. The 'mayor' explained that the citizenry of Tinytown was quite diverse, including several European immigrant families, a good number of veterans, and an overall highly patriotic population.

Subsequent interviews involved a school teacher, the town barber, a minister at the protestant church, the desk clerk at the hotel, the pharmacist, a homeowner who worked as a salesman, a housewife, the physician's assistant, the school Principal, two veterans, and three high school students, a White boy and girl and a Black boy. As Walt watched the interviews, he recognized the background and variable opinions of people he had discussed with the students.

Walt thought the scripting was clever, especially how the background and avatars showed the diversity of the people interviewed, including the unpredictability of their answers to the other questions.

Not all the voiceovers were of Joey or Hal. Walt thought he detected at least two other male voices and three women's voices, only one of which was Bella's. As each person interviewed gave their personal history, the interviewer, Bobby Blatant, would emphasize any connection they might feel toward the Hungarian Revolution, such as recent immigration from Eastern Europe or personal involvement in the recently concluded World War. Walt found the most compelling part of the scenes was the logical manner each person provided a believable framework for their position; in the end, the position most approved by the people of Tinytown was for America to play no active role in support for the revolutionaries. The minority opinion for involvement was accompanied by harsh criticism of President Eisenhower.

In the program, after Bobby Blatant signed off, there was a spinning collage that ended with an aged Bobby watching as the collage spun into a contemporary television set. The 'older' Bobby then said, "That was then, and this is now. Twenty years later, we have definitive information concerning President Eisenhower's decision not to support the Hungarian Revolutionaries. First, here's what happened to those who spoke with us twenty years ago."

The film then showed short clips about some of the previous interviewees. Each was appropriately twenty years older and often no longer living in Tinytown. The Mayor gave information about jobs in the oil fields drying up and the town contracting in size, the barber moved to Florida, the Principal to a neighboring district, and the doctor joined the Veterans Health Administration.

But for Walt, the three key presentations were those of the high school students. One of the boys had gone to the state university, then to law school, and joined a large firm in Kansas. The girl explained that she had married and now worked as a secretary in a large construction company in Big Town. The third interview was with the other boy, the Black one. He explained how unsure he felt of his place in life at graduation, so he enlisted in the Army. He went on to say that the Army taught him programming, and he was able to retire from service with a job in programming for a shipping company. He said while on active duty, he heard a briefing about the Hungarian Revolution that explained why the U.S. Government did not make any effort to support the revolutionaries. The issues were logistics, since the U.S. had no troops nearby and concern about an escalated conflict with the Soviet Union.

Old Bobby Blatant summed up the message: Americans have individual positions on major events, sometimes without all the facts. We, the people, need to listen carefully, gather the facts that can be found, and continue to make our thoughtful opinions known without creating conflict in the country. The film faded to black, and credits began to roll.

Walt looked at Sandra with tears in his eyes. She nodded and said, "Exceptionally good, Walt. They say it's all you."

"It's true that I told them much of what was in there. But I didn't think it would turn out so clearly. I don't think it was clear in my mind until I heard that briefing, years later."

Sandra handed him a tissue from her purse and turned off her laptop, preparing to put it in her purse. Walt asked, "Who has seen this?"

"Well, I'd say almost all the 400 or so that attended the History Fair, especially the seven judges that awarded it Best in Fair, the School Board had a special presentation and every teacher at the school. That's all, I guess." She smiled at him.

"They certainly did a bang-up job."

Sandra finished her lemonade and put their glasses in the sink. She patted Walt on his shoulder and said, "My thanks to you, old friend. You helped me generate more interest in the History Fair than ever before. And you know that Maddy would be proud of it, too."

After she left, Walt sat at the table, replaying the closing scenes of the students' project in his mind's eye. *Those students! What a crew.*

# CHAPTER 51

06/08/2020 WEDNESDAY

Walt continued sitting at the kitchen table, thinking about his interaction with the students. He remembered Joey changing from aloof to engaged, Hal's initial hesitancy and questioning everything. Bella seemed a bit of a cipher from the outset, throwing out complex questions and quietly writing everything anyone said in her notebook. Walt smiled to himself that none of the discussions he had with the boys about cars made it into the final program. They must have kept that discussion from her.

He went back to the garden patch and spent the next hour pulling grass clumps. Before returning to the house, he checked each of his planting areas. The tomatoes were starting to shoot up; one plant even had a single bloom on it. His pepper plants were also filling out their cages nicely. He had planted cucumbers at the base of an forty-five degree angled wire fence section; the plants were shooting out runners to help them climb the fence. Walt smiled at this because the cucumbers would hang down through the openings in the fence and be easy to harvest. Last, he checked on his lettuce. Like his father, Walt planted three kinds of lettuce in two five-yard rows. Even at this early stage, the plants gave him hints of their mature appearance. Walt judged he would soon have garden salad for dinner.

After making these rounds, Walt washed his hands in the kitchen sink and again sat at the table, thinking about the students' program. He wondered who the students had modeled the avatar students after: his friends Andy, Charlie, and Jan, or more on themselves. *Perhaps a mix of the two.*

Sandra had come after school, and now the sun was fading. Walt pulled a casserole from the refrigerator and heated a bowl of it. He finished the lemonade, rinsed off the dishes, and thought about making his coffee and sitting on the porch. But something caused him to go to the liquor cabinet instead. He stared at the partially filled bottles and decided to have gin. He had purchased some small bottles of tonic water and used one of them to make a tall drink of gin and tonic. Walt did not have any limes to cut up for the drink and instead put a few drops of lemon juice in the glass before taking it to the porch.

Sipping his drink, Walt let his memory run over the students' video again. The avatars were a nice touch and added color to the presentation. Walt wondered how they had convinced other students to play some of the roles in the project. But then he thought that Bella and Joey would likely be very persuasive. Just as Charlie had been; he could talk anyone into being a part of his pranks.

Walt's thoughts about Charlie merged with more memories about the Philosophy Group, about Andy as possibly a teacher, and, of course, of Jan. What could have happened to her? Would she have stayed? Or would they have gone to Billings or Bozeman to start a marriage? As much as Walt did not want to think of Jan and Billy together, he knew that was unfair to them both. He had left Whealton, developed a career he had never really planned for in his own future, married a wonderful woman, and had a fulfilling life. Why should he not want something like that for Jan?

Without easy answers, Walt sipped on his drink more vigorously, and pushed his mind to think of other things. An obvious choice was Graduation Day from Whealton High. Walt's graduating class was only thirty-two students, and two others left in the last two months as their families relocated for other construction work. It was a sunny day, and the Principal allowed the ceremony to take place on the grassy lawn in front of the school. The Principal made some remarks, but Walt could not remember what they were. Nor did he remember what the valedictorian said in her speech. He remembered he tried to catch Jan's eye throughout the ceremony, but she would not look at him.

Even then, Walt had a growing feeling that she was pulling away. After the ceremony, Walt tried to talk to Jan, but she maneuvered away, and he was left talking to Andy and his parents. Walt's mother was very proud of him for graduating; there was no pressure from his parents for him to pursue higher education. Although that lack of pressure was somewhat comfortable, Walt knew that he needed to have some kind of future in mind and he needed to work toward it. And it suddenly looked like there was no hope for Jan to be involved in that future.

Charlie had gone to university, and Andy was accepted at Montana State. Walt could not remember whether the Group had ever pressed him for a long-term goal, but he knew he didn't have one and, as best he could remember, neither did Jan. Maybe she did, and she's about to go off pursuing that, and Walt would never see her again?

Walt remembered that feeling on Graduation Night at the class party on the sandbar. Of course, Jan wasn't there, and Walt had visions of her leaving before he could talk to her. Looking back, Walt now knew how juvenile his fears were and how they led him to his Army career.

Walt tossed down the final bit of his drink and returned to the kitchen to rinse his glass, turn out the lights and make his way upstairs. But not to sleep. He was again troubled by demons in his sleep. They came as realistic dreams, real people making rational conversation but tuning into horned demons that chased him until he was awakened, often by a shotgun blast, trembling and soaked with sweat. Walt had tried the sleeping pills, but they were of little avail. More often Walt tried to drink himself to sleep. That's what he thought might happen this time.

Walt was woozy from the gin and tonic; he didn't even try to put on pajamas, falling into the bed after taking off his shoes. He pulled a cover up to his chin and was asleep within three minutes.

The sleep was not restful or peaceful. Walt kept seeing images that were either indistinct or frightening in sharp focus. He saw bus crashes and houses on fire, and people he knew were dead trying to talk to him. He woke once in a sweat but couldn't get out of bed. Walt tried rearranging his clothes, fluffing the pillow and finally got back to sleep. This time his dreams involved Jan, her mother yelling at her, and Walt driving out into the grassland. It seemed he drove for hours, not clear what he was seeking. Then he stopped the car and took his shotgun, and began walking. Suddenly many other men were walking around, and each one had a shotgun on his shoulder. Walt began to feel anxious; he turned his head to watch the other men and almost stumbled on something.

Walt looked down and saw a bloody shirt at his feet, and his panic rushed to his head. All the other men were staring at him, so Walt began to run, but he forgot where he had left his car, and behind him, he heard shotgun fire.

And he awoke, startled, heart pounding, chest aching, and feeling slightly nauseated. He swung his legs over the side of the bed, and sat there until his pulse was slower and his breathing was controlled. Walt decided he would not be sleeping that night, so he dressed. Downstairs in the kitchen, he stared at the coffee carafe for several minutes before turning on the fire under the kettle.

When the coffee was ready, Walt pushed the filter down and poured himself the first cup. He added a dollop of half and half and carried the cup and the carafe out to the front porch. Recognizing the chill in the air, he ducked back inside and grabbed a coat and scarf. Suitably wrapped, sipping his coffee, Walt Dell sat in his chair and watched the new day dawn, keeping his thoughts in the present and refusing to let his memory take hold.

# CHAPTER 52

## 06/29/2020 TUESDAY

Three weeks later, Walt walked into the barbershop. Henry Ellison was sitting in one of his chairs with a novel. He looked up as Walt entered and said, "Glory be, the man with the worst hair in town has finally come to see me. Do come in, Walt. You want a perm or a dye job?" Henry was a lanky man, six feet tall but weighing only 175 pounds. He carried a perpetual smile, and the shock of unruly white hair on his head seemed a poor advertisement for his barbershop.

"Keep your seat, old man," Walt said, closing the door behind him. "Since you have no one waiting, how about letting me buy you a cup of coffee?"

Henry looked at Walt for a moment, and then said, "I think I can take a break from all this work. You wanna go someplace in particular?"

"No, I don't. In fact, maybe we could just stay here."

"We can," Henry allowed, "And I'll just put out the sign "Henry's Coiffure Consultation Room is occupied." He turned the card in the doorway from 'Open' to 'Closed'. "And, as you probably know, I have a new coffee maker in the back."

"And, as you probably guessed, I'm not here for coffee," Walt said as he took a seat in one of the barber chairs.

Henry proceeded into his back room, commenting, "Your choice, Walt. But I have got to have my cup as a prop during any consultation."

"Well, then make me one too. Two creams, no sugar."

Shortly the two old friends were facing each other, sitting in the barber chairs. Walt made a gesture of clinking his cup with Henry, and they each took an initial sip.

Henry said, "You first."

Walt sat his cup down on the counter and started his story. "Nobody knows some of the stuff I'm about to tell you, Henry. And I ask that you be very discreet about letting it out."

"Gotcha. Are you really an axe murderer, Walt?"

"Be serious, Hank. It's almost that bad. But I need to give you some background to understand how it all happened."

"Okay."

"There was this girl ..."

"Did Maddy know about her?"

Walt lowered his head and stared at Henry from under his eyebrows.

"What?"

Walt held his glance, "I said this is serious."

"Okay. Okay."

"There was this girl in high school. The funny thing was we had been friends for a couple of years, and then I wanted to be more than that, and she didn't. Had her sights on another kid, Billy."

Henry gestured with his cup for Walt to continue.

Walt proceeded to give a string of facts about Jan and Billy until Henry signaled he was aware that Walt was dodging his point. So, in painful detail, Walt told about the Prom, Billy asking the girl with the big chest, Jan being disappointed, and Walt asking her to be his date, and his surprise and happiness when she agreed. Walt's story about the night of the Prom was increasingly uncomfortable, delayed at times by minute detail of Jan's dress, the decorations, etc.

Henry finally interrupted, "Look, Walt, either something happened that night or not. Is there a point to your story?"

Walt nodded and picked up his pace. He explained about the sandbar, the bonfire, and the blankets. He was particularly graphic in explaining to Henry how he expected Jan to go off hunting for Billy. And, he told how excited he was to find that she wanted to lie with him on the blanket, both of them in their swimsuits. Henry was a little embarrassed when Walt told the event that happened next; how Jan had initiated hugging and kissing and more. Still, Henry was astonished when Walt explained how she slipped her hand into his swim trunks and more so when she rolled on top of him and moved her hips rhythmically. In less than a minute, it was all over; Jan rolled off and snuggled at Walt's side. Walt reported he remembers how he felt, acutely aware that Jan was not a virgin, incredibly flushed, and wondering what she meant by the act. He did not remember what either of them said.

Henry nodded and commented, "It is not unusual, you know, Walt. Lots of guys have their first with an experienced woman."

"But I had no idea she was experienced, Henry," Walt said plaintively. "She was a kid, like me, someone I had known for several years. Someone I never would have thought …"

Henry nodded and said, "Someone you were holding up as a Dream Girl, right?"

Walt paused and then reluctantly nodded, "I guess so."

"Guess so? Walt, you got it hanging out all over you. She was your first love. And the sandbar incident was confusing because she was yours, yet she had been someone else's first. Of course, you were confused, probably wondering what this meant for the future."

"Spot on, my man. I know I started to build castles in the air, thinking that Jan was now mine and she was no longer Billy's. My future began to look better than ever."

"Right. I can see that. But why bring this up all these years later? You said Maddy knew about this affair, right? So, why tell me?"

"Because, Henry, that's the very moment everything started to go downhill."

"That doesn't sound good."

"It wasn't, and it isn't. Let me tell you what happened next."

Henry held his hand up and said, "You look like it's a long story. We're going to need more coffee for that." He took Walt's cup and went into the backroom while Walt sat hunched over his knees until Henry handed him another cup of coffee.

Henry took his chair and said, "Well, what did happen next?"

"She disappeared."

"What?"

"She just wasn't around. Not in any of the usual places. I looked for Billy Parks but she wasn't with him, either. The next time I saw her was a couple of weeks later, at graduation. She showed up at the last minute wearing her gown and cap. She looked like she'd been crying. She dodged me, and we had to march. I tried to catch her eye, but she ignored me. And after she got her diploma, she walked out of the auditorium. Didn't hang around to congratulate people, and she didn't show up for the class party on the sandbar."

Henry nodded and agreed, "That certainly sounds suspicious."

Walt said, "Things got a little clearer a week later when Jan's older brothers came in town to find Billy Parks. When they did find him, they beat him severely, using only their fists. Really mashed up his face."

"Did they say why?"

"They didn't say anything. They just grabbed him, hauled him into the street, and whaled away for four or five minutes. Then they got in their car and left before anybody could think about stopping them."

Henry shook his head in disbelief, but he said nothing, wanting Walt to continue his story.

Walt had stopped talking, however, and seemed lost in reverie. Minutes later, he lifted his head and said, "So, that night, I went to her house."

"Hmm," added Henry without judgment.

"Yeah, they lived a little bit out of town, and their street didn't have a street light, so I got up the driveway and almost to the front porch without attracting attention. Then I heard voices from the back of the house, and I went back there. The voices were from Jan and her mother. They were in the kitchen and the window was open." Walt stopped his narration and needed a few seconds to catch his breath.

When he resumed, he told Henry that everyone at graduation had seen Jan and decided she was pregnant. That explained the beating of Billy Parks. Walt wondered why Jan had not mentioned his name to the brothers and had no good answer. But he desperately wanted to see her, and peeking through the kitchen window, he caught a glimpse of her face with a large bruise and a black eye. At that point, Walt realized he would not be welcome in the Berryton home. He sneaked back down the driveway and went home.

Walt looked at Henry and spread his hands helplessly. "She was beaten in her home, Henry. By her father. And I left her there and ran away."

"I'm not sure what you could have done, Walt."

"Well, I know what I did. A couple of days later, I was in the general store and heard Mr. Berryton buying shotgun shells for rabbit hunting."

Slowly, Walt told how he followed Berryton out in the grasslands north of town, confronted him, and the aftermath ended with Berryton lying on his back and his plaid shirt welling up blood. Walt took his time telling the story, partly from hesitation to let things be known but also because he choked up at several points. Henry let him finish everything he wanted to say, even to the announcement Walt made the following morning that he was going to enlist in the Army.

The two friends sat and regarded each other silently for several minutes before Henry opined, "Sounds like a mean SOB, Walt."

"Yeah, but so what?"

"Did you go out there to kill him?"

"I don't think so. I intended to threaten him, though."

"With your shotgun?"

"No, with revealing to the town that he beat his daughter."

"Why are you telling me this, Walt?"

"I'm not sure, but I think somebody ought to know."

"Why me?"

Walt smiled for the first time and said, "Because I trust you to do the right thing. And because I just met with my lawyer and appointed you as the executor of my estate."

"You don't have an estate, Walt."

"The lawyer says I do, and you will be the executor. I want you to liquidate everything and donate it to the school in Madeline's name."

"That I can do, and willingly, old friend. What now?"

"Now I got to get back home. There's papers and stuff I want to get organized. You know, so's it won't cause my executor any trouble."

# CHAPTER 53

## 11/22/2022 TUESDAY

Sandra Postella had finished her lunch and was placing papers on each desk in the classroom, readying herself for the first class that afternoon. She had just finished distributing the papers to a row and was heading back toward the front of the room when she heard someone come in the door to the room. Thinking her afternoon students were early, she turned and was greeted by Hal and Bella bursting through the opening saying, "Hey, Ms. Postella!" Both wore broad smiles.

Sandra smiled and welcomed them with open arms. Joey Symes was right behind them, somewhat reticent about his entrance but not hesitant to join a group hug. Sandra greeted them by name and inadvertently looked at the wall clock.

"Hey, don't worry," Hal laughed at her. "We won't stay and get in your way with the class."

"I know," she said, with a slight shake of her head. "I heard you guys were back and I hoped we could get a chance to talk, but …"

Bella hugged Sandra again and replied, "We just wanted to say hello and set up a time when we could tell you all about everything."

Sandra looked questioningly at Joey, who said, "Not everything, of course. But, you know, highlights and like that …"

Sandra said, "Well, you are aware that class starts in less than ten minutes and I will be busy from then until shortly after four. If you come back then, I'm sure we can find a place to sit and talk."

Bella and Joey took the hint and began moving back toward the doorway but Hal insisted on making another observation. "Sure," he said. "We want to run out to see Walt, anyway. We already planned to spend the afternoon with him. I want to tell him how his little discussions turned out for me. Plus, you know, I'm coming up on the end of my enlistment. Yep, it's been two years, and I'm thinking maybe it's time to do something else. I want to ask him about whether to re-enlist or make an application to college." Watching Sandra's face as he finished this speech, Hal's voice slowed and decreased in volume.

"What's wrong?" Bella asked coming back to the teacher's side.

"Walt Dell died several weeks ago," Sandra said, looking sadly at each of them.

The news was obviously a shock; individually they all turned to look at each other and no one spoke. Sandra reached out and touched each of them and said, "It was all very peaceful. One of his neighbors went by to check on him and found him sitting on the porch with a cup of coffee. Stone dead and smiling at the sunset."

Bella's eyes began to water and she said, "I wanted him to know what that project did for me and how it helped me get into college."

Sandra nodded and said, "Actually, he did know. I told him what had happened to each of you."

Joey sniffed very loudly like he was having trouble with fluid in his nose. Hal said, "He was responsible for me signing up for the Army and becoming a Ranger. Did he know that?"

"I don't know what all he kept up with," Sandra said, quietly. "But, I do know he was aware that you had enlisted."

Then the classroom door opened again and several students entered, talking among themselves. They stopped abruptly when they saw the visitors and recognized the somber look on everyone's face.

Sandra quickly regained her composure and greeted the incoming students. "Come on in. Take your seats. These are some of my former students who just dropped by to say hello." She made gestures to the current students and ushered the three former students toward the hallway.

"We can talk more after class," she said.

Joey, Hal and Bella stood still and unmoving outside the classroom, wondering what they would do with their afternoon.

# CHAPTER 54

## 11/22/2022 TUESDAY

Sandra entered her front door and kicked off her shoes. She hung her bag on the coat hooks inside the doorway and plodded barefoot to the kitchen. This routine had been set for several years. Kick off the shoes, turn on the burner under the kettle, reach into the cabinet for the teabags, and put two of them into the china pot on the right side of the stove.

Then she went to the sink, picked up the cup she had used for her breakfast coffee, and rinsed it out before drying it with the tea towel hanging on the rack behind the sink.

She could hear the sound of the water heating in the kettle as she took the tray from the drying rack and placed it on the table. Sandra opened the refrigerator, took out a small tin of cookies, and placed them on the tray. Then, carefully handling the teabags, Sandra looped the string and tag from each teabag around the teapot handle before pouring the hot water from the kettle. She replaced the teapot top, pinning the strings and tags outside, and then picked up the tray and went out onto her front porch.

The tray found its usual place on the chair side table, and Sandra sank thankfully and easily into the cushioned Adirondack. She put her feet up on the footrest and sighed.

Those kids! They had been right there at four o'clock, ready to talk and, with a little encouragement, to listen. Sandra was normally tired at the end of a teaching day; this had been no different. But the enthusiasm and energy of Hal and Bella were hard to contain. Even the usually laconic Joey Symes was leaning forward and occasionally interrupting someone to speak.

Of course, they first wanted to know all about Walt Dell's death. They even wanted to hear about the funeral; who was there and whether anyone spoke about his past. Sandra had replayed the event for them as best she could, but her discomfort was obvious, and the young people allowed her to change the subject and start talking about them.

Hal eagerly told them gory details about basic training and how he wrangled a tryout with the Rangers and made it through their rigorous coursework.

"It's like the Seals," he said. "Only without the risk of drowning." When Hal seemed to have run out of steam, Sandra looked at Joey. He looked at her for a long moment and then smiled as he said, "You know, if it weren't for Specialist Bingham, I wouldn't know anyone in the Army, Ranger or not."

Hal rejoined, "I told you, I'm not a Specialist. I'm a Private First Class. That Specialist stuff depends on whether I re-up or not. And, I would have to take a course in leadership and stuff. I told you that."

Joey nodded, "You certainly did. So many times." He turned to Sandra to explain. "This guy sent me a postcard every week telling me what he was going through. It's like he thought I was his mother or something." He was grinning as he made this comment and obviously had welcomed the information and involvement in his friend's life.

"Yeah, well, you said you didn't know anyone in the military, and I kinda thought you'd like to know what it's like. Right?"

"Right, Specialist Bingham. Absolutely right, or, as you guys say, 'spot on'."

Hal noted to Bella, "I think he wants me to re-up and keep him in the loop so he can enjoy life in the military without getting dirty - or shot at."

"Are you going to re-up?" Bella asked.

"I don't know. I've got a couple of weeks to decide. I really wanted to talk to Walt, you know?"

"Yes, Hal, we know. We all wanted to talk to him again."

"Well, you know, he talked me into the Army, and I wanted to know what he thought."

"No, he did no such thing," Bella said laughing. "We were all right there when he talked with you - and us about the military. He said it was right for him, and he thought it was right for many others. Especially kids like you who had no idea of what you might do in college. He didn't talk you into anything. You talked yourself into it; he just agreed."

"Yeah, well, maybe."

Joey nodded vigorously, "No doubt about it, buddy. Bella and I talked about it after you enlisted. It was your decision, all the way."

"You were talking about me behind my back?"

"Couldn't talk to your face. You were in some Camp doing pushups."

Bella interrupted before Hal could respond. "We all changed our minds about some things because of Mr. Dell. I know I did."

Hal asked, "What did you change? Aren't you still the bleeding heart you always were?"

Bella laughed slightly at this terminology, and said, "Of course I am. But now I no longer think you guys with guns are my enemy. And that's a big change for me."

Sandra clapped her hands quietly. The trio looked at her, and she said, "This is what a noted politician said years ago: if you're under thirty and not a liberal, you have no heart. But if you're over thirty and not a conservative, you have no brain."

Joey added, "You know, listening to that old man for all those weeks, I think we all gravitated to a more central political position. I certainly now see a reason for some of the beliefs at both ends of the political spectrum."

Sandra observed, "That's what happens with maturity, young man."

"Well," he said, nodding in agreement, "perhaps it's maturity. But, now I know to ask my professors 'Why?' and 'How do you know that?' far more often than I would have before spending so much time with Walt Dell."

"And how do your professors respond?" Sandra asked.

"Some of them, well just a few anyway, actually seem to like it. They get into the question and answer thing right there in class."

"And the others?"

"Well, one or two seem a little puffed up, and try the old 'Because I said so' explanation. But that no longer persuades me."

"Good for you," Sandra responded.

As she sipped her tea and looked at the far horizon from her porch, thinking about the disappointment the students had expressed about Walt's death, Sandra remembered the visit she had from Henry Ellison right after Walt's funeral. The man was nervous and hesitant about talking but not willing to leave without telling her his story.

Walt had come to him several months previously and confided in him over coffee. Walt said he had a dark secret in his past and wanted to tell someone. At that point, Sandra tried to halt the proceedings. She didn't want to know any dark secrets, and besides, the man was dead. Ellison persisted, however, and she ended up with the whole story.

Walt had explained about his crush on Jan during high school and her disregard for that affection because of her infatuation with the drummer boy, Billy Parks. So, when Billy asked someone else to the Senior Prom, Walt asked Jan to be his date. She agreed but insisted that it was only to irritate Billy that she agreed to attend the dance at all. And that was the way the evening went. Walt said they danced, but her conversation was all about Billy, even for the final dance of the evening, a slow one for everyone to enjoy their date. Walt also remembered how Jan had ended that dance prematurely because Billy and his date, the girl with the large chest, had left early. Jan insisted that she and Walt go even before the lights in the gym came up.

Walt went on with his story and told how surprised he was that Jan wanted to stay with him and go to the sandbar. They were aware of plans for a bonfire on the sandbar where there would be no chaperones. As Ellison related, Walt did as he was asked and took Jan to the sandbar, expecting to be left alone at some time. But Jan acted very differently once they spread their blanket and lay down. Each of them had changed into swimsuits for a late run in the river, but she showed little interest in the water or others around them. Walt told how she initiated contact and kissing.

Walt told how uncomfortable he was with her amorous activity at first, but he had decided to play along and enjoy the rest of the night. Even so, he was surprised when her hands became engaged inside his swimsuit and even more so when she pulled him out and rolled on top of him moving her hips rhythmically, but he found himself committed to the involvement. Even at that time, Walt said he became aware that Jan was not a virgin. He also realized that she was taking revenge on Billy, and she had not developed a sudden affection for him.

Henry paused, somewhat embarrassed about the details he had shared.

Sandra thought the story had ended and said, "Well, Henry, that wasn't as bad as I thought."

But Ellison indicated that he had also thought Walt was unburdening himself solely of the blanket event, but he looked at Sandra and shook his head. He said, "That's when Walt told me, 'and that's when everything started going downhill.' " Henry took a breath and went on with the story, mentioning that several weeks after graduation, Jan's brothers showed up at in town one afternoon and beat Billy Parks with their fists until he was unconscious. Billy spent ten days in the area hospital and required extensive facial surgery.

Jan disappeared, but she had been around enough that everyone soon was aware of her pregnancy. Walt said he felt responsible even though it seemed that the Berryman family had settled on Billy Parks as the culprit. Walt wanted to speak with her anyway, and one evening went to her house. The Berryman home was a little away from others and down the block from a streetlight, so the yard was dark as he approached. Walt said he heard shouting from the rear and walked around there. He found an open kitchen window and could glimpse Mrs. Berryman yelling at Jan. He could see that Jan had a facial bruise and a black eye, and he overheard her mother say, "mind you, now, or your Daddy'll hit you worse than the last time and will prolly break some bones. You stay away from them boys." Walt left without trying to speak to Jan.

According to Walt, several days later, he was in the general store when Mr. Berryman came in and bought two cartons of shotgun shells and said he was going rabbit hunting. Walt made plans to follow him out in the countryside. He followed Berryman's car at a distance and went past where the older man parked before turning around several miles later and coming back to park nearby. Then, taking his shotgun, Walt slowly began tracking Berryman into the mildly undulating grassland. An hour later, he crossed a small ridge and found Berryman ahead of him by less than a hundred yards; the man had paused to drink from his thermos.

Walt got within thirty yards of Berryman before being noticed. "Hey," the older man said. "What you doing out here?"

"Huntin'. Same as you."

Berryman stood and watched as Walt walked right up to stand about three feet away. "Yeah? Well, this field is claimed. Go on back."

"I wanted to talk to you, anyway."

"What about?"

"About you hitting on your daughter."

"Who the hell are you?"

"I'm Walter Dell. I'm one of …"

"Oh, yeah. I know about you. You're just as bad as that Parks kid!"

"Why are you beating your daughter?"

"Why? 'Cause she's knocked up, that's why. What business is it of yours, anyway?"

"I don't like you hitting on her."

Walt noted that the older man's right hand gripped the barrel of his shotgun as it rested, butt on the ground, at his right foot.

"Well, I don't care what you think. Get out of here." Berryman's grip tightened on the barrel of his shotgun.

"I want you to stop hitting her."

"Really? What are you going to do about it?" Berryman asked, as he raised the shotgun, grabbed the barrel with his left hand, and swung the butt at Walt's head like a baseball bat.

Walt's reaction was swift and effective; he lifted his shotgun in front of himself and blocked the butt of Berryman's shotgun. At the moment he heard the sound of the two weapons colliding, Walt said he heard the boom of Berryman's gun firing. The collision had caused Berryman's gun to fire as he was holding it, like a bat, with the barrel pointed at his mid-chest.

Walt stood, momentarily transfixed, and watched as Berryman's face went from rage to surprise and then to fear as he took a step or two backward and tumbled down the side of a small rise to settle on his back in a small ravine.

Walt stepped forward, looked down at the man, and watched the growing stain of blood on the man's shirtfront. Then, he turned and started back toward where he had parked his car. By the time Walt reached the car, he was running and had tears on his cheeks. He had to calm himself before driving back to town. Walt went to bed without supper that night; the next morning, he announced he was enlisting in the Army. He filed his paperwork that afternoon.

Henry Ellison ended his recitation with a sigh and then slapped both hands on his knees. He made a tight grin at Sandra and stood up to leave.

Sandra looked him in the eye and said, "And, what? That's it?"

"That's what he told me."

"I don't get it. What happened was this Berryman's fault, an accident."

"Not the way Walt has looked at it, I guess. He believed he killed that man, and he spent his life trying to dodge the law and do enough right things to somehow make up for it."

Sandra asked, "I wonder why he chose to tell you the story."

"Probably because he also made me executor of his will."

"Really? How nice."

"To a degree. Walt donated everything to the school in Madeline's memory."

"That's really nice."

"Yes. But being executor means I had to go through his papers and such."

"And was that not nice?"

"Well, at least I know why he felt guilty all those years," Henry said as he carefully extracted a yellowed old newspaper clipping from his pocket and handed it to Sandra.

She carefully unfolded the fragile clipping and saw a three-column head reading, "Local Man Killed While Hunting". She quickly scanned the article and looked at Henry. "This says the Sheriff thought this man was murdered by someone, and they were seeking the killer and asking for assistance."

"That's right. But I believe they soon figured out it was his own gun that killed him and changed their story. But that newspaper went out of business several decades ago. I can't find a retraction."

Sandra shook her head. "All those years, poor Walt thought he was a murderer, afraid the law would catch up with him at any minute."

Henry nodded, "That's right. And I imagine that's why he was smiling when they found him in that rocker on the porch. He thought he had finally gotten away with it."

Sandra smiled a half smile, "I prefer to think he finally figured out he wasn't guilty after all."

I want to thank my wife and children for their encouragement during this writing process. Their feedback, support, and encouragement were positive factors in me finishing the original manuscript.

I also want to recognize Elle Murray for her faithful and frequent efforts to clean up the manuscript and to assist me in getting to the right place in decisions about format, artistry, and pagination.

Any errors that escaped these screening activities are mine alone.

Galen Barbour
Alexandria, Virginia
January 2023

Two totally unexpected deaths seemingly unrelated in New City Hospital are very upsetting for chief of staff Tom Bolling. He is recently new to the hospital and already struggling with a negative review from the Joint Commission endangering the hospital's affiliation with the local medical school. Tom asks an old friend, homicide detective, Ron Looney to assist in finding whether these deaths were murders.

Ron surprises Tom with findings that indicate that the unlikely connection between the deaths actually exists.

## Excerpt

"Ms. Harding?"

"Yes sir?"

"Would you take these files on the Geterman merger and organize them?"

"Yes sir."

Patricia Harding took the files to her desk in the cubicle just past the junior partner's office and put them on the left hand corner. Left hand corner is the 'in' box and she intended to work the files from left to right. She sat in her Herman Miller chair and thought, briefly, how lucky she was to have this paralegal job. She had been working here at Tillson and Martin for nearly three years and she felt respected and highly thought of by the partners. Of course, that couldn't be said of all the other paralegals. But there's just no accounting for some people; at least that's what her mother used to say.

Further, this would really fit in well with her long-range plans. As that thought crossed her mind, she smiled and looked at the screen saver on her computer. It showed a panorama of the desert near Four Corners – a place of quietude, still air and low humidity. Being there would also fit in with her long-range plans.

The lawyers in the firm trust her work. She had been given some of the more 'desirable' cases to work on several times – especially by that one associate. And at least one of the partners has been supportive of her newfound desire to go to law school herself. Things were working out for her here at the firm.


Patricia had actually discussed this with her friend Elaine, at lunch. "I'm really thinking about law school," she said after the first bite of her salad.

"Good for you. When?"

"Well, that's the thing. I don't think we have the money right now."

"Can't you get a loan?"

"Sure, if we want to be in debt for the rest of our lives."

"What about your folks?"

"They might help but Benjie is another issue."

"Because?"

"Well, he isn't working and we're living entirely on my income."

"But, he's looking isn't he?"

"Sure. But you and I both know that market has passed him by. He would have to go get a degree himself to get back in the game."

"Why isn't he doing that?"

"Still the money, Elaine.  Even at the Cincy State campus here, the cost is over our head."  In her head she briefly thought of the many different times she and her husband had come to that topic over the past few months.

"So, what are you gonna do?" Elaine pressed.

"I'm actually working on something.  But the safer and better way would be to get Benjie back in the ranks of the employed – even if it's not the programming job he wants right now.

"So, doesn't he grasp that?"

"Well, we can't really talk about it.  He keeps bringing up having kids, too."

"Is he not paying attention?"

"Really."

"I mean, unless he can get a job, there's no way you guys can afford kids right?"

Patricia thought of the last conversation she had had with Benjie on that topic.  They had been finishing breakfast just that morning and he was excited about a plan for a baby crib he had seen on the Internet the night before.  Benjie was convinced that he could make the crib by himself and save considerable money.  Patricia had tried to talk him out of the project because their finances were too cramped to take on the unneeded crib construction and Benjie had looked like she had hit him in the face.

"Unneeded!  How can you say 'unneeded'?  Do you expect me to allow our baby to sleep on the floor?"  Patricia had seen how irrational he was and tried to walk the conversation back by saying, 'Really, Honey, there will be plenty of time for you to do that when I am actually pregnant.  We just don't have the money right now."

Benjie responded, "That just keeps coming up, doesn't it?  We don't have the money for this or that – and it's because I don't have a job, right?" And he slammed his fist on the tabletop and stormed out of the room shouting, "I'm looking every day.  Every damn day!  It's gonna happen.  But in the meantime, I just wanted to do something for us, you know?"  He was still closed in the bathroom when she left for work.

"I have tried to tell him that but he just says, 'I'm gonna get a job pretty soon, I know it.' And then we're back at square one," Patricia said to Elaine. They fell silent and worked on their food for a few moments.

"Have you talked with the partners?" Elaine asked.

"Yes. Well, with Mr. Hall. He thinks I should do it – go to law school – but he doesn't know about our finances."

"Do you think the firm would help you?"

"I don't know why. It's not like I could pay them back or anything soon." Another period of silence.

"You going to eat that?" asked Elaine.

"You know I never eat the pickle. Take it."

Patricia had been just picking at her pasta salad and Elaine knew that meant she didn't want to continue this line of conversation, so she asked about whether they should get into the office pool on March Madness. Patricia had actually won a little money last year and maybe she could do that again.

They lingered over dessert, splitting an apple turnover with ice cream. Then they walked back to the Starbucks across the street from the office and Patricia ordered a macchiato to take back to her desk.


And now she was just back from lunch – the pasta salad was really quite good – and would like to put her feet up on the desk for a brief spell but she knows that would not be a good example of the type of employee she wants to be. So she sipped at her macchiato and reaches for the first file. Before opening the file, Patricia looks again at the screen saver and smiles to herself about her plans involving the Four Corners.

About thirty minutes later, Elaine Johnson in the next cubicle heard a brief cry and the sound of something hitting the floor as files went tumbling around. She stood, peeked over the cubicle wall and saw Patricia lying on the floor beside her desk with files scattered all around, over and under her.

"Help, something's happened," she hollered to the room as she scurried around the to enter Patricia's cubicle but when she got there all she did was stand and stare.

Other people came running and started bending over Patricia and calling her name, "Pat! Pat! Can you hear me?"

"Call 911!" someone yelled and three people grabbed at their phones.

Patricia lay still and unmoving with short gasps of breath and her co-workers stood around and watched while one of them bent over and lifted her head and put his jacket underneath for support. Two of the women crouched nearby and rubbed her hands and someone else started picking up all the files and straightening them on the desktop and knocked over the cup of macchiato. That led to several cries of dismay and more scrambling around, this time for towels to mop up the mess.

The legal staff was helpless in the face of a medical emergency. They had some minimal knowledge of the Heimlich maneuver but each of them felt this was obviously not a situation that called for such intervention.

They were feeling more and more agitated as they stood around doing nothing; the two women tried again to rouse Patricia with hand rubbing and calling her name but there was no response. The women looked up and around at the coworkers hoping someone had a better idea.

And then the EMTs arrived and began their assessment. They easily moved everyone back and began checking Patricia's vital signs.

"Anyone know her medical history?" asked one.

No one answered.

"Is she diabetic?" asked the lead EMT, looking up and making eye contact with each pf the people standing around their fallen coworker.

"I don't think so," someone said.

"Has she eaten recently?" the Tech asked, zeroing in on the speaker.

"Yes, we were at lunch together." Elaine volunteered.

"Does she take any medications?" The EMT shifted his attention to the new source of information.

No one knew.

"Is she epileptic?"

No one knew. They had all worked together for three years, had lunch and coffee together and no one knew anything about her medical history - or really anything about her outside of work. They looked at each other, expecting one of them to know the answers to these questions. But no one did. Elaine slumped back against the desk feeling like she had betrayed her friend. She remembered times she had asked Patricia about her earlier life and

Patricia had dodged the issue but Elaine had not pushed in follow-up.  Now she thought, "I don't know how to help her!"

The EMTs pushed the observers back some more and slipped a couple of ECG leads on her chest and arms and legs.

"Looks like VT" said one, looking at the monitor.

"I'm ready to shock," said the other.

They shocked her. Twice, and then one said, "OK. Back to normal sinus. Let's get her to New City." And they pulled out their gurney, unfolded it and lifted her up on it, quickly strapping her small body on the frame and then, almost without looking, picked up all their gear and equipment and headed for the door.

The space around Patricia's desk was littered with pages from some of the files and with wet and dry towels.  The workers stood around for another minute just staring at the now empty space before someone said, "Anyone know how to call her husband?"